Praise for *The Kassa Gambit*

"Layers of intrigue unfold in this star-spanning tale of a far-flung humanity."

—Paul Melko, author of *Singularity's Ring* and *The Broken Universe*

"Combines space operatics with mystery. . . . *Pride and Prejudice* and space opera and spies."   —*Locus*

"A great contender for any science fiction fan who enjoys intriguing characters, a fast-paced plot, and an expansive universe that offers the potential for many more strong stories of a far-flung human race!"   —*Examiner*

"A most impressive debut."

—Dave Duncan, author of the Seventh Sword series

"The plot is fast moving and coupled nicely with political intrigue, a dash of thriller, and a nice layer of interstellar space opera–type travel. Things move forward at a fast clip, and at times there is little occasion to catch your breath before the next thing happens. . . . A fast, fun read."   —*Bookworm Blues*

THE KASSA GAMBIT

M. C. Planck

A Tom Doherty Associates Book
New York

For Sara

THE KASSA GAMBIT

Copyright © 2012 by M. C. Planck

A Tor Book
Published by Tom Doherty Associates, LLC
175 Fifth Avenue
New York, NY 10010

www.tor-forge.com

Tor® is a registered trademark of Tom Doherty Associates, Inc.

The Library of Congress has cataloged the hardcover edition as follows:

Planck, M. C.
    The Kassa gambit / M.C. Planck. — 1st ed.
        p. cm.
    "A Tom Doherty Associates book."
    ISBN 978-0-7653-3092-5 (hardcover)
    ISBN 978-1-4299-9283-1 (e-book)
    1. Human-alien encounters—Fiction.   I. Title.
    PR9619.4.P56K37 2013
    823'.92—dc23

                                        2012026480

ISBN 978-0-7653-3093-2 (trade paperback)

Tor books may be purchased for educational, business, or promotional use. For
information on bulk purchases, please contact Macmillan Corporate and
Premium Sales Department at 1-800-221-7945, extension 5442, or write special
markets@macmillan.com.

First Edition: January 2013
First Trade Paperback Edition: May 2014

Printed in the United States of America

0 9 8 7 6 5 4 3 2 1

ACKNOWLEDGMENTS

Thanks to my wife, Sara Creasy, for inspiration; my agent, Kristin Nelson, for heroics; and my editor, Stacy Hill, for catching my missteps.

ONE

Falling

Dropping out of node-space, Prudence instinctively knew there was trouble. Seconds later the computer complained there were no navigation beacons, and after a moment, that there was no radio chatter at all. But she already knew.

She flipped the switch and shut off her own radio signature. Should have done it when the feeling struck, but she hadn't wanted to believe. Hadn't wanted it to be real.

"Pru, the link is down." Jorgun took off his headphones. They always looked amusingly delicate on his huge frame. "I was trying to call Jelly but the link is down."

He had made friends here. They all had, and Jorgun didn't make friends easily. Not true ones who wouldn't take advantage of his simpleness.

Prudence did not make friends easily, either. It would just hurt more when she had to leave. And she always had to leave.

She flicked on the intercom and broadcast throughout the ship. "Battle stations." Jorgun's eyes went wide at her clipped tone, but she had no comfort for him yet. The inexplicable silence of the planet below promised worse to come.

Jorgun drew in his trembling lip and began strapping himself down. Melvin stuck his head in the bridge hatchway.

"Did you say—"

"I did. Don't power up until I tell you to."

"Fucking uncool. Uncool." Melvin was constitutionally unable to perform his job—or for that matter, his life—without a running commentary. It was just one of the many quirks Prudence had learned to live with. She couldn't recruit her crew from Fleet academies.

At least he would do his job. She could hear him cussing all the way to the top deck. The *Ulysses* was a commercial trading vessel, of the smallest economical class, and thus unrated for combat of any kind. But Prudence was a woman of extreme caution and deep paranoia, and thus had made a few modifications. The "mining laser" bolted to the top of the ship was wired in a most unorthodox fashion. It was only good for thirty seconds of operation before something burned out, but two seconds from the amped beam would cut an unarmored ship in half. The left cargo pod carried a rack of missiles. And she had six chaffers bolted to the hull, disguised as auxiliary fuel pods. Hopefully, it would be enough.

She had to trust to hope, because she had no experience. Despite the hardware, constant drills, and obsessive planning, she had never been in combat. Such vigilance had made her the butt of many jokes and the object of her crew's displeasure, but it had always kept her out of even the hint of a fire fight.

She didn't intend to break that record now. Running quiet, the *Ulysses* presented almost no signature. Too small to impinge on any grav fields, at least until she turned her own gravitics on, and with only life support operational, there wouldn't be enough emissions to pick her out of the void.

Aside from Jorgun broadcasting their presence the minute they'd dropped in, that is.

"What's going on?"

The voice of Garcia, the super-cargo, rattled through the intercom with his peculiar and sometimes unintelligible drawl. He claimed it was an ancient heritage, like his fiery cooking, but Prudence was sure simple orneriness was an adequate explanation.

"There's no radio signal from Kassa."

As usual, he didn't bother to figure out the meaning of the last answer before asking the next question.

"Some kind of malfunction?"

"Right, Garcia. A whole planet, fifty thousand people, with a full satellite crown and a C-class spaceport. And they've all gone on the blink."

Perhaps this was not the best time for sarcasm. Still, it made Garcia stop and think.

"What the hell are we gonna do?"

"We're going to run." What she always did when things got bad. Perversely, it was also what she did when things got good. When she'd made enough margins long enough, and had a hold full of high-value trade goods, she would set her crew down in the biggest spaceport she could find and offer them a choice.

Get off, or go Out.

Sometimes they stayed. Sometimes they took their bonus pay and left. Sometimes she found other adventurers, stragglers, wanderers to replace them. And then she would run, hard and fast, hopping from node to node, until either they ran out of fuel or ran into a planet that had the local nodes locked down tight. Then they bartered, bribed, and begged their way into whatever passed for a commercial license in those parts, and started all over again.

The rumblings of Altair imperial politics had hinted it was time to run. The quiet of the planet below screamed it. Idly she wondered which of her crew would go and which would stay. Idly, because she couldn't afford a long dry run yet. Idly, because she couldn't face losing any of them. For all their faults, they were part of her life. Trapped on the tiny ship, constrained by the necessities of space travel, they had learned to get along despite their differences, to support one another and even enjoy each other's company. Together, they were no more dysfunctional than the average family. Or so she assumed; her experience with family had been cut short.

Garcia interrupted her musing. "There might still be people down there. We gotta find out what happened." Since when did he care about anything but a profit margin?

"That's not our job. We'll report the situation to Altair Fleet, and they can investigate. After they call it clean, we'll come back for the delivery." They had to. The colony below was an anomaly, growing its food outdoors instead of in hydrotanks. No other planet that she knew of would want a hundred mechanical threshers. She'd bought the machines as surplus from a factory that used to do something else with them, but had changed production methods. So she couldn't even take them back for a refund.

Without this deal, the ship would be perilously close to bankrupt. That might explain Garcia's solicitousness.

"And for a visit." She flashed a smile for Jorgun's benefit.

If there was anything left to come back to. What kind of disaster could silence an entire world? Prudence didn't know, and she didn't particularly want to find out.

"So what are we waiting for?" Melvin asked over the intercom, from his station in the laser pod.

"Grav." She shouldn't have had to explain it to an engineer, but then, he already knew the answer. He just couldn't stand to be left out of a conversation.

A gravitics engine manipulated gravity; but that meant there had to be gravity to manipulate. Something the size of a planet was an ideal source of gravity. But right now Kassa was a million kilometers away. At that range, the influence it exerted on the *Ulysses* was minuscule.

The *Ulysses* had come out of the node exit with a high nominal velocity, expecting to cut the long trip to the planet down to a few hours. Now that energy hurtled them toward the distant planet, and it was still too far away to push against. Only when they were within a few hundred thousand kilometers would the *Ulysses* be able to change its course, undo all the velocity they had brought with them from the node. They would have to get closer to get away.

She started programming a course into the computer, a slingshot around the planet. One quick pass and they would be back out again. If they were silent, if they were lucky, they would be gone before anyone knew they had come.

A light on her console blinked, and Prudence lapsed into a rare swear word.

"What? What is it?" Garcia was audibly nervous. Prudence had threatened his life once without resorting to swearing.

She thought about hiding it from them. They didn't need to know. It would be her decision, whatever happened; her responsibility, whatever they did. She had to balance the interests of her crew against the duties of basic humanity. That was why she was captain.

Jorgun made the decision for her, glancing with curiosity over at her console and puzzling out what the insistent, dire little light meant.

"A distress beacon," he announced.

"Just one?" Garcia, practiced at the art of deception, was instantly suspicious.

Her console told her Melvin was panicking, trying to do a radar sweep despite her direct orders. But she'd already disabled his console, so he would get no further than another complaint.

Counting breaths, she waited for it.

"Pru, I'm gunning blind up here. Turn on the targeting system."

"For what, Melvin? What are you going to target?"

"I don't know." He did exasperation very well. "If you turned on the system, I'd know what there is to target."

"Not yet," she said. "They might not—"

Another light.

Nobody thought to ask who "they" might be. Whoever did this. Whoever was still out there, and was now coming for them.

"Powering up, Melvin. We have company." She routed her detector into his targeting display. Someone out there had turned on their gravitics. Something was moving. And they weren't coming from the planet. Whoever or whatever it was had been lying in wait, in deep space.

She was still too far out to do anything meaningful. Right now the *Ulysses* was little more than a comet, falling inward.

"I don't see anything on the targeter." For once, she found Melvin's commentary deeply interesting.

"Then it's not a ship."

"Maybe it's Fleet. I heard they have a cut-out signal that disables standard targeting systems." Garcia believed every trick and cheat he heard about.

"We don't have a standard targeting system," she reminded them. Her ship had not been built on Altair. It had been built on a planet so many hops away that no one on Altair had ever heard its name.

It was a testament to the laziness of man that her Altair-trained engineer could maintain the ship despite its foreign origin. The basic designs, refined into perfection over untold centuries, no longer evolved. Only the electronic protocols changed, like dialects of the mother tongue. The computer could learn to translate those quickly enough, so that was rarely a problem. And sometimes, like now, it was a benefit.

"If it's not a ship . . ." Garcia was still waiting for her to fill in the blanks for him.

"Then it's a mine," she said. Let him stew on that.

Melvin started swearing again.

Her gravitics detector wasn't accurate enough to tell her if the mine had locked on to them. She might still be able to slip away, but without knowing what signal it was using to track her, she didn't know if it was safe to turn on her own gravitics.

Garcia's gossiping might be helpful here.

"What's the standard signal for Altair defensive mines?"

"Grav," he answered immediately. "For Earth's sake, don't turn on the engine."

"I haven't. And it's still coming. What are their secondary triggers?"

"Uh. Maybe thermal . . ."

Altair was a technologically sophisticated system. They would use the best. But she had passed through worlds with plenty of tech, and a lot more interest in combat than Altair had. The chaffers were supposed to be proof against all known targeting systems. Hopefully targeting technology was as stagnant and unchanging as the rest of the space-faring designs.

She launched one of the expensive pods. It floated off of the ship, out into space, pretending to be the ship itself. It used gravitics to drive itself, and to fake a mass signature. It put out the same amount of heat. It generated internal static to appear as typical radio-signal leakage from electronic circuits, including canned intercom communications with Prudence's voice announcing bogus course changes. If the black-market dealer who had sold it to her was to be believed, it even faked cosmic ray scattering. She had believed him. She'd paid enough for competence and honesty.

Five minutes later, when the gravitic detector said the mine hadn't changed course, she stopped believing.

"Why isn't it showing up on targeting? How can it see us and we can't see it?" Melvin was outraged at the unfairness.

"Maybe it's not locked on." Garcia said, looking for the easy out.

But Prudence was used to things being hard and unfair.

"Less chatter, more ideas. I'm going to try a course correction. Hang on."

She brought the engines online and slammed the controls hard to starboard. Her warning was wasted. As far out as they were, she couldn't feel the motion through the ship's passive grav-plating.

Cutting the engines, she went back to silence and waiting. Two minutes and the console gave its answer.

"It's tracking us," Melvin squealed. She was sorry she'd left his display wired into the gravitic detector.

"Come on, boys, think. What else is it locking on to us with?"

"Screw that," Melvin cut her off. "Bring it up on target, so I can shoot it."

The laser beam was a half centimeter wide. The mine was probably less than a meter broad. At a range of a million meters, even a computer wouldn't be able to make that shot.

"Seriously, Pru. Let me defocus the beam and spray it."

"Defocus to what, Melvin? A kilometer across?" At that level of spread, the laser wouldn't even give you a suntan.

"Just a meter. It's worth a try, damn it."

No it wasn't. Melvin didn't understand even the most basic physics. Defocusing the beam more than a few centimeters would weaken it to just a bright flashlight. And if the mine was hardened to military grade, even a tight-beam hit from the laser might not matter.

"Wait till it's closer, Melvin."

No point in measuring the distance in meters. All that mattered was time until impact. Her future had been reduced to ten minutes.

At five minutes she set off two more chaffers, to no effect. She hadn't expected any.

At three minutes she turned on the engines and started evasive maneuvers, a complex series of course changes. Each one extrapolated to a unique vector, but the sum total of them all was the real path the ship would wind up taking. If her random number generator was smarter than the mine's random number predictor, they might throw it off.

For this pass. It would turn around and come after them again. But at these velocities, that would buy them more time. Time to get closer to the planet, where she could really maneuver. Or possibly hide in the atmosphere.

"Stop jerking the ship," Melvin shouted through the intercom. "Let me aim."

At what? She could see his targeting display was still clueless. But she had promised him his chance. She turned off the random autopilot. The detector showed it wasn't confusing the mine, anyway.

"Go ahead, Melvin."

"Are we gonna be okay?" Jorgun asked. He'd been so quiet she had forgotten about him.

"We'll be . . . fine. Just close your eyes and count to . . ." She looked at the readout and its bleak display: sixty seconds to impact. "Count to sixty-one."

Over the whisper of his chanting, she heard the hum of the laser. It drained power at a phenomenal rate. Because of its modifications it bypassed the usual circuit breakers. The lights went out, and life support shut down.

Jorgun was trying not to cry. That was no way to spend your last sixty seconds as an ordered collection of molecules, before poofing into atomic plasma. She got out of her chair, went over to Jorgun's, and held his hand.

"It's all right," she told him, with a smile. It would be quick. Instantaneous, even.

This was not how she wanted to die. In space. She wanted to die on a planet. On a place she could call home. She wanted to make that one last landfall someday, come to rest on a dirty rock and never leave. As young as she was, she had thought she had more time to find it. But all of her searching had led only to deals. Negotiations, not acceptance; contracts, not trust. Even the few men she had taken to her bed had been dealers, of one kind or another.

With her free hand, she touched the medallion that hung around her neck. Just another dream that would fail, dying silently and unfinished in the black of space and blinding fire.

The hum of the laser went away and the lights returned. As life support began pumping air, she could smell the burned silicon.

Thirty seconds.

Out of habit, she kept trying. From Jorgun's console she flicked the engines back on. No more time for random dodging: she pushed the ship into as steep a turn as it could pull from this distance. Not much, but at least she could feel it.

The gravitics display went blank, its crude accuracy incapable of distinguishing mine and ship at this close range.

Ten seconds.

She really didn't want a damn countdown, but Jorgun faithfully whispered the numbers.

"I think I got it." Melvin's voice was jarring. "I defocused the beam a lot, at the end. I'm sure I hit it."

If he had succeeded in damaging it, why hadn't it self-destructed? At this range the blast would probably have killed them anyway. But she took pity on him, as she had on Jorgun, and let him believe.

Jorgun stopped counting.

"Are we safe now?" he asked.

"Sure," she told him. It would be good to see him smile one last time.

He turned on the intercom.

"We're safe, guys. Prudence says we're safe now."

"Jorgun, you half-witted genetic cesspit—" Garcia unloaded a lifetime's bitter frustration into the nearest target. Prudence flicked off his intercom.

"Garcia sure can swear, can't he?" Jorgun said with a grin. "Like you told me, Pru, we all have our own special talents."

Jorgun was a giant, seven feet tall and well proportioned. He could crush Garcia like an eggshell. But Jorgun was incapable of violence. The best he could do was to glare silently from behind dark glasses. It had worked a number of times, browbeating port officials into being less obnoxious, but if he forgot his role and took off the shades, they could see his eyes were laughing. It was just a game to him.

Now he thought the game was over. He was trying to raise Jelly on the comm again.

Prudence held her breath, involuntarily.

The gravitics display winked on. The mine had passed them, was still sailing blindly out into space.

Melvin really must have hit it somehow. The odds were impossible; not merely astronomical, but impossible. Far more likely the damn thing had malfunctioned on its own, but Melvin would never accept that. The man would be impossible to live with now.

She laughed at the irony. Complaining about living conditions when you expected to be dead was Melvin's shtick, not hers.

Turning on the intercom, she shouted over the noise.

"Shut up, Garcia!"

The swearing stopped.

"We're safe. It missed, and it's not even slowing down. It's on a dead run."

"I told you I hit it," Melvin crowed.

Garcia, a rational person despite his cavalier attitude toward the truth, was too stunned to say anything. At that moment Prudence remembered what they shared, why she had kept him on the ship so long. They were the only two with a shred of common sense.

The distress beacon was still calling.

Sighing, she pushed caution aside, and entered a course for planetfall.

The *Ulysses* floated out of the sky on a cushion of gravity. Prudence sat at the helm, her fingers twitching, ready to spook and run at the shadow of a threat.

The beacon lay in the middle of a burnt field, whining plaintively. A village was over the hill, or had been, once. Now it was a smoking pile of rubble.

Nothing stirred below; the field was quiet and still. On this silent world, it seemed like a warning siren.

"Melvin, give me a targeting sweep."

The comm panel told her he was trying. It also told her the result.

"There's nothing down there made of metal. 'Cept the beacon."

"Sweep the horizon," she said. Melvin tended to think a little too directly.

"Hang on—I got something out in the woods. Aft of us. Light metal—it's bouncing up and down!"

Reflexively, she touched the controls. But left them unmoved.

"Tell me if it starts coming at us."

"It's gone now," Melvin complained. "How can I tell you if it's coming, when it just blinks in and out?"

She sighed. Melvin was used to space, where things were neat and clean. Planetside, there were always obstructions and distractions. She sighed because she sympathized with Melvin. Space was better.

Gently she rotated the ship until it faced the mysterious woods. Hovering for a moment, she stared at the view-screen, trying to pick out details. But the trees yielded no secrets.

The thought of landing twisted her stomach into knots. Anything could be buried in that innocent field: plastic explosives, a magnetic grapple, electrifying cables. The *Ulysses* belonged in the sky, the only place it was safe. If somebody out there wanted her attention, they would have to play their cards first.

Very slowly, she started going back up.

The watching woods parted. A figure stepped out into the open and waved both arms in a universal, timeless signal.

Over here.

"The metal's moving again—now there's more! What the hell is going on, Pru?" Melvin was obviously too absorbed in his radar screen to look at his visual. At least he couldn't panic and open fire. The laser was dead.

"Somebody down there is asking for our help, Melvin. But they're not alone, and they're not stupid. The metal you're detecting must be hand weapons."

"Weapons! Don't go down, Pru. Get us out of here," Garcia's voice demanded through the intercom. He hated being strapped into the passenger lounge, but there were only two seats on the bridge. Prudence had had the other two removed years ago, one of the best decisions she had ever made.

Melvin voiced his opinion by aiming the defunct laser at the woods.

But Jorgun cast the deciding vote. "Is it Jelly?" he asked, and Prudence's heart wrenched.

"No, Jor, it won't be her. She lives in Baliee, a thousand klicks away."

"Oh," he said, disappointed. Too simple to understand that meant hope for her. Too innocent to guess that hope was all there was.

Prudence took the ship down again, heading for a spot halfway between the woods and the beacon. The tiny figure watched her.

She punched up the zoom on the visual display, brought the man into focus. Dirty, bearded, disheveled. At this range, his face was inscrutable.

The feet of the *Ulysses* touched ground, unsteady with the tension between mass and apparent weight. She left the gravitics on, ready to spring up, to safety.

The man waited, unmoving. Her turn to play a card.

"Jor," she said, hating herself for using him. "Open the boarding hatch. But stay on the ship. Do not get off, for any reason. Just let them see you, okay? Wave to them." She had to use him. He was huge, intimidating—from a distance. They would take his size for strength. If it was a trap, they might change their minds and flee. If they attacked, then Jorgun was the only crew member she could afford to lose, the only one who could not use a weapon.

While he was stepping out of the bridge, Garcia stepped in, carrying a short, stubby gun. The splattergun was designed to repel boarders. Its projectile disintegrated into a hundred tiny particles when it left the barrel, which made it less likely to puncture hulls and more likely to hurt people. Prudence hated the crude weapon. It was, like Garcia, undiscriminating in picking its targets.

"Where's he going?"

"To make friends," she answered.

"I came up here to tell you to escape while we still can. Not to watch you send Jor out to die."

"Shut up, Garcia," she repeated. Despite his protestations, he didn't go running after Jorgun to stop him. Instead, he stared at the zoomed image on the display.

"That guy hasn't been eating well." Trust Garcia to notice something like that. He never missed a meal.

Carefully they watched the display, looking for clues. They heard the boarding hatch open. They heard Jorgun's shouted welcome. Then, and only then, the man relaxed, his shoulders sagging. With his hands raised, he stumbled toward the ship.

Behind him, faces appeared, peering out of the foliage. Scared, tired, hungry faces.

Prudence met the man at the boarding hatch. Standing at the top of the gangway gave her power, rendered him a supplicant at the foot of the throne. A simple trick, but it had worked on more than one dockside petty official.

"Thank Earth you're here," the man said.

"Captain Prudence Falling, of the *Ulysses*," she introduced herself. The formalities were there for a purpose. They gave structure to the negotiations, reminded everyone exactly where they stood. "And you are?"

"Brayson James." There was no argument in his voice, only despair. "A pumpkin farmer. Or I was. Until we were attacked."

"Attacked by who?" Garcia whispered fiercely from where he was hiding behind a bulkhead. "It freaking matters, don't you think?"

It did matter, rather a lot. Knowing which planet launched the attack would tell them where to flee. "By who?"

Brayson shrugged.

"Burn Earth if I know. The bombs just fell out of the air. No warning. If I hadn't been out in the field, trying to fix an irrigation line, I'd be dead with the rest of my family. They dropped a bomb right on my house, Captain. They aimed for us."

"And those people?" Some of the crowd coming out of the woods were carrying weapons, but they no longer looked dangerous.

"Refugees and survivors. We haven't eaten right for a week. Too afraid to go near town for any supplies that might be usable. They didn't leave right away, Captain. They stayed and hunted us for days. We only figured it was safe now because you weren't already dead."

"Nice that you were thinking of us," she said, but without heat. She would have done the same in their shoes. "You set the beacon?"

"Yes. And the seven before it. This is the first time a bomb didn't fall out of the sky on it."

"What do you want me to do?"

Someone in the crowd answered with a shout. "Get us out of here!"

The *Ulysses* was a freighter, not a passenger liner. Its life support couldn't keep a hundred people alive for the four-day trip through node-space to the next colony, let alone the long journey to Altair.

"I can't take you to off-planet," she said carefully. Unhappy crowds were not prone to listening to reason.

But Brayson stared at her, his face set into ugly hardness, like badly poured concrete that could never be smoothed over. "We're not running away. And we're done hiding. Take us to the capital."

TWO

Secrets

The *Launceston* came out of node-space fast, silent, and ready for anything. Regulations called for battle stations when exiting any node, since one was necessarily blind to local conditions on the other side, and "surprise" was a dirty word in military-speak.

Lieutenant Kyle Daspar had his own reasons to expect shenanigans. Following up on an anonymous tip wasn't really what an up-and-coming police detective with political connections was supposed to be doing. But his orders came from on high, and plenty of hints had been dropped about how it might be important to the League, so there had never been a chance of saying no. His instincts told him there were unseen angles to the situation. And he didn't like surprises any more than the military.

The trip had been miserable. Three nodes and twelve days out from Altair, on a small ship with six angry soldiers. They looked down on him for being a civilian, they despised him for being a League officer, but they hated him because their captain did. And their captain hated him for a perfectly good reason: the papers Kyle carried from the League gave him command of the ship.

You can't make a captain a servant on his own ship, not even a patrol boat the size of the *Launceston*. Not without making him hate you and everything you stand for. The heavy-handed blundering of the League was its own worst enemy.

But the League had other enemies. Some of them were political, like the Alliance, the chief opposition party despite its sheer ineffectiveness. Some of them were vocal, like the vid celebrities and their talk shows, although equally ineffective. But some of them were secret: deep, dark, and biding their time, working from within to expose and destroy.

Like Lieutenant Kyle Daspar.

But that was a thought too dangerous to dwell on for a man as deeply undercover as Kyle was.

"Orders, Commander?" Captain William Stanton had been icily formal from the first instant his gaze had lighted on Kyle's armband, back in the Altair spaceport. Kyle had hoped the man would at least swear out loud while reading the orders that had seized his ship, but he had been disappointed. Stanton had simply become colder. If Stanton had made an outburst, Kyle could have forgiven him, and then at least they could have had a human interaction. But the captain was too well trained. He folded up the orders precisely, handed them back to Kyle frostily, and proceeded to follow them literally.

That was part of the problem. Too many people followed orders without raising enough fuss. Furious that Stanton was going to make the trip unbearably difficult for him, Kyle had leapt into his role and played the tin horn to the limit. Theoretically, he meant to push Stanton to the point of rebellion, since making enemies for the League was part of his secret mission statement.

So much contempt crammed into the tiny confines of a patrol boat made for a very miserable trip indeed.

"Contact Kassa spaceport and get clearance to land." Kyle could hardly admit he had no clue what to do next. All the tip had said was "Go to Kassa." He still had a million kilometers before he had to come up with a new plan.

"Sir," said the comm officer, "there's no radio traffic from Kassa. Not even a navigation beacon."

"What? That's a violation of code, isn't it? They can't turn off their nav beacons." Kyle was disgusted by the thought that he had come all the way out here to write somebody a maintenance ticket.

But Captain Stanton's disgust had a more immediate target: Kyle. He could see it written all over the man's face. It was an active kind of disgust, not the passive contempt he'd come to take for granted.

"Do you have something to say, Captain?"

Stanton answered in precise, clipped tones, each word carefully enunciated. "I believe the commander does not understand the full import of comm's data."

Kyle translated that in his head, from military language to ordinary speech. *I think you're a fucking idiot. And I hate you. Idiot.*

"Feel free to fill me in, Captain." It must be something important for Stanton to have brought it up at all, instead of just letting Kyle make a fool of himself.

"There's no radio from the colony. None at all."

"Why would they be trying to talk to us? They don't know we're here." That was the point of coming in silent, wasn't it?

Gritting his teeth in frustration, Stanton tried again.

"Commander. There is no radio traffic on the planet. No one down there is talking to each other."

A blip appeared on the console in front of Kyle. He didn't know much about spaceships, but he knew what that blip meant.

"Well, they're sending someone out to talk to us."

That finally cut through Stanton's ice-block reserve. He leapt to Kyle's side, stared down at the console, and reached out for the controls.

At the last instant, he stopped, a testament to the rigidity of his training.

"Permission to assume the helm, Commander."

It wasn't really a question, but Kyle was too relieved that the man had finally asked to be picky.

"Granted, Captain." Kyle stepped out of the uncomfortable chair. Stanton sank into it, his hands and eyes already fully engrossed in the task at hand.

"Not emitting standard FOF, Captain. Permission to query." It was the first time Kyle had heard the comm officer speak without sneering. The crew was too busy with the current threat to remember they hated him.

Captain Stanton answered instantly, assuming the authority he should have had all along. "Granted, comm. Gunnery, you are live."

The other two men on the bridge silently took up their duties, slipping goggles over their eyes. Stanton put on his own. They would see the battle from any of a dozen different angles, hopping between the external cameras and computer-generated displays, but all Kyle would get to watch were several men in funny glasses talking to each other. Not the excitement one expected from a space battle.

"Query is negative." The comm officer didn't sound worried. He was too professional for that. But Kyle was a professional at listening to what people didn't want to be heard.

Unable to bear being completely out of the loop, he ventured a question. "What does that mean, Captain?"

Stanton flicked him a pitying glance, no mean feat considering his face was obscured by goggles.

"It's not one of ours. Or anybody that we know."

"An unregistered ship?" It wasn't unheard of.

Stanton spared him one last comment before forgetting about him completely.

"It's not a ship. Targeting, report."

The gunnery sergeants spoke for the first time.

"DF negative."

"T negative."

They carried on like that for another thirty seconds, speaking their Fleet jargon so fluently it almost sounded like a real language. If it hadn't been for the urgency in their voices, Kyle would have thought they were just putting him on.

Then Stanton reached for his console, pausing only long enough to direct a comment to Kyle.

"Hang on."

To what? Instinctively Kyle went into a wrestling crouch, expecting anything. Stanton's fingers moved, and the atomic engine flared into life, throwing Kyle to the deck with its force.

He slid to the back of the room, where he could at least latch on to a stanchion. Gravity moved under him, changing direction, made his stomach feel like it was pushing up to his mouth. The ship went both forward and up.

Stanton killed the engine, returning the world to normal. The grav-plating in the deck said down was down again, comforting Kyle's whirling stomach.

A few seconds of tension, and then the comm officer made his pronouncement.

"NavProj says it's null-vee."

The words were gibberish, but the tone said victory. The men in the room relaxed, and Kyle relaxed with them. Stanton, perhaps rendered giddy with relief, offered Kyle an explanation without being asked.

"It's a mine. But it's powered by gravitics, not thrust. It can't match our vector. This far from a planet, it maneuvers like a pregnant cow."

Kyle paused, trying to formulate just the right response to show his legitimate respect without blowing his cover as a petty political hack. The delay cost him his chance.

"Captain! More bogies!" The comm officer, so recently urbane, now sounded perilously close to panic. "Five—six—seven!"

Stanton tried to focus his officer, get him back to thinking about his job instead of his possibly short future. "Mines or ships?"

"Too small to be ships, Captain. But . . ."

Kyle's stomach got light again. Fleet officers were not supposed to say "but." It wasn't the kind of word you ever really wanted to hear. In the context of a space battle, it was positively ominous.

The comm officer paused for an agonizingly long time before continuing. "Only one is on an intercept vector, Captain. The others are . . . spreading out." The officer punched at computer buttons furiously. "They're ignoring our decoys, and blocking us. All possible escape routes are covered." He sat back in defeat, disbelief written on his face. "One of them is even covering the node entrance."

Stanton stared straight ahead, reviewing the situation through his goggles. Then he took them off and faced Kyle.

"You should begin preparing your final report, Commander. Our optimal course predicts approximately twenty-seven minutes before impact."

Kyle was amazed at the captain's sangfroid. "You're giving up? Already?"

"I am not giving up." The ice was back, all the more noticeable for its brief absence. "I am explaining the expected outcome. The *Launceston* is a patrol boat. Our chief defense is maneuverability. I foolishly revealed our maximum thrust while avoiding the first mine. Now we will all die because of my error."

Putting the goggles back on, he began determinedly punching buttons on his console. Kyle could almost see him mentally paging through the Fleet tactics manual, trying every trick in the book. If they died here, it would not be from a lack of training.

"Why?" Kyle asked.

Stanton did not answer.

"Why did you reveal that information?"

Yanking the goggles off of his face, Stanton turned and all but snarled at Kyle.

"Because I am human and capable of error would seem to be an adequate explanation. Sir."

Kyle didn't believe that for a minute. The man was too much like a machine to claim to be human now. Even with his life expectancy reduced to less than half an hour, Stanton wouldn't break protocol and *actually* snarl at a superior officer.

Following his hunches was what had got Kyle to where he was today. Not that being on a spaceship doomed to destruction was a particularly laudable destination, but it was too late to change methods now. "Did you break some kind of regulation when you took that first evasive maneuver?"

"No, sir, I did not. But I have already accepted blame for the situation, so I do not understand the commander's line of inquiry."

"Why isn't there a regulation against what you did?"

Stanton stared at Kyle. Obviously he didn't think it was an appropriate time to discuss Fleet regulations.

But the comm officer had been listening in, and now demonstrated that someday he would earn a command of his own. Assuming he survived this one, of course.

"Sirs . . . no known mine system would be able to take advantage of that information."

Kyle could see Stanton's face slowly changing from choleric to puzzled.

"You said it before, Captain. It's nobody we know." Kyle didn't know how this information would help them, but he was sure it was important. He had to make Stanton realize that.

The comm officer interrupted. "Captain—I'm picking up another ship. An independent freighter, registered from Altair. Merchant class A, identifies as the *Ulysses*. It's in low-orbit around the planet—just broke atmosphere."

Stanton frowned at this new piece of the puzzle. "Maybe it's someone *they* know. Give me a channel, comm."

Kyle didn't want to pull rank now that the captain was finally treating him like a human being, but he had to. Whoever had sent him on this mission had sent him for a reason. If that freighter was League-friendly, a League officer would have to make the call.

"I think I better handle this, Captain. It might be politically sensitive." That was the most hint he dared to give.

Stanton paused, but only briefly. "Comm, give the commander a line." Although it was what Kyle had hoped for, it still bothered him that even the suggestion of politics could scare off a Fleet officer so easily. Stanton went back to abusing his console, trying out new strategies.

Kyle went over to the comm officer's console and accepted a headset.

"*Ulysses*, acknowledge. This is the Altair Fleet vessel *Launceston*, demanding acknowledgement."

"And hello to you, too, Captain."

A woman's voice. Subtly exotic, with an accent he could not place. Cool, but inviting; assertive, but not aggressive.

Oddly tongue-tied, Kyle fell into a bad imitation of Fleet-speak. "Negative, *Ulysses*. This is Lieutenant Kyle Daspar, League officer and temporary commander of the *Launceston*."

The voice hardened. Some part of Kyle, deep in the back of his mind, regretted that. "Acknowledged, Commander. This is Prudence Falling, captain and owner of the *Ulysses*. We're glad you've finally shown up."

His knowledge of Fleet jargon deserted him. "What do you mean?"

Apparently his ability to speak like an intelligent adult had gone with it.

"We've got a disaster on our hands, Commander. Perhaps you noticed? I've spent the last sixteen hours ferrying refugees, but there's more broken here than I can fix. We need a hospital ship."

"What happened down there, Captain? Give me as many details as you can."

The voice paused. "Why don't you come down and see for yourself?"

She was a suspicious one, all right. From one clue she had deduced that there was something important he wasn't telling her. She was wasted as a freight-hauler; she should have been a detective.

"We are currently under attack ourselves, Captain. You wouldn't know anything about that, would you?"

The voice turned curt and direct, ignoring his implication. No more gamesmanship. "A mine?"

"Seven of them, actually."

"I'm sorry to hear that." A hint of real pity. "We were only tracked by one."

How could a freighter escape a military-grade mine? Even to Kyle that seemed unlikely. "Then why are you still alive?"

"It malfunctioned. Gave us a miss." Just the lightest hint of amusement. Not a chuckle. That voice would never chuckle. But she appreciated the irony of his question.

Every bone in Kyle's cop body twinged. This was the point in an ordinary interrogation where he would sit down next to the subject, shake his head sadly, put his hand gently on their shoulder, and quietly explain that lies would only make it worse. Much, much worse.

But this interviewee could not be intimidated. Kyle wasn't looming over her, with the power of the State and a few burly beat cops behind him. Whatever truth she was hiding, he would have to lure it out of her.

"Your luck seems providential. Remarkably so, wouldn't you agree, Captain?"

She surprised him, giving up without a fight. "I would agree. My engineer fired on the mine, with a mining laser defocused to a meter spread. But that seems far less likely a source of miracles than a malfunction. I should also note it evaded several decoys, which I was assured were fully effective against all known targeting systems."

For a tramp freighter, the *Ulysses* sounded remarkably well armed. It was like stumbling onto a murder scene and finding a hot-dog seller loitering in the area with a grenade launcher hidden in his cart. It tended to make one suspicious.

But the comm officer had been listening in with one ear, and had found something interesting enough to intrude on their conversation. "*Launceston* comm here, Captain. What model were those decoys?"

She answered him immediately, the bond between spacers obvious now that she was talking to a real one. "Nonstandard. Not from Altair, but Fleet grade. Supposed to work on gravitics, thermal, radio, and cosmic ray detection. I don't have any better specs for you."

"What evasive action did you take, Captain?"

"Random vector generation. But it didn't help. Running silent didn't either. We never figured out how it was tracking us. And then it just stopped trying."

"After the laser? But you can't crack the hull on a lifeboat with that kind of spread, let alone a mine." The comm officer hounded down the stray fact, cutting past all the boring, unhelpful, well-behaved ones. Kyle watched the officer worrying it like a bulldog, trying to squeeze out the answer by brute force.

"What's missing?" Kyle asked, trying to help. "How can a laser stop a mine without breaking through its armor?" He had no idea what the answer was. He just knew it was the right question.

The comm officer silently counted on his fingers, eliminating possibilities. He started over, on the other hand, and then froze.

"Tracking. Captain, it has to be an optical tracking system. That's why all the other mines came after us when we turned on the fusion engine—we were the brightest thing in the sky. That's why the decoys failed—they don't *look* like us. And that's how the *Ulysses* escaped—it *blinded* the mine."

Stanton spoke up, his voice coming to Kyle both through the headset and from across the bridge. "Captain Falling, could you give us an estimate on your laser's output?"

A brief pause before she answered. "Twenty megawatts."

"Acknowledged, Captain." The delay was a clue that there was something interesting in her answer; the dryness of Stanton's reply confirmed it. That they were trying to hide this from Kyle just made it all the more interesting.

Stanton cut his link to the conversation, and addressed his bridge. "Gunnery, calculate luminosity for a twenty-meg beam at one meter, and then tell me how wide we can get and still match it."

He took off his goggles to face Kyle. "Commander, I have a plan. I intend to make a vector directly for one of the mines. At the last minute we will disable it with laser fire. This will allow us to slip through their screen. Do I have your permission to proceed?"

Kyle suspended his call to the *Ulysses,* also. He didn't want the enigmatic Captain Falling in this part of the conversation. "And if the laser doesn't work?"

Stanton didn't even bother to shrug. "Then we die. In six minutes, instead of twenty-one."

"Don't you think you're staking an awful lot on a brief conversation with a woman you've never met?"

The contempt was back, deep in Stanton's eyes. Obviously, he felt no mere police officer could understand or appreciate the fraternity shared by all true spacers. But Kyle was unable to dredge up any sympathy. Kyle had plenty of experience with the alleged fraternity of professions, from cops to robbers to politicians and every shade in between. It had left him severely unimpressed with unwritten codes of honor.

"Do you have any other suggestions, Commander?"

If this was what the League had sent him for, then the woman was a League agent trying to save his life. Unless she was a plant, sent to make sure he died. He had enemies in the League—everyone in the League had enemies—and one of them could have arranged this, given the woman this clever story to lure them into making the wrong choice.

He hated having to make decisions without adequate evidence, but in this case, it was easy. There weren't any other options.

"No, Captain, I do not. You may proceed at your discretion."

"Then find a place to hang on, Commander. You have thirty seconds."

Kyle retreated from the bridge, fleeing to his private stateroom. Over the intercom he asked the comm officer to let him know when the last possible moment to launch a report capsule would be. Strapping himself into a chair, he tried to compose what might be his final message.

What should he say, and who should he say it to?

His allies in the police force, the shadowy handful of men and women that sought to thwart the seemingly unstoppable rise of the League, would receive all the message they needed from his death. Anything he might say or even hint to them could only increase their risk of being discovered by the League.

His father would also be content with the mere fact of his death. They would tell the old man that his son had died in the line of duty, serving the police, the League, and the glory of Altair. That would be enough; that was all his father had ever expected. All he had ever wanted.

In this last moment, all Kyle had to reach out to was the League. And if they wanted him here, then they didn't want him recording indiscriminate facts without knowing who would hear them. If he lived through this, he would need their favor. He had to continue to act like a loyal apparatchik. Even now.

The taint of self-pity disgusted him. He took his hand away from the console, and leaned back into the chair.

To wait.

THREE

Bonds

Prudence watched the patrol boat touch down without envy. Sleek and lean, its lines appealed to the uninitiated eye. It *looked* fast, and the array of weapons and sensors it sported made it appear as prickly dangerous as it really was. Its skin was finely painted, smooth, and angular. As a craft of war, she could appreciate it for what it was.

But what it could never be was a home. It could never offer refuge from a hard day's work, never be a place where friends gathered for a meal. It could never earn its keep, make people happy with its promise of new goods, bringing presents from faraway places. It would never attract a curious and happy crowd with its mere landing.

Even now, under these terrible circumstances, its presence only garnered relief. And anger, for its lateness. The refugees waited sullenly for the ship. The weapons it brought were too little, too late.

She watched as the officers of the *Launceston* were deluged by the bitter demands of Kassa's survivors. She had struggled with the angry crowd past the point of pity. They had been in shock, still grateful for any help, any friendly face from the skies. Now that they were beginning to grasp the full extent of the disaster, their personal dismay would be translated into global outrage.

Prudence would share their outrage, when she was not tired beyond feeling. Nothing electrical was left functioning on the planet. Hardly any buildings were still standing. The extent of the dead was unknown. It would be months before everyone was accounted for. The only good news was that Kassa had prided itself on its outdoorsmanship, almost as if they were primitives. The bulk of the population would still be out there, hiding in the forests. Of all the worlds she had visited, Kassa was perhaps the best capable of surviving a hit-and-run raid. Any dome colonies would have suffered total casualties. Even Altair would have lost vastly more, their densely packed cities sitting ducks for orbital bombing runs.

Of course, Altair had a fleet of warships that stood between its vulnerable cities and the threat of attack. Not that there ever had been any credible threat of attack before. The nearest planet with enough population to think of itself as competition was too many hops away, too embroiled in its own internal politics to project its power across the tiny stepping-stones between there and here.

Kassa was one of those tiny stones, too small and poor to be worth stepping on. Kassa had defended its freedom with a volunteer police force and a single fusion-powered rescue boat, and that had been enough, because there was nothing here worth a conqueror's time.

But this enemy had come to kill, not to conquer; to destroy, not to possess. The survivors, terrified by this irrationality, shouted at the officers of the *Launceston,* whose uniforms were the only visible sign of authority and reason left on Kassa.

"Tell them to pay us." Garcia was quick to accept the authority of the uniforms, as well. "For our fuel, at least."

"Why would they, Garcia? This isn't Altair soil. They don't owe Kassa the time of day."

Garcia looked over the angry crowd with a new appreciation. "It looks like he's telling them the same thing. And they don't like it any more than I do."

"He" would be the man in the police uniform. The captain of the *Launceston* stood behind him, deferring to him. Prudence felt an immediate pang of sympathy for the captain. His government might have the right to seize his ship and hand it over to a political hack—after all, they paid the bills—but it was still painful to watch.

She couldn't work up anything but contempt for the cop, though. True, his job right now was as hard as the captain's—he had to stand there and explain to the Kassans exactly what the price of their freedom was—but the armband he wore trumped her natural sympathy. Law and order were fine things, but what he offered was something else.

Garcia found something amusing in the scene. "If he's recruiting League members, this is the right place to do it. Plenty of those farmboys will want to dish out a whipping now."

"Against who?" The refugees had seen nothing but bombs. They had no more idea who their attackers were than Prudence did.

"Do you think they care? They just want to hit somebody back."

The officers had finished with the crowd and were making their way over to the *Ulysses*.

"Now it's your turn," Garcia said.

"Don't you mean our turn?"

"Nope. Them League guys give me the creeps. I'll be belowdecks. But don't forget to ask them for money. It can't hurt."

Garcia scuttled away, abandoning Prudence to face the uniforms alone. Jorgun was asleep in his bunk, exhausted after carrying and lifting supplies and injured people for a double shift. Melvin was AWOL, probably locked in the gunnery pod and stoned out of his mind. All of this misery was too much for him to bear. It detracted from his ability to whine about his own suffering.

That was unfair, she reflected. He'd done what he could, for the first twelve hours. It was only when it became obvious that nothing in his power would be enough that he had given up. Garcia was the one who cared the least, and thus was least scarred by the pain around them. Jorgun was protected by his simpleness. But he kept asking for Jelly, and sooner or later Prudence would have to find an answer for him.

Knowing what the answer had to be, she had not looked for it.

She wondered when she got to give up, stop caring, or just trust someone else to take charge. But she silenced that feeling before it grew into a whine. This was the price of command. This was the price of her freedom.

"Captain Falling. Thank you for your assistance earlier." Captain Stanton clapped his hands to his side and performed a half-bow. The gesture was entirely unnecessary, but mildly romantic.

"I'm glad we could help." Stanton was not really her type. Fleet guys never were. But she could certainly appreciate him as a fellow spacer.

"May I introduce the commander, Lieutenant Kyle Daspar."

She was amazed at how much seething hatred Stanton could inject into such a simple sentence.

"A pleasure to meet you, sir." Formality seemed to be the appropriate tack. A spacer might appreciate her for her merits, but a civilian, promoted to authority on political strings, would expect to be deferred to and flattered.

"Please. Just call me Kyle." He seemed flustered, uncertain. In his face Prudence recognized a familiar suspicion. Authority never trusted the tramp freighter, never understood why someone would hop from system to system unless they were running away from something. The idea that someone might be running to something never satisfied them. Prudence's dream, her restless search for something better, only sounded like escape to them. They never looked forward, only behind; never up, only down.

She sighed, resigning herself to the coming interrogation. Curiously, his eyes flickered, and for a moment she thought he was disappointed. Perhaps she was seeing things. After all, she was tired, and there was enough disaster here to throw anyone off their game.

"Captain Falling, I have a few questions I need to ask."

He was beefy, in a compact way, like ten kilos of steak packed into a five-kilo bag. His jaw was set in perpetual defiance, expecting hostility even while his stubborn eyebrows projected innocence. But he wasn't as hard as a soldier. His curly black hair was short and neat, but not severely so. She could, with a generous stretch of creativity, imagine his lips pouting in a cute, boyish way, a depth of feeling that most spacers and soldiers had beaten out of them long before they became old enough to interest her.

As much as she detested the uniform, she could still admire the physical package. Languidly she let her eyes communicate this ambiguity. He responded with more contradiction: instead of swelling under her unspoken compliment, or following up its implied half-invitation, he seemed to be struggling not to blush.

But Captain Stanton had no patience for their emotional fencing match. "Perhaps the commander would like to start with the formalities. We have a narrow window if we wish to capture one of those mines."

Daspar was unhappy with being rushed. His face flashed a grimace, which she assumed indicated violent outrage, given how tightly he had a lock on his emotions. She could feel his repression, like you could feel the energy of a tight spring just by looking at it. It was a state she was all too familiar with.

Just to provoke him, she played into Stanton's hands. "You're going after a mine?"

Stanton nodded. "Thanks to you, we disabled all seven. Once blind, they went on null trajectories. Capturing one and dissecting it constitutes a level-one military goal. We need to know who did this, how they did it, and what else they can do."

Noticeably missing from his list was "why" someone would do it. But she couldn't really hold it against him. He was Fleet. "Why" wasn't part of his domain.

"You need to get some rescue operations here, too," she reminded him.

"Yes," he agreed, "but that constitutes a level-two humanitarian goal. We don't even have a mutual defense treaty with Kassa."

She ventured a tiny piece of bait. "After this, you might get one."

Reassuringly, he didn't take it. Looking at her with a slight narrowing of eyes, he said, "I don't think that is particularly relevant, Captain Falling. I'm just pointing out that it's not a level-one problem. The populace here is not in immediate danger. My military goal will delay humanitarian aid by no more than a few hours."

"Thank you, Captain Stanton." She let her real gratitude inflect her tone.

He responded with a ghost of a smile. Probably the closest a Fleet officer was allowed by regulations. "I'm offloading what medical supplies we have. I can also offer you two armed guards. You're the only operational vessel on the planet right now, which puts you at an undue risk. Especially while you're flying relief missions for strangers."

No doubt he thought he was being generous. But she didn't want a couple of goons hanging around. "That's not necessary, Captain Stanton. We're known to these people, and we trust them."

"As you wish, Captain. Now, if you'll excuse me." He stood there, waiting to be excused.

"Captain Falling," Daspar said. "My directives do not overlap with Captain Stanton's. I understand your ship is legally registered out of Altair?"

Daspar was reaching into his jacket for papers, terrible papers that would place her ship under Altair's orders, while Stanton waited eagerly. All of Prudence's sympathy for the captain of the

Launceston evaporated. The bastard wasn't being nice to her, he was just happy to get rid of the cop.

"I've busted my ass helping these people," she snapped, "for sixteen hours and no pay. I've dumped a cargo to help them. You are not going to commandeer my ship *now*."

"I have the authority to do so." Daspar tried to hand her the papers. In disgust she knocked them out of his hand, and they fluttered to the ground.

"No," she said, fighting back tears. It felt too much like being trapped, too much like being chained. Too much like losing everything. What the League took, it might never give up again. That was its way.

"Captain, I must insist," Daspar said, and his tone was not what she had expected. Hard, yes, but underneath, something else. Something striving to reach out to her, make her understand. "At least this way you can get paid for your efforts. I can make sure Altair reimburses you, for time lost, for fuel, for expenditures."

Casting about for a way to control her emotional reaction, she thought of what Garcia would say. That mercenary bastard would never let emotion get in the way of money. "For our cargo?"

Daspar paused, thinking. With a little surprise, she realized he was not considering whether or not it was worth it, but whether or not he could pull it off. Not whether she deserved the promise, but whether he had the authority to make it.

"Yes. For your cargo, if it's unrecoverable."

It was a good deal. It was a deal she had to take, both by the law of Altair and by the law of economics. But it still made her insides clench in terror to say the words. "Accepted, Commander."

"Please," he said, "call me Kyle."

They flew hops for another sixteen hours. Kyle used his authority on the refugees, cutting through the sea of complaints to find the ones that needed help now, the ones dying or without water, instead of the merely injured and without food. He browbeat those who had plenty into sharing with those who had nothing, threatened the aggressive and comforted the meek, appointed officers and managers, and assured everyone that Altair Fleet was on its way. With no more than his voice and his badge, he brought order out of chaos.

Prudence would have been impressed, if she had been able to think about anything other than how tired she was.

Standing on the bridge, he watched her fly. The scrutiny made her nervous, vaguely, but the blanket of exhaustion muffled everything.

This was the last trip they would make tonight. An arctic research station had gotten a radio working and called for help. Bombed out of their installation, they would freeze to death soon. They'd already burned what was left of their building for warmth.

Garcia had stayed at the refugee camp, organizing the distribution of supplies. Prudence had cajoled the rest of her crew into one more flight.

"Melvin," she said over the intercom, "give me a heading." They were using the targeting system to home in on the radio signal. Without GPS, it was like finding a snowflake in a blizzard. But GPS depended on global satellites, and those had been the first things destroyed by the attack.

"Left three degrees . . . Wait. There's another one. There's some kind of radio source out there, to starboard. And it's close!" Melvin was exhausted, too. He slipped into panic without any resistance.

"Is it moving, Mel?"

A pause. "No . . . I don't think so."

Kyle was helping Jorgun with his console, working the communications system like an old pro. He'd said the police system wasn't that different. Now he pointed out something Jorgun would have missed. "It's not another colonist. The signal is wrong—it doesn't plug into our comm protocols."

She resented his automatic suspicion. That was her role. "Maybe they jury-rigged a system."

"No," he said, contradicting her without hesitation. "It's too regular. I can't decode it, but it's repeating. It has to be a distress beacon. It has to be one of theirs. The enemy."

Jorgun offered his best to the conversation. "If they're in distress, we should help them. It's the right thing to do."

"They might not want our help, Jorgun." Kyle was surprisingly gentle with him. She hadn't expected that from a man wearing a League armband. "But I agree with you anyway. We should help them into the brig."

"Are you kidding?" said Prudence. "My ship is unarmed." All they had were rifles and handguns.

And the hidden pod of missiles, but Prudence was not about to reveal those. The miswired laser had been a regulations violation. The unregistered missiles were a crime.

"I'm not kidding." His voice was hoarse. He'd spent hours talking, bullying, persuading. "These are the people that did this. They need to be held to account."

"Letting them freeze isn't good enough for you?"

Gray with fatigue, he stared at her.

"No. It's not good enough."

His eyes were like flames behind smoke: hot and black. She recognized the look of stubbornness, the spirit that would not back down. It was like looking into a mirror.

Casually, disguising the action as merely flipping the intercom switch to contact Melvin in his gunnery pod, she began the arming sequence for the missiles. Outside, the hatch panels would slide open; the electronic brains of the missiles would come awake, sniffing for a target, eager to be released on the hunt.

The sound of grating metal was washed away by the windstorm.

"Melvin. Direct us to the new signal."

Melvin argued with her. "Why? Because the tin-horn sheriff says so? Screw that! Screw him."

She was too tired for insubordination, too tired to stroke her crew into doing their jobs. "If you don't, I'll send him up there to take your place."

"Whatever. See if I care." Even while he dismissed her threat, he caved in to it. "Go right, five degrees. And down."

Visual was worthless. The cameras, so finely tuned for empty space, were blinded by whirling flecks of white. They hovered a hundred meters above what the radar claimed was ground, and crawled slowly forward.

"Can we even see it this far up?" Kyle was obsessed.

"They'll see us long before we see them." Prudence kept trying to change his mind, mostly out of habit. She knew she would fail. "What if they shoot us down? It's not just us that dies. That arctic team won't last the night."

"Land a kilometer away and we'll walk in, if you're worried about getting shot at."

It was tempting: the walk would surely kill him, and that would be the end of her problems. But then she almost certainly wouldn't get paid.

"Stop, Pru! You've passed it." Melvin had become conscripted to the cause by sheer curiosity. "Radar says metal, but not ship-sized . . . it's a boat or something."

She sent the ship down, drifting through the white sky. If the enemy hadn't fired yet, they weren't going to.

"How do we know it's not a mine, waiting to explode when some fool comes out to investigate?" she asked. It was the sort of thing a paranoid person would do. Like herself, for instance.

"Nobody would put a trap out here. They would have left it where it would matter." Kyle was looking around, searching for something. "Where's your suit locker?"

"Next to the air lock," she said, trying not to sound too exasperated with his ignorance.

"I'm going out there. If I lose radio contact, take off immediately."

A thrum, deep and distant, sounded in the far recesses of her mind. Her suspicious nature, flaring up despite the exhaustion.

"I'm going with you."

He stared at her, shocked. "Don't be foolish. Send one of your men, if you want. But you can't leave the bridge."

"Can I go, Pru? I want to see it." Jorgun was grinning with simple excitement at seeing something new. How easy it would be for Kyle to pull one over on him, set up whatever trick he'd come all the way out here to prepare.

"We'll all go, Jor. Suit up."

This had to be what Kyle was here for. This had to be what all of this was about.

"What if something happens to you?" Kyle stood in her way, adamant as a wall. "Who else can fly the ship? We'll all freeze out there."

"Then you better not let anything happen to me." She would not let him get away with it. Thousands had died on Kassa, and she was going to find out why.

"You can't tell Pru what to do," Jorgun explained patiently. "She's the captain. She tells us what to do."

"You're being stupid." The anger in Kyle's voice was leaking out.

He wasn't in real danger. In a few weeks, Altair Fleet would be all over this planet. He would be safe on the ship until then—its life support could sustain people in deep space, it could certainly protect them from a blizzard. His Fleet would come and get him. He didn't really need her.

She decided not to point that out.

"If you get off this ship without me," she promised, "you won't get back on it. I'll leave you out there. Take us all, or stay here. Your choice."

He surprised her. Even though she could feel the heat of his anger, he surrendered.

"Fine. Have it your way."

Kyle fit into Garcia's suit, albeit badly. Both men were thick, but in entirely different ways.

Melvin was complaining bitterly, but Prudence ignored him. She wanted as many eyes and guns as she could get around Kyle. She even gave a rifle to Jorgun, although she made sure it was unloaded. He would be useless if Kyle turned on them; but Kyle might not have figured that out yet.

Kyle had brought over two mag rifles from the *Launceston*, military-issue assault weapons. They were vastly more intimidating than her civilian equipment. With the imitation of perfect innocence, he even offered her one.

She accepted, gracefully. When his back was turned, she swapped them, taking the one he had set out for himself.

Her last precaution was to remove the medallion she wore around her neck. It was small, three centimeters across and a millimeter thick, but it was the most valuable thing she owned. Worth more than even the *Ulysses*.

It was the only link she had with her mother. A trinket, passed from mother to daughter, but the one tangible thing that had come from her hand to Prudence's, from her exotic world to the cramped apartment Prudence grew up in.

Reflexively, she squeezed the medallion. It had taken her years to learn the trick, just the right pressures in just the right places. As a child she had struggled for hours a day to master this skill, to be worthy of her mother's gift. Her father could only manage it one try out of ten.

The medallion unfolded in her hand, stretching out into a

handle, and the blade sprung free. Ten centimeters long and as light as a feather, it was the sharpest edge Prudence had ever seen, heard of, or read about. Her father had claimed it was a single molecule thick. It would cut through hardened steel as easily as through water.

A ridiculously dangerous object to give to a child. But her father had trusted her, had known she would treat it with the respect it deserved.

Letting it collapse into a disk again, she dropped it into a pocket of the suit, where she could reach it in a hurry.

"Are we ready?" Kyle was eager, despite his exhaustion.

She responded by punching the air lock release.

FOUR

Discoveries

Standing in the air lock, he checked the magazine on his rifle. Visibly, so she would see him doing it. Letting her know he had a functional weapon might prevent her from trying anything stupid. Her switch-up had been smoothly done, but he'd memorized the serial numbers of both weapons. An old cop habit, born out of the fact that professional-grade weapons imprinted their serial number on every round they fired. Knowing who had shot who was the sort of thing cops liked to know.

Call it lessons from cop school. Making sure everyone knew the consequences of starting a fight was the best way to stop one. Making sure everyone understood they would be held accountable for every shot they fired was the best way to make them shoot carefully.

Of course, that was on Altair, where squads of SWAT goons were a panic button away and forensics teams would pore over every square inch of the crime scene. Out here, on a primitive planet in the middle of an arctic blizzard, the rules might be different.

The lock cycled, exposing them to the outside. The big one, Jorgun, reached up to toggle his helmet mike.

Kyle put out a hand and stopped him. "Radio silence. Don't let them know we're coming." He had to shout over the howling wind. Jorgun nodded, accepting the rebuke without reacting to it.

They trudged outside, sinking up to their knees. Jorgun stared up at the sky, entranced by the swirling patterns of snowflakes. Melvin was hardly more effective, wading clumsily through the snow.

But she slipped out of the lock, alert and aware, her eyes scanning the horizon carefully, looking up to make sure nothing had crept onto the ship above them.

As tired as he was, he found himself grinning. They should have hired a better actress. Instead, they'd sent a special operative to make sure he did whatever it was the League wanted him to do out here. She was good at her job; too good. She'd given herself away with her industrial-strength wariness, the trained habits of the professionally suspicious.

He'd do whatever they wanted, play his part to the hilt. He had to: she wouldn't let him get away with anything less. He just hoped that they wanted something other than him dead.

Gripping the mag rifle, he reflexively glanced at the magazine indicator, checking it again.

They spread out into a short line and struggled ahead. She'd given the handheld locator to Jorgun, so they all followed his lead. At first Kyle had thought that was rather coldhearted of her to put the dumb guy in front. But now he saw why. Following him, she could watch over him while still searching for any threat. If he was behind her, trying to keep track of him would just be a distraction.

She managed her crew like a well-trained team. Which surprised him, given that they clearly weren't operatives themselves. The big one might be putting on an act, pretending to be stupid, but the other one, Melvin, was just plain clueless. Nobody could act that vacuous.

Jorgun was going too fast. The giant plowed through the snow, his eyes locked on his locator unit, unaware that no one could keep up. Kyle flipped up his faceplate to yell at him, but the wind whistled in and drowned his shout. He pushed harder against the snow, but the giant was leaving them behind.

Kyle started thinking about breaking radio silence. It would be better than losing anyone out here in this blizzard. The suits were rated for the cold of space, but that was when they were insulated by the vacuum. He could feel his feet going numb as the clinging snow leached the heat out. A few hours out here would be fatal.

Something flew past him. Instinctively he dropped, spinning to see where it had come from, bringing the rifle to his shoulder.

Prudence was making another snowball. She glanced at him curiously before throwing it. This time her aim was better, and it hit Jorgun in the back of the head.

The giant turned around, and Prudence made a very simple hand signal. Kyle could guess it meant "slow."

It was too simple. No operative would have such an obvious combat signal. No self-respecting soldier would have charged off without checking on the rest of his team in the first place. It was almost like they were just ordinary people, just a ragtag crew under a young but fiercely determined captain.

Kyle had not survived this long by taking things at face value. There was always a hidden catch, always another angle. There had been a time when he trusted people, but then he'd become a cop. Now he just assumed the hook was there, and didn't stop searching until he found it. So far, he'd never been disappointed.

He looked back reflexively, checking behind, and froze. They couldn't have gone more than fifty meters, but the ship was already hidden in white-flecked gray emptiness.

Rapping the rifle against his helmet made a metallic clink that carried through the wind. Prudence heard, glancing over to see what his problem was. Pointing the way they had come, he shrugged a question.

She waved a hand, dismissing his fear, and kept moving.

Damn, but she was a cool one.

Up ahead, Jorgun had stopped. He stood like a tree, the most visible element in the landscape. Melvin floundered up to him and stopped, at the edge of a crater, staring down.

Prudence came close enough to touch helmets, the old spacer's trick. He could hear her through the vibration of her faceplate on his. "Looks like they found something."

Even through the weather, the suits, the plexiglass of the faceplate, his body thrilled at the intimate proximity. She was beautiful, in a thin, unusual way, but that wasn't it. He'd been close to pretty women before.

It was her attitude, her deep confidence masked by extreme caution. She thought about everything before she did it, treated every act like a carefully chosen move in a chess game. It was a way of life he had learned to embrace, once he had gone undercover against the League. A game where one wrong move could spell detection, disaster, and death.

He wondered if the stakes were as high for her as they were for him.

She was waiting for him, patiently. Waiting until he realized he had to go first. She already had committed her crew. She couldn't join them, stand there in a tight knot where a single burst of autofire could kill them all.

So he had to go up there. He had to put himself at risk. And if the crew were just mooks, if they were expendables hired to die with him, whose only role was to get him to commit himself, then he would be dead in the next thirty seconds. Either the enemy lying in wait would blast him out of existence, or she would cut him down with a spray of needle-sized bullets from the mag rifle he'd given her.

Regretfully, he wished he'd only borrowed one rifle from the *Launceston*.

He didn't have a choice. He had become used to doing things without choices, but it was difficult to pull away from her, to have to walk forward without seeing her face. If he was going to die, he wanted to see the face of the person who killed him. Or maybe he just wanted to see *her* face. Too tired to puzzle out the difference, he trudged forward mechanically, continuing on his chosen course long after he'd forgotten why he'd chosen it.

When he got up to where the other two were standing, he knew he was going to live. The wreckage in front of him changed everything.

The ship was small, no more than ten meters long. Battered and cracked like a child's toy dropped from the sky, but still in one piece. It looked like a bizarrely elongated snowflake: six fat tubes stacked together hexagonally on the inside, and outside a ring of six thin tubes. At the rear was what had to be a fusion nozzle. At the front was a glass pod, like a huge insect eye, multifaceted and staring, shattered on one side. The vessel was still and quiet, but it radiated menace.

Not the menace of a warship, even though it almost certainly was one. The *Launceston* was far more intimidating, with its bristling gunports and racks of missiles. But the *Launceston* was solid and sleek, every surface polished and smooth. This ship was like a spider web's nightmare, the struts and spars that held it together as gnarled and lumpy as wood, unsettlingly organic in their texture.

Alien.

The word came to mind, unwelcome but undeniable. The ship in front of them shrieked it in the sheer incomprehensibility of its design.

In all the centuries since Earth, on all the planets and moons intrepid explorers found and conquered, mankind had never met its equal. Or even the equal of an ant colony. Life was common enough: simple bacteria, plants, the occasional mollusk. But nothing organized. Nothing *social*.

Man stood alone as a sentient race, looking into the mirror of the universe and seeing only his own reflection. A miracle without explanation, a blessing of no competition or a curse of loneliness, depending on your point of view. Was it improbable that no other planet had been climatically stable enough long enough to make society, or was the improbability that Earth had? Philosophers argued, scientists washed their hands of the insolvable, and ordinary people relaxed in the knowledge that the closet was empty: there was no bogeyman hiding in the dark.

But here the broken eye of alien intelligence stared back at him. And it was hostile. First Contact had come in the form of a lethal attack.

Jorgun shouted above the wind, childish wonder in his voice. "Who made that?"

A fine question, even if the answer was obvious: *not us*. But Kyle's mind was obsessed with a different question. A subtle question, one that an untrained or merely unsuspicious mind might have overlooked.

Who had given the League that anonymous tip? The one that had sent him out here, on a twelve-day trip, just in time to discover an attack seven days old.

The tip had been given before the attack had taken place.

Someone human knew this attack was going to happen. Someone human had sent him out here to discover the aftermath. Someone human knew the answer to Jorgun's question. And they weren't sharing.

Prudence had come up behind him, and was staring down at the wreck. He studied her face carefully. But the operative was gone, replaced by a frightened young woman. She glared back at him accusingly, demanding that his badge and his authority make sense of the tragedy that lay in front of them. The same look so many victims had given him over the years. No actress could fake that heartbroken glare, that shattered innocence, that instinctive need for someone to explain how ordinary life had suddenly become nightmare. He'd nailed a dozen murderers simply because they had failed this test. When confronted with the body, they could fake the loss, the grief, the sorrow, but they couldn't fake the outrage that their predictable world no longer made sense. They could pretend to lament the deceased, but not the death of meaning.

She didn't know the answer.

"Fucking aliens." Melvin screamed over the blizzard. "Aliens! Pru, what the hell are we gonna do?"

"Is it the Dog-Men of Ophiuchi Seven? Because I thought their ships were shaped like giant wolves." Jorgun was talking about some space-opera comic show that ran on the low-grade entertainment channels. From a normal man, Kyle would have suspected irrationality born of fear; from a clever mind, satire from much the same source. But Jorgun's voice was smooth and even. Of all the people here, he was the only one who did not shudder. Protected by his Zen-like innocence, while the rest of them teetered on the brink of the unthinkable.

"This isn't a fucking vid show, you idiot!" Melvin's outrage didn't sting. It wasn't directed at Jorgun, but at the alien ship, the war-shattered colony, the entire universe itself. Even the simpleminded giant could tell that. He didn't flinch, but just asked his next question, obviousness having been transformed into insight by the impossibility of the scene.

"Are you sure? It feels like a vid show."

Yes, Kyle thought, it did. It felt like one of those prank shows, where people were put in ridiculous situations and secretly filmed for their comedic reactions.

Except a lot of people had died to set up this gag.

Prudence's voice was carefully neutral. "What *are* we going to do, Commander?" She watched him patiently, wearing a ghost of a smirk, challenging his authority, mocking his confusion, demanding that he lead, follow, or get out of the way.

The men who ran the League would mark her out for that, put her name on the list of Undesirables. The list of people to silence, while they took control. The people to make disappear, once they had it.

That list that was already too short, depopulated not by threats and subterfuge, but by bribery and innate laziness. Sometimes he wondered if anyone would notice when the League finally won and seized absolute power. If the price of a vid and a beer didn't go up, would they even care?

Prudence was an attitude he had stopped expecting to find. Complacency was easy on a rich world like Altair. Looking the other way when the price of looking deeper got too high. Letting someone else take care of things because they'd always done such a good job of it before.

In the presence of her piercing eyes, entranced by the shapely lips that almost smiled but not quite, trembling as if they could burst into laughter or disdain at any instant, he could not stop his mask from slipping. He spoke honestly, from the heart, without calculation.

"We're going to go down there and take a closer look."

Like he could trust her; like she was on his side. Always it was "I" or "the Department" or "the League." Never "we." Never himself and another, partners and equals, peer to peer.

A subtle slip, but his life had become a pirouette on the razor's edge, and subtlety had become the only flavor left.

Trudging down the crater's edge to the alien ship, he resolved not to make any more mistakes.

Melvin screamed something, but the wind took it.

Kyle turned his helmet mike on. "No point in radio silence now, people. But consider this a crime scene. Don't touch anything. Do I make myself clear?"

Melvin's voice rattled in his ear. "We're not bio-sealed! How do you know it's safe?"

Prudence answered, the voice of spacer wisdom. "Melvin, we can't get sick from aliens. For crying out loud, we can't even eat native plants."

Everything the human race had, they'd brought with them from Earth, or made since then. Life was a complex orchestra, and one wrong note made it incompatible. It wasn't just the molecular composition of proteins: it was the shape they folded into. Sometimes the local flora was poisonous, but usually it was just inert, like eating cardboard. The dreaded space-plague was a feature of science fiction, not reality.

Kyle added his own reasoning, trying to reassert control from that one foolish moment he'd let it slip. "If they had a biological attack vector, they would have already used it. None of the colonists were dying from disease."

Even while he spoke, a thousand warnings rattled through his mind. There were so many ways this could end in death: automated defense systems, a wounded but still living pilot, a booby trap, or just industrial hazard. What if the fuel source was toxic? What if the ship was on fire, internally, and about to explode? What about radiation?

He worried about these things, but he didn't stop walking. Curiosity and the proverbial cat. Thinking about cats made him think about Prudence, so delicate and reserved in repose, but feral in movement.

He turned to look at her, coming down the slope after him with Jorgun in tow.

"The locator doesn't read any signal other than the distress beacon," she said over the radio. "There's no distortion in our communications. And the snow hasn't melted. This wreck is cold."

She had done more than just think about the dangers. She had looked for them.

"Good," he said, because he couldn't think of anything else to say.

"Quite brave of you to assume it was safe." She was mocking him again.

"No, it was stupid. I'm tired. Don't let me make any more stupid mistakes."

Melvin was still standing at the top of the crater, holding a rifle. She wasn't making mistakes.

"This whole expedition is stupid," she told him. Floundering in the snow, she leaned on the big Jorgun for support, let him help her through the drifts. Kyle was seized with a completely unreasonable pang of jealousy.

"Then why are you down here?" he asked.

The two of them had caught up to him, close enough that he could see her face.

"I had friends here," she said softly.

"I have friends on Altair," he answered. Not that it was strictly true. He had comrades, acquaintances, and enemies. But he was loyal to Altair's millions of citizens in the abstract, in the sense of duty to the innocent, even if he wasn't personally attached to any of them as individuals. "Imagine Altair like this. Imagine fifty million targets, not fifty thousand."

"You have a fleet."

She put a lot more stock in Fleet than he did.

"Altair would be down by one patrol boat if it weren't for your assistance. Unless you're volunteering to be admiral, I'm not sure we should rely on Fleet."

Jorgun laughed. "Admiral Prudence! Does that mean I get to be a captain?"

Kyle wanted to laugh with him. The image of this slight young woman in full regalia shouting at lines of hardened spacers was incongruous. But the facts were more incongruous.

How had Prudence known how to defeat the mines?

She returned his suspicion. "I can't take the credit. I'm sure you would have figured it out on your own." Suave, even dismissive.

She had saved his life, and he couldn't even thank her for it, because she thought he was playing a game. That he was pretending to have asked for help, to make a radio record that looked like he hadn't already known what to expect.

But that was absurd. The League would never broadcast its own incompetence as a cover-up. How could she be so sophisticated but not understand that basic fact? Unless she was playing deep, making cover stories for herself. If she kept accusing him of conspiracy, it meant she wasn't the conspirator.

He closed his eyes in weariness. Too much double-dealing, too many possibilities and secrets. Over the years it had worn at him, grinding him down, stripping away everything that was not deception or counterdeception. Here, in the presence of aliens and beauty, in the shadow of violence and strength, it was too much.

He envied Jorgun. For the giant, everything was as it seemed. Too stupid to be suspicious, he could trust—and be trusted. No wonder Prudence had picked him. The perfect tool for the perfect operative.

"Are you all right?" She managed to make her voice sound like real concern.

"I'm tired." In so many ways. "Let's see if there's a body."

The three of them cautiously advanced on the shattered cockpit. Well, the two of them. Jorgun strode up to it eagerly, while Prudence and Kyle followed.

"Don't touch anything," he warned the giant again.

Jorgun peered inside, and shook his head. "I don't think this is a Dog-Man ship."

Kyle pushed up against Jorgun, trying to gently shove him out of the way. He might as well have pushed on a tree. Instead, he settled for slipping in front, and leaned his helmet forward to stare into the alien vessel.

Again, Jorgun asked the simple and the obvious. "Where does the pilot sit?"

There wasn't a chair. The cockpit was a welter of unfamiliar dials and levers all along the edges, but there was no central chair.

"Maybe he doesn't sit." Prudence reached with her hand, inside.

"Don't touch anything," Kyle repeated automatically. Like she was a child. Or a green recruit.

She didn't bother to retort to his pettiness. "Put your hand in there, Commander."

Chastised, he did so. Their arms together, hands almost touching.

"What do you *not* feel?" she asked.

Dumbly, he shook his head. What he wanted to feel was her hand in his, her warmth and smoothness. But through the insulation of the suit, he couldn't feel anything at all.

"That's right. No grav field." She seemed to think that was significant. Maybe to a spacer, it was.

But Kyle saw something that was significant to a cop.

A blue stain, on the cockpit floor. On the glass. More on the control panel resting on the snow.

"Who flies without passive grav-plating? Even in a tactical craft." Prudence was shaking her head in disbelief.

"Who has blue blood?" Kyle asked her, pointing to the stains.

She stared down at the little patches of color, silenced.

Jorgun had been thinking his own thoughts. Now he leaned over both of them, reached deep into the cockpit, grabbed part of the floor, and pushed.

It spun, floating freely, a wheel within a wheel. An outer track remained stable, and in the contrast, the pattern leaped out at them.

Eight resting places. Eight kickplates. Eight legs.

Kyle glared at the big man, his suspicion flaring out of control. How could simpleness have seen what they had missed?

Prudence explained, her eyes sparking with secondhand pride. "That's what he does, Commander. He sees patterns. That's why he's on my crew. He can plot a multihop course more efficiently than a computer. They used to call it idiot savant. He's not stupid. He's just wired different than the rest of us."

"Like you told me, Pru, we all have our own special talents." Jorgun smiled.

"Tell me what you see, Jor."

Kyle could tell from her voice that she already knew the answer. But she was letting him go as far as he could. Pushing him gently.

"Eight." Jorgun announced, but then fell silent. That was all it meant to him, but Prudence nodded in agreement.

"Eight places to put your feet. Whoever flew this ship had eight feet. The absence of passive grav-plating tells us they don't suffer from inertial sickness. And that they're strong—that fusion nozzle must be capable of at least two or three G acceleration. They could stand up through that acceleration, spinning around, looking for visual contact—that's why there's so much glass. Which tells us they have impossibly good eyesight, too."

"Who has eight feet?" Jorgun asked, confused.

"Nobody we know," she said.

"Fleet needs to see this." Kyle found himself hoping that authority would know what to do about it.

"The *okimune* needs to see this." Prudence used the old word for the collective human realm, the sum total of civilization, wherever and whatever it might be. A normal person would have said "the world," meaning his own planet; a sophisticated person would have said "Altair," the biggest society around. But Prudence thought in wider terms. Like an outsider.

For the first time in his life, Kyle felt provincial, a country rube fresh off the farm. The feeling wasn't pleasant, but the novelty of it was astounding.

"Fleet first," he said. "We can't just put this on the evening news. Can you imagine the panic?"

"Maybe people should be panicking."

He stared at her. "How would that help?"

She waved her hand, in no particular direction, indicating the ruined world around them. "How did this help?"

"Running scared won't make it better. You know that." Was this their plan? To plunge every world within a hundred hops into mindless terror? Oppression always followed fear, like rain after the lightning. He'd studied enough history to know that.

"We don't know that, Commander. We have no idea what we are up against. This wreck could be the blow that frightened them off, made them retreat in such a rush they only stopped to grab the pilot. Or it could be such an inconsequential prick that they haven't even noticed it's missing yet. Maybe running scared is the only thing anybody can do. Maybe Altair is already dead."

"What about Jelly?" Jorgun's face was creased with worry and concern. The death of civilizations meant nothing to him, only the death of individuals. Kyle was struck by the difference. There were no individuals for him to mourn. Only the ideal of community, not the fact of it.

"I'm sorry, Jor. We haven't found her yet. I don't think we will." She broke the news to him while he had this shiny new toy to distract him, like a mother to a child.

The giant puzzled over her words, his lower lip trembling, but he did not cry. Like a boy trying to be a man. Kyle started to reach out to comfort him. Like a father, he stopped.

Let the boy show his strength. Let him grow into it.

"Did they take her?" Jorgun asked. "Did they take Jelly?"

But this child would never grow any taller.

"No, Jorgun." Kyle used his most reassuring voice. "They didn't take her. They didn't take anyone." There had been no reports of sightings from any of the refugees. The attackers had been as insubstantial as ghosts. Bombs from the sky, but no follow-up; destruction, but no looting.

It was inhuman. But that was the point.

"I'm fucking freezing up here." Melvin, complaining again over the radio. "What the fuck are we gonna do?"

"Can you fit this in the cargo bay?" It was the first thing Kyle could think of.

Prudence stared at him. "How? We don't have any loaders here. Are you going to fly it in? And then fix my ship when it decides to melt down or self-destruct?"

"If it blows up in the ship, wouldn't that be bad?" Jorgun didn't get sarcasm.

"We can't leave it here. If this beacon turns off, how the hell can we find it again?" Kyle waved his hands at the blizzard. It was getting worse. In a few hours the alien ship would be buried under clean white snow. The evidence would be lost. A cop's worst nightmare.

"That's not my problem." Prudence cradled the rifle, like its weight was unfamiliar in her hands. "If your Fleet can't find one dead fighter craft on a planet's surface, what good will they be against a host of live ones?"

That wasn't the point. He was sure Fleet had the ability to find this ship again, if they really wanted to. It might take days or weeks, but they could just scan the entire continent with short radar.

The point was that he didn't know if he could convince them to try. What if they didn't take him seriously? What if they brushed him off as delusional? A snow-vision by an exhausted cop, a flighty girl, and a simpleton.

"Screw Fleet. What if those aliens come back and find us?" And a paranoid stoner. Even filtered through the helmet speakers, Melvin's whine was annoying.

Kyle would be laughed out of the prosecutor's office if this was all he could offer in a criminal trial. Altair Fleet would need half as much reason to ignore a League officer.

While he was trying to think of another plan, he saw her move.

Subtly, out of the corner of his eye, the casual swing of her hand. But she was dropping something in her pocket, not the other way around. She was taking, not leaving.

He let it slide. Better not to confront her now, in the snow, with her men and so many guns. Better not to let her know he knew at all.

"Then what do you suggest?" he said, giving her the chance to advance whatever plot she and her unknown bosses were trying so hard to make happen.

"That arctic research station has a transmitter. If we give them a ride out, maybe they'll let you have it. And we can drop it off here on our way."

"What if the beacon fails in the next five minutes?"

"We can have the autopilot backtrack by dead reckoning. For a short trip, it should get us close enough."

She'd prepared for everything. Shown him just enough, channeled his every step. He could wreck her plans, search her pockets and seize whatever she'd had to steal to make this whole scheme fly.

But she probably had a plan for that eventuality, too, and it might require his being dead. Better to play along for now.

Like he always did.

"Okay, Captain. We'll do it your way."

FIVE

Records

He was so passive it was scary. At every turn he let her suggest the solution, and went along with it. How could anybody have predicted her actions so well?

It was almost like he wasn't following a master plan, but just winging it.

Watching him with Jorgun, she wanted to believe that. His gentleness was born out of respect, not pity. She could not reconcile his behavior with the armband he wore and its rhetoric of perfection. Kyle Daspar was a cargo bay of contradictions, and it bothered her.

But she didn't dare stir the pot. These people played for keeps, and they already had their claws into her ship. She had to keep her head down, play stupid, and hope they forgot about her.

What she had done out there, at the wreck, had been foolish. He might have seen. But she couldn't walk away from the most fantastic artifact in human history empty-handed, not when she expected bureaucratic security clearances to bury it more effectively than any mere blizzard could.

One quick flip of her nanosharp blade, and a sliver of glass with a smudge of the strange blue blood was in her hand. They wouldn't miss it. Nobody would put the shattered cockpit glass back together to find the missing puzzle piece. Even if they did, they would just assume it had been lost in the snow.

Let them put on their stage show. She would play whatever part they wanted, and wait until they shooed her off for the main act. She had her own breadcrumb now. She could pick up the trail after they stopped watching her.

Cycling through the air lock, she took off her helmet and breathed the warm, familiar air of her own ship.

"How long before we're airborne?" Kyle was in a hurry.

She was, too. "Thirty seconds after the air lock door opens." The sooner they got to the end of this charade, the sooner she could get him off her ship.

And out of her life. She didn't like his contradictions. She didn't like the way part of her kept wanting to trust him, to turn to him for support. She didn't like the way his unflappable confidence laid over constant tension, like a tiger perpetually ready to pounce even while it purred. She didn't like the way it made her feel.

Not because it made her nervous. But because it made her lonely.

Unzipping the suit, she encountered a problem. How to empty the suit pocket without his noticing? And she couldn't leave it here—he could come back and search the suit locker while she was on the bridge.

The instant she paused, he turned away. Like he was giving her privacy to undress. It was silly. It was just a space suit, and in any case, spacers hardly expected privacy even for showers. Ships were just too small for such formalities.

It was silly, but it was also touching. Again it sparked uncomfortable feelings. She wasn't used to being treated like a woman. She was used to being treated like a captain.

It was easy to pocket the sliver of glass while his back was turned. So easy she almost felt guilty.

"Liftoff in thirty. Be ready," she snapped at her crew. Running down the passageway, retreating to her citadel of power, where she could mask her feelings in the necessity of command. Where she could be in control again.

"Melvin, get a reading on that arctic station." Barking over the intercom while she powered up the gravitics. The ship felt heavy under her fingers, the weight of snow tangible.

"It's not working. Fuck, something's wrong. Somebody sabotaged the radar!" Melvin slipped back into panic. Maybe he'd never left.

"Calm down, Melvin. It's probably just ice clogging the detector vanes. We'll go orbital and let it cook off." The boiling point of water in a vacuum was zero. Latent heat from the vanes would melt the ice, and space would do the rest. They could go straight up without losing their position, and then come back down to find the arctic station. A few minutes above the atmosphere and the *Ulysses* would shake off the touch of the planet.

But space had its own touch. As soon as they were clear of the sheltering blanket of air, the comm beeped insistently.

"*Ulysses*, confirm. This is the *Phoenix*, hailing the vessel *Ulysses*."

The *Phoenix* didn't have to identify itself. The comm station did that, signaling in large red letters that it was an Altair Fleet cruiser.

"Fleet's finally here," Prudence muttered, and put her hand on the comm switch.

"Wait." Kyle's voice leapt across the bridge to stop her.

Turning in her chair to face him, she waited.

"Don't tell them about seeing the alien ship."

What kind of game was this? Why show her the evidence, and then tell her to keep quiet? Surely her role in their plot was to validate the alien attack. She would play the straight man, the hardened spacer veteran on the evening news talking with wide-eyed excitement about the aliens. An independent witness, interested only in the truth. A seed of rumor, spreading fear and panic.

And now Kyle warned her to silence?

"They'll interrogate you. This whole thing's a cluster fuck, Prudence. There's dead people everywhere, and an impossible alien warship. Nobody knows what to do. So they'll do everything. They'll impound your ship, strip search it for clues, and lock your crew in a holding cell for a month. I don't think you want that."

It wasn't about what she wanted. It was about what she feared. Jorgun would be putty in their hands, manipulated to whatever ends they needed, broken and discarded when they were done. And none of her crew were citizens of Altair. Fleet wouldn't be particularly concerned about their legal rights.

If they started asking questions about the *Ulysses*, what would she tell them? That a dying old man had given a young girl a starship, charmed by nothing more than the romance of her quest to seek out her mother's world?

She had survived this long by going unnoticed. She was certain her future depended on it. But why would Kyle know that? Why would he care?

"Let me get this straight. You want me to lie to Altair Fleet?"

"Not lie, exactly. Just don't tell them everything. There's nothing in it for you, Prudence. Direct them to the signal. Let them find it themselves."

She stared at him. He was as close to unnerved as she could imagine him being.

Flicking on the comm, she answered Fleet's call. "This is the *Ulysses*, responding to the *Phoenix*. How can we help you?"

There was a pause, as if that simple response had confused them.

A different voice on the speaker. More nasal, and laden with the expectation of obedience. "You can start by explaining what's going on down there." Not a spacer's voice. Apparently, commandeering ships was in season.

Prudence flicked a glance at Kyle and was startled to see his anger. He obviously recognized that voice, and he didn't like it.

"There's been some kind of attack, *Phoenix*. A week ago. We've been in-system for about thirty-six hours, and running relief operations for most of that. Any assistance you can render would be greatly appreciated." She shouldn't have said that, shouldn't have baited the unknown authority on the other end of the line with her dry sarcasm. But the look on Kyle's face paid for it. He almost smiled.

Subconsciously, she'd known he would. That's why she'd done it. In the sixteen hours they had spent together, he had been scrupulous about not flirting with her. She'd never been around a man, single, married, or homosexual, that hadn't risked at least one bantering comment for her approval. And now she was performing for his.

Deeply annoyed at herself, she returned to business.

"You didn't get a message from the *Launceston?*" But of course not. The timing was wrong. They would have passed in node-space, silenced by the inflexible laws of relativity.

The voice changed direction, avoiding the question. "*Ulysses,* put your captain on the line."

Prudence had dealt with this a thousand times, but it never got any easier.

"This is Captain Prudence Falling, owner and operator of the *Ulysses.*" Straining to keep the annoyance out of her voice, all she achieved was to drive the irony deeper.

But the voice didn't care. It was immune to subtleties. "Captain, we are on an important diplomatic mission to Bierze, and we can't be diverted. Give us some GPS coordinates to rendezvous and we'll transfer our medical supplies and staff."

She answered without thinking. "*Phoenix,* this planet is in shambles. There's nothing left standing but hungry, scared people. Whatever stuffed-suit meeting you're rushing to can wait."

Too tired. Making mistakes, losing control of her feelings. Kyle was part of the problem. She wanted to hate him as much as she hated his armband, but he wouldn't let her.

Now he stepped up to save her. The voice had just begun squawking, working itself up to a fine outrage, when he walked over to her console and put his finger on the transmit button.

"This is Police Lieutenant Kyle Daspar, command leader of the League. I have the honor of addressing District Leader Rassinger, do I not?"

Miraculous silence from the comm. Then curiosity, although it tried to hide under polished indifference. "Daspar? How are—what are you doing out here?"

"We're not on a secure line, Leader, so with your permission I'll spare you the details. I came out here on some League business, but that's obviously been superseded by what's happened."

Prudence blinked her eyes, jolted by yet another facet of the enigmatic Kyle Daspar. She would never have imagined such diplomacy from that jutting jaw. She could not reconcile those proud eyes with this bureaucratic subservience.

"What are you doing right now, Command Leader? What is your current status?"

"I've commandeered the *Ulysses,* and we are on a polar flight to rescue some research station personnel. However, there is a matter that I feel might exceed my competence, and I would appreciate your advice, Leader."

Prudence stared at him. He looked like he meant it. The act was perfect, his sincerity unquestionable. If she had not seen him at the alien wreck—if she had not seen his confusion, anger, and gentleness—she would have been convinced.

But she had. And now she could not guess what this role-playing was costing him. How could his spirit survive, buried under that? Under the weight of the League.

Carefully, she pulled herself back from the edge. She had seen many strange things in her short life. She had learned that appearances can be deceiving, on every level. Kyle Daspar might be exactly what he seemed: a true believer. A person whose soul was given over to a higher power, allowing him to be a man at one moment and a slave at the next, without even noticing the change.

In this case the higher power would be more odious than most, but in her experience, it never really mattered what you sold your soul to. In the end the result was always the same.

"What is this situation, Daspar? Are you sure it's that important?" Rassinger's voice wrestled with itself. In the space of a single vowel, she could tell the man was annoyed at Kyle's urbane competence, but unable to find a reason to complain.

"We have located an anomalous signal, Leader. It's deep in the arctic circle, and the research staff assures us they have no teams or equipment in that sector. It's possible that it could be an artifact of the enemy. If so, that would constitute a level-one military goal, which would supersede my current mission. Should I divert from the rescue mission to investigate this signal?"

The answer was quick—too quick.

"No, Daspar, do not divert. If it really is a level-one priority, then it supersedes our own mission. I'll take the *Phoenix* and investigate. Can you give us a coordinate for that signal?"

Kyle paused, looked at Prudence. So he was going to let her help. If she played her cards right, uber-leader Rats-ass would not remember her earlier slip, only her useful assistance afterward.

She leaned over the microphone. "I'm afraid not, sir. Without GPS satellites, we're operating off of dead reckoning. But I can transmit a solar vector. Your nav officer should be able to get close with that, and we can tell you what frequency to look for once you're in the area."

The pause was brief, but long enough to confirm that Rassinger was no spacer. He was waiting for someone to verify her words.

"That will be acceptable, Captain. How close to this signal did you get?"

No pretense, no lure, just a straight-up trap. It was like a hangman tying a noose and casually asking how much you weighed.

"We're really pressed for time and resources, sir, and my crew is pulling its fourth straight shift. We just want to bail this research crew out and get some sleep."

Only after the weaseling misdirection had left her mouth did she realize how much like Kyle she sounded.

Rassinger was satisfied. "Understood, Captain. We'll take care of it."

And that was that. The biggest find of human existence, the greatest discovery since fire and the wheel, was out of her hands. Scooped up by a politician who would use it to boost his repulsive career. And she had Kyle Daspar to thank for it.

So why did she feel so relieved?

They finished the run in silence. Even Melvin was quiet, speaking only enough to guide her into the research station. It wasn't entirely due to the subtle menace of the *Phoenix* and its tyrannical commander. While his authority was frightening, it was also a relief. Let him deal with the alien problem.

The *Ulysses*'s mission had been reduced to rescuing the research personnel, and the crew was tired enough to be glad of it.

"Attention, arctic station, we are coming in for landing," Prudence announced over the radio. "Please look up and let us know if we're about to squash anything important."

"It's *Station Zebra*." The voice on the other end was difficult, like a child on the edge of a tantrum. Prudence was weary of faceless voices.

"What the Earth are you talking about? No, don't tell me, I don't care. Get outside and walk us in."

"*Station Zebra*. That's our call sign. It's a tradition. Arctic stations are always called *Station Zebra*."

What was a zebra? She almost asked, before remembering she didn't care. "Coming down now. Last chance to back us off."

She let the ship drop, perhaps faster than prudence dictated. But only the soft thump of snow crunching under the skids sounded through the ship.

"Go ahead, Jorgun," she said over the intercom. He and Kyle were already suited up and waiting at the air lock.

Flipping to a different channel, she addressed Melvin in his gunnery room. "Melvin, you have the bridge. Don't let anybody on unless I'm with them."

Words she could never have imagined uttering. Turning her ship over to Melvin. It was possibly more unnerving than the discovery of the alien spaceship.

But nothing grated her nerves as much as Kyle Daspar. She could not fathom his game. That he was playing one was obvious; but every stone she cast into its depths disappeared without a trace. His appearance on the scene had been remarkably well timed, except for the mines that would have killed him. His armband gave him the authority of intimidation, even on Kassa, but he had only used it to create order. And then leading them to the alien ship, only to turn it over to Rassinger.

She could not make sense of it. That's why she was crawling into a space suit, following him and Jorgun out into the snow again. To keep an eye on him. Not knowing what to look for, all she could do was watch his every move.

Outside it was cold, even worse than before. The snow-covered wreck of a building was bleak and sorrowful when it should have promised warmth and safety. She had been outside in space a thousand times and never felt this cold.

Movement caught her eye. Thankfully the blizzard had not reached here yet, so she could see something other than snowflakes. Jorgun was waving to her.

Trudging over to the collapsed wall he stood beside, she looked down to see what he had found. A door in the ground. Freshly moved.

"Kyle went down there," he said. Somewhat unnecessarily, since two men's tracks led here, and none led away.

"Let's join him," she suggested.

"I was waiting for you. I wanted to open the door for you."

At some point Jorgun had latched on to this old romanticism, and he used it whenever he could. Jelly had found it ridiculously cute when Jorgun would run ahead to open even automatic doors for her.

The remembrance pained Prudence. Biting her lip, she could only nod and wait while Jorgun pulled on the heavy steel door.

Steps down, into a dark basement. She wished she'd brought a gun. Spiders lived underground, in caves and tunnels. What if the pilot of the alien vessel had sought refuge here?

A flicker of light in the distance, a cry of pain. She started to back up the stairs, and collided with Jorgun coming down.

"Kyle went ahead," Jorgun said, his voice booming in the darkness. He stepped past her, moving forward.

She tugged at his arm. He had walked into danger for her enough times on this run.

"Jorgun, wait," she whispered, but he pulled out of her grasp and went on, oblivious.

"Kyle went ahead," he repeated, and then he disappeared into the murk.

More light from across the room: Jorgun's great frame outlined in the flashes. A woman was sobbing somewhere. Hushed murmurs as the people hiding with her tried to silence her.

Prudence remembered hiding in the dark, from monsters. Monsters that wore a human face, but were inhumane: once people but now possessed by a foul spirit that had dogged man's footsteps even from Earth, followed men and women into the Out, hiding in their shadows until indifference and contempt gave it form.

Creatures of unreason, immune to pity, compassion, or even bribery, who fed their neighbors into the machinery of insanity.

And Jorgun walked into it, unaware, unheeding. Prudence tried to call out to him but her voice died in her throat, strangled by helplessness, by the certain knowledge that nothing she could do could save anyone but herself. The walls rushed in and Prudence's world shrank, spinning in shades of black, and the fire at the end of the hall flared hungrily into life, like it always did in her nightmares, again and again and again.

"Jorgun, grab that corner. Have you got it?"

The sheer normality in Kyle's voice was disorienting. In her world of madness, upside down and inside out was escape, and she let it wash over her. Blood pounded in her temples, and the vision passed.

Jorgun was backing up, his arms full. "I can carry her. I'm strong."

"Keep the blanket on her. Keep her warm, man! She's lost too much blood." The voice from the transmitter, shrill with exhaustion and urgency.

"It's a short trip." Kyle, being reassuring.

Brilliant light swept the room, disappeared. The beam on Kyle's helmet, revealing her before he aimed it down to spare her eyes. "Prudence! Come give us a hand."

Feeling foolish, she reached up and flicked on her own head lamp. The eerie darkness dissolved into a thoroughly trashed storage room. Jorgun was carrying a woman wrapped in gray cloth. A white-haired man hobbled behind him, cloaked in gray and leaning on Kyle's shoulder.

She advanced into the room, met them halfway.

"There's three more. We're coming back for them once we get Dr. Sanders onboard, and can spare these drapes." Kyle, being in charge, as usual. But then he paused and narrowed his eyes. "Are you all right?"

"I'm fine." She was, now. "Just tired. Go on, I'll watch the others."

Grateful for the escape, she turned away and headed into the sheltering alcove at the far side of the room.

They had built a fire, but it was dead now. Two young women stood, trying not to shiver, while a handsome young man stretched out on the ground and tried to be macho. His leg was bound in strips of clothing. He looked up at Prudence, and flashed a pained smile.

"No thanks, I'll wait for the big guy. Looks like a smoother ride."

The girls giggled.

"Thank God you're here," said one of the girls. Tall and willowy, with long blond hair and an incongruous tan.

Prudence pointed at the man's leg. "What happened?"

He looked up at her in mild surprise. "A building fell on me. Why, what did you think? A skiing accident?"

Prudence had still been thinking of giant spiders.

"Did you see anything?"

"No," the other girl said. "We woke up in the middle of the night when the station blew up. We ran to the basement, because it was the only thing not on fire. When we got here, Fletcher noticed Dr. Sanders and Dr. Williams were missing, so he went back up for them." She was shorter, plumper, and much more composed than the other girl.

"Did you find Williams?" Prudence was surprised at her own hardness, but the presence of the alien ship made every fact matter.

"Not until two days later," Fletcher said. "The radar array was directly above his quarters. The bomb took out the main support column . . . Well, anyway, we were stripping the meshing from the dishes to make blankets. After the first few layers, we found him."

"That's how Fletcher got hurt." The blonde again. "Trying to reach Dr. Williams."

"I went down after him, but something shifted. Then the

building . . . well, you know that part." Fletcher grinned, telling his story of danger and sacrifice winsomely.

The blond girl filled in the heroic details. "Fletcher had to climb out all by himself. With a broken leg. We couldn't even find a rope to help him. Daphene and I couldn't do anything but watch." Her eyes were very earnest. The shorter girl nodded in agreement.

Fletcher ignored them, his eyes focused on Prudence. "But now the beautiful Captain Falling is here to rescue us. It was quite a morale boost to hear your voice on the radio, Captain."

Handsome and cheeky. No doubt he found her exotic, a change of pace from his college-age harem. Although they probably weren't that much younger than she was. But they had lived sheltered lives. They were still soft and dewy. Unscuffed, like new shoes.

Well, until now.

"Are you aware of how bad it is out there?" she asked. Not because she wanted to deflate them. But she was already hiding the truth for Jorgun. That was all the lying she could bear.

Fletcher winced. "Nobody came looking for us. So we figured it can't be good."

"What about Klakroon? Is it okay? That's where my parents live. We tried to reach it on the radio but the satellite link was down. It's just a little village . . ." The blond girl was trying not to whimper.

Daphene, the smart one, didn't ask.

Prudence sighed, more for their benefit than for hers. She was beyond emotion, but they still needed it. "The whole planet looks like this." She waved her hand at the wreckage. "I'm sorry."

"Who?" Fletcher, steely-eyed. The men always wanted to know who. The women sometimes asked why, but the men always wanted a name. A target to strike back at.

"Nobody knows," Prudence said, and winced. For almost two days she had been saying that, but this was the first time it had been a lie.

Sounds from the entranceway. Kyle and Jorgun were returning.

Too late Prudence remembered her strict instructions to Melvin. But the two men were alone, their passengers safely onboard. She could always rely on Melvin to screw up a direct order.

They came into the little room and distributed the blankets. Fletcher tried to turn his down, but Kyle insisted.

"You've been lucky so far. But if your system takes too much stress, that leg could get infected. It's a short trip. There are enough blankets to go around. The girls will be fine."

The girls were collecting something—data pods. The plastic bulbs were spilling over the ground like jellybeans.

"For crying out loud, Brenna—don't lose that one." Fletcher pointed at a bright blue pod rolling across the ground. "That's the latest data." Glancing at Prudence, still trying to impress her, he explained. "Cosmological telemetrics for the last few weeks. Probably the same boring star-stuff we've been collecting for years, but who knows? It might have a clue about what happened. We haven't been able to analyze it yet." Then Jorgun lifted him, cradling him gently, and Fletcher turned into the scared young kid he really was, forgetting about everything else.

Prudence understood. Being carried by Jorgun was psychologically debilitating. It made you feel like a baby again.

"Let me help," Kyle said, bending down to chase after the little rolling pods. Prudence tucked the blanket around Fletcher, getting him ready for the blast of cold.

But she saw.

Out of the corner of her eye. Not the switch, exactly, but the too-casual fluidity of Kyle's hands. He helped Brenna wrap the pods up in a fold of blanket and squeeze it tight. The bulge was safely sealed for the trip through the snow.

Yet Prudence knew if she opened it now, the bright blue pod would be missing.

SIX

Separations

Kyle already knew what was on the data pod he'd swiped. Trouble.

Either it showed something about the aliens, which meant that their human allies would stop at nothing to get it away from Fletcher, or it didn't, which meant the kid would be wasting people's time. And Kyle didn't think anybody was going to be in a forgiving mood for a while.

So really, he was doing the kid a favor. Not that Fletcher would see it that way. Kids his age never did. Certainly Kyle hadn't. His father had tried to guide him past the rocks a dozen times, given him sage advice on when to shut up, salute, and look the other way. He'd always ignored it, done things the right way, the direct way. He'd worn the resulting scars like a badge of honor.

Until one day he'd seen the light. Not the light at the end of the tunnel, but the other one, the bad one. The one you were supposed to go toward. The one that came after your life flashed before your eyes.

It had started as a simple traffic stop. Being assigned to traffic duty was already punishment, for having pointed out a senior officer's inability to add two columns of numbers and get the same answer. The officer had been collecting unearned overtime for twenty years; the resulting financial penalty had bankrupted the man and cost him his house. That it was the kind of house a working cop shouldn't have been able to afford didn't really spare Kyle any unpopularity. Everybody likes a straight shooter, from afar. That doesn't mean you want to work with one.

So Kyle was driving an unmarked ground car, alone, writing people tickets for driving too fast. For being too eager to get home to their families, or out to nightclubs, or any of the thousand places that people want to get to in a hurry. But he really was a straight shooter, all the way down. He didn't take his humiliation out on the public. Most of them appreciated that, after they cooled off a bit.

This one was different. From the start he knew it would be bad. It was one of those ridiculously expensive sports models, making an illegal turn. Kyle flashed his lights, sent the cut-out signal from his car to the other one, causing its engine to cycle down to a whisper and forcing the driver to pull off the road. Walked up to the window, expecting some stuffed-shirt executive or underdressed socialite, and wondered how much they were going to yell at him.

But the driver was calm and polite. As befitted a man of his station—Veram Dejae, the mayor of Altair's largest city.

"What seems to be the problem, officer?"

Such a simple question. With a simple answer. Kyle explained it all, in simple words. He remembered what came next with jagged clarity.

"I can't get a ticket. I can't . . . be here. Do you understand, officer?"

By this point in his career, Kyle had already been in several gunfights. He'd already done undercover stings on mobsters and juicers. He knew what fear felt like, recognized its peculiar tang, the heightening of sensation coupled with the shrinking boundaries of awareness. He knew the smell of death, the look in another man's eyes when you had crossed a line that could not be uncrossed while one of you was still alive.

In that moment he was more afraid than he had ever been.

Dejae was not angry or threatening. The politician was merely . . . distressed. Uncomfortable with what was going to happen.

Kyle had known with absolute certainty that Dejae was uncomfortable with what was going to happen to *Kyle*.

He had lowered his data tablet. An act of weakness: submission to fear. Even now it gnawed at him, shamed him. It would have destroyed a younger Kyle, shattered his vision of himself. But this Kyle was older and wiser. This Kyle was not prepared to die for a traffic ticket.

"Not even a warning, if it will leave a record. You have to . . . forget. You never saw me."

Kyle had manufactured an excuse. One that sounded good to himself. Mumbled something about state secrets or mistresses. Pretended it was okay for a politician to make a minor mistake and cover it up by threatening murder.

"I won't forget you, Officer Daspar."

And Dejae hadn't. A week later Kyle had been reassigned. A month later, the first promotion, one of many. After a year, the invitation to become a League member.

Surreptitiously Kyle had scanned every news article, crime log, and database he could find. Careful not to let even a whisper drop to his fellow officers, he had run his own private investigation. And come up empty-handed. No murders, no smuggling, no embezzlements had surfaced. No foreign dignitaries had gone missing, no off-world treaties suddenly signed. He had never found a whiff of a hint for why Dejae had to not be seen that day, in that place.

But he had discovered just how powerful the League was. Just how deep it had its claws into Altair government. Still in investigation mode, he went along with the League's requests. Fixing parking tickets and the like, little things, tests to see how deep his loyalty ran. Those malfeasances didn't bother him. They weren't done out of fear, merely part of his undercover act. He wanted to see where all of this led.

He knew he was on to something really important after the second year. After Veram Dejae was elected prime minister of Altair.

And now, three years later, he was still unraveling the threads. This little blue data pod might be one of them. If it wasn't, then he wasn't stealing anything valuable from the kid. If it was, then Fletcher did not want to find the spider on the end of that thread.

So many rationalizations. They had become habitual now. He hated that about himself. The only way he could cope was to add it to the ledger he kept in his head. The list of crimes that the League would someday be held to account for.

Bitter memories to bear while trudging through the cold snow. But they had reached the ship now, and he had to put his public face back on. Smiling at the girls, he helped them through the air lock.

"We need to get settled in, quickly. Dr. Sanders is in bad shape. We have to get her out of here fast." Subtly herding the girls, keeping their minds off the data pods, he guided them to the ship's lounge. It had enough chairs and couches to seat them all. A more comfortable journey than the cargo hold, where the larger groups of refugees had ridden on hard metal floors.

"Will she be okay?" Brenna kept asking if things were going to be okay.

"We have some medical facilities back at the capital." An ambiguous answer, but the most hopeful he could offer.

Prudence stalked off, turning back into the captain now that she had passengers onboard. He watched sadly. With the *Phoenix* here, he would lose his hold over her. If he tried to keep her ship commandeered, Rassinger would just wind up running it. So he would let her go, and she would fade out of his life, into the background of faces and events that streamed past him without really touching him. He would go on alone, as always.

It was what was best for her and her crew. They had to run far, far away, before they got entangled in this web of treachery. Especially now that Rassinger was on the scene.

Rassinger. Of all the rotten luck. Why couldn't his ship have beaten them here? Then the mines would have paid their respects to District Leader Rassinger, and the universe would be a better place.

But of course, it wasn't luck. Rassinger had shown up on cue to collect his shiny prize. Sure, there probably was a diplomatic meeting waiting for him on Bierze. They would have made their cover story airtight. And the disinterest he'd shown in the disaster— Rassinger was the perfect man for that. Anyone who knew him would have no trouble believing the man was prepared to sail on by.

Then, ever so conveniently, the *Ulysses* had located the biggest discovery of all time, and turned it over to District Leader Rassinger. On a snow-covered platter. The League would make hay with this. Bales and bales of it, stacked to the barn roof. In the panic of an alien attack, money would flow into the government's hands. They'd double the Fleet. They'd recruit scared young men from off-world, men who wanted to fight aliens but weren't citizens of Altair. Men whose first loyalty would be to the government, not to the people.

And they would pass laws, laws intended to block spies, to increase security, to protect. Laws that gave the government power to do things in a hurry, and in secret. Laws that would be carried out in dark rooms at the end of silent corridors.

Rassinger and his ilk would be there, in those rooms. The League's thugs would be creeping through those corridors. The fist that reached out to strike the alien threat would never unclench, and Altair would suffocate in its grasp.

But there was a flaw in their plan. Lieutenant Kyle Daspar.

Someone on Altair had dispatched Kyle out here, before the attack had taken place. They needed him here for something. That gave him power. And they had known in advance. That meant the aliens had been negotiated with.

Politics.

This was an arena Kyle could hope to affect. A war was beyond the scope of any one man to significantly influence. But a secret only needed one voice to expose it. If Kyle could find the League's link to the aliens, he might be able to avert the war.

Even if he couldn't, he could at least destroy the League. If Altair had to fight for its survival, he might at least give it a chance to preserve what it was fighting for. To remain free, and democratic. To remain Altair.

Assuming he could survive his own private battle with the League. Which made him realize he'd been thinking of Prudence as an innocent, not as an operative. If she was working for the League, he might see her again after all.

But the thought was not comforting. There were only two conditions under which he would be exposed to such a skilled operative a second time. The first condition was if she was trying to kill him.

The second condition was if he was trying to kill her.

Settling into a chair next to Fletcher, he leaned back and closed his eyes. Maybe if he pretended to sleep, they wouldn't pester him with questions. But he didn't have to pretend.

After so many hours on the ship, after so many flights, he could tell now when they broke atmosphere. It was a subtle difference. Spaceships were always humming and vibrating, always alive under your touch. But in space the animus was internal, the turbulence of air no longer drowning out the heartbeat of the generators and the breath of life support. He fancied that he could feel a difference in acceleration, even through the passive grav-plating of the deck. The ship no longer weighed down by earthly concerns, but floating free under its own power. He could see why Prudence preferred being in space. It was insulating.

Sheltered in the comfort of vacuum, he fell asleep.

At first he didn't know what woke him. The rest of the passengers were asleep, too, lulled into unconsciousness by warmth. The room was silent and still.

But they were going down. Sinking back into the grasp of the world, the fears and demands of others clutching at them, pulling them down.

He rubbed his eyes, still gray with fatigue. It had only been forty minutes. Not long enough.

But too long for Dr. Sanders. He'd seen enough dead bodies to know, even from across the room. The old white-haired scientist was sleeping next to her, his arm across her body. Kyle let him sleep. A few more minutes of peace.

He got up and went to find the bridge.

Prudence sat in her chair, alone. Kyle looked around for Jorgun, automatically. He had become that accustomed to the giant's presence.

"I sent him to bed," Prudence said, without looking around to see who had come in. Showing that he could not sneak up on her. A spider demonstrating her total control over her web. He wondered if she had tagged him, put some kind of local radio tracker on his clothes at some point. Or if the ship had internal sensors that could distinguish individuals.

Or perhaps it was just her superb operative training.

"Now what?" he said, because he couldn't help himself.

She looked at him then.

"Now we're going to offload these people, and then I'm going to turn my ship off and get some sleep. What else did you have in mind?"

What had he meant? So much more than that. More than just the next few hours, the next few days. More than just the aliens and the coming war. He had meant the future, beyond all that.

He had meant what would happen between them.

The realization was startling. He had come to depend on her in the last day, not just to fly the ship, but to make decisions. Like at the wreck, checking for radiation. Or misdirecting Rassinger. Even while he had thought of her as the enemy, he had relied on her strength and ability. Taken it for granted.

"You're not going to get involved with . . . Rassinger's mission." He didn't know himself if it was a statement or a question.

"No," she said, looking away again. "I'm going to collect my pay and get out of here."

"These people will need help. Off-world help. That means lots of transport. There'll be work for you here." Why was he trying to change her mind? Selfishness. He wasn't prepared to let her disappear from his life.

"We've done enough. Every time we come here, Jorgun will ask for Jelly. And every time, I'll have to tell him all over again. No amount of transport fee is worth that."

Her voice was bitter, but Kyle almost laughed at her. He had seen through her. So much effort wasted, so many futile precautions. Prudence had bound herself to nothing planetside. Her concerns were only for her ship.

But the crew was part of the ship, and the crew was human. And they did not have the iron discipline of their captain. They had become contaminated by the ground, and now they laid their burdens on her secondhand.

Kyle knew exactly how she felt. All of the relationships in his life were secondhand, too.

He gave her what freedom he could. "I'll sign a blank voucher. You can fill in the amount. But if you ask for too much, they might ask questions. I don't think you want that." The blank voucher would earn him plenty of questions, too, difficult ones; but Prudence had earned it, regardless of what it might cost him. She was what he had sworn to protect from the League: the good and the innocent. Even if she was the only person he could name who fit both criteria.

He put his hand on the back of Jorgun's chair to steady himself. He had momentarily forgotten that she was a mercenary sent to destroy him in some Byzantine and nefarious plot. He was too tired for this, emotionally and physically drained from the last few days. The last few years, even.

Again she looked at him, with those dark eyes asking questions all by themselves. "That's generous of you. And by extension, Altair. Will your government be as generous to Kassa?"

He shrugged, honestly. "I don't know, Prudence. I'm a cop. I don't even work for the planetary government, just a city."

"And the League." Whispered. He wasn't sure if it was a question or a statement.

"And the League," he agreed, because he had to.

Silence between them. Stretching painful, and complete.

"Who was Jelly?" he asked. Not just to hear her voice again, but because he wanted to know.

"A local girl. She suffered from Tay-Sachs disease. The condition is treatable, but the medicine is delicate. It has to be prepared fresh on a daily basis. It needs complex machinery. It requires electricity."

Outside, the refugee camp below them was lit only by fire.

He wanted to say he was sorry, but the words sounded trite and inadequate. He didn't know her well enough to share her grief. "Was that why she got along with Jorgun? Because of the disease?"

Prudence's voice was so cold, so far away. "Yes. Complications, from childhood. They were alike in that way. Not . . . perfect. Not candidates for your League."

The League preached strength. The League had tried to make

terminations of abnormal pregnancies a requirement, not just an option. Kyle had never been a parent, never even thought about being a parent. He didn't used to have a position on the issue. Now he had another crime to add to the list.

Automatically, he pretended to defend them. "It wasn't the League that killed her. This wasn't the work of the League." Even as he said it, the crashing realization that he might be wrong rattled him. Maybe there weren't any coincidences. Maybe he was supposed to get here first in the *Launceston* and absorb the mines, thus clearing the way for the *Phoenix*. The mines that had been left to make sure no one else found the alien ship before Rassinger. Maybe the only unexpected factor was Prudence Falling's survival.

He had been prepared to accept that the League was taking advantage of this, but he hadn't gone so far as to suspect them of *arranging* the attack.

Breathing heavily, he tried to order his thoughts. If she was an operative, then this was a test. He had to defend the League's reputation, to maintain his own cover. And if she was innocent, then it was even more important to defend the League. So that she would go away. Far, far away where they couldn't find her. In a war between aliens and imperial politics, a tramp freighter captain would be crushed like a blade of grass under the feet of mighty gladiators.

"The League . . ." he started, but she cut him off.

"Spare me your rhetoric. I know my place. Now get off my bridge."

He went. It was what he had wanted. The best possible result. She would be safe, his cover was intact, everything was going according to plan.

Then why did walking away from her feel like surrender, all over again?

SEVEN

Running

She had thought it would get easier, but four days in the cocoon of node-space only made it worse.

Surprisingly, they had let her go. "They" being the *Phoenix*, of course. Kassa didn't have any way of stopping her. Short of guilt, which they had certainly tried. But she had explained that they needed things from off-world to survive the next few months. Things that Fleet would not be bringing. And Fleet wasn't going to be eager to share the news about what had happened here. They'd want to lock everything down until they knew exactly what was going on—and that could take a very long time.

So she had offered to go out and spread the word, tell every captain she met what Kassa would buy. The tramp freighters would swarm to Kassa, like flies to a corpse. They would overcharge, but they would bring the necessities of life. And the sooner they got started, the cheaper it would be for Kassa.

In any case, there was little more the *Ulysses* could do for them. The various pockets of refugees had radio contact now and the most isolated groups had been brought into larger settlements. The *Phoenix* had lent Kassa its launches, so they had functioning aircraft. All she had left to offer was convenience, not survival. The Kassans had believed her, and let her go without resentment.

But Garcia had been livid enough to invade the bridge while they were lifting off.

"Are you insane? We know exactly what Kassa needs. We could charge premium prices. For crying out loud, Pru, I've spent days crawling through stinking dockside bars trying to ferret out good cargoes, just to keep us floating. This kind of information could make us rich!"

She took his outrage with a grain of salt, since she happened to know he enjoyed hanging around in those stinking bars. After all, that's where she'd originally found him.

"We are not going to get rich off of Kassa's disaster, Garcia."

"At least tell me you'll *sell* that list." He was whining, which was unlike him. Usually he blustered or threatened when money was involved. Prudence decided he was developing a conscience. Given his past, it was almost certainly a painful process.

"We're going to do everything we can to prevent anybody else from getting rich off it, too. The news goes out on a public broadcast as soon as we reenter normal space." It was the best thing she could do for Kassa. The more freighters that knew about it, the less any of them could gouge.

Melvin had been next, paging her from the gunnery console.

"The laser's still broken, Pru." He said it like it was her fault. Melvin had become increasingly volatile since his exposure to the wreck. "We're unarmed. What if we get attacked?"

What good would a stupid mining laser do? They had been lucky the first time. Just a dumb mine. If they met a real combat ship—even one of those little fighters—they would die in the first pass.

"We won't be attacked, Melvin. There will be Fleet swarming through all the hops between here and Altair."

Garcia rolled his eyes and muttered under his breath. "Assuming they haven't already destroyed Fleet." She'd told him about the alien wreck. She had to; he was part of her crew. He deserved to know.

"What if they've already blown up Fleet?" Melvin asked, his voice rising.

She snapped at him through the microphone. "Then we're better off running, instead of waiting here for them to come back and finish the job."

Silence from the intercom. He'd turned it off, the most insulting thing he could imagine. That being cut off from him was a relief to everyone else was not the sort of thing Melvin would understand. He couldn't bear to be unheard, so he assumed no one could bear to not hear him.

Garcia walked out, and left Prudence with Jorgun. For a moment she wished she was still arguing with Melvin.

"Will we come back and see Jelly?" Jorgun asked.

She had already told him the truth, but he kept asking. She could not determine how much he understood, whether he was in denial or simply expressing his grief, holding on to her memory with the only thing he had left. In either case, there was only one thing she could do now.

She lied. "When we can, Jor. When we can."

It was a double lie. They would never see Jelly again; they would never come back to this planet. She would never put her ship where Kyle Daspar's impressment papers could reach it.

He had left her bridge when she had told him to. He had left her ship when they landed, running to the whistle of his master on the *Phoenix*. He had let her go in silence.

All the way out to the node-point, she had pushed the edge of safe velocity, eager to escape before he called her back. She had congratulated herself on slipping out while the *Phoenix* was too preoccupied to realize its mistake.

But in the seconds before they entered the node, in the last instant that they could still interact with the outside world, she had discovered a part of herself waiting for the comm board to light up. Hoping for a word from him, even if it was only "good-bye."

A curious desire to hold toward a man she despised. A man that represented her worst nightmare. As much as she detested his authority, she still missed his competence.

Now she sat on the bridge, preparing to reenter the universe. Not entirely certain of what she would find out there, and four days of worrying about it gnawing at her belly. Melvin couldn't take the strain; he'd snuck off somewhere and hid, no doubt stoned again. Garcia pretended indifference, claiming fate was in the hands of some nebulously defined supernatural entity, but she had seen him drinking heavily in these last few hours. Only Jorgun was immune. Jorgun could not comprehend his own death any better than he could comprehend Jelly's. He was asleep in his bunk, oblivious.

Prudence had other concerns to occupy her mind. She'd entered the node too fast. An emotional decision, fleeing from the reach of Daspar's papers, but also a tactical one. Halfway to the node they had already built up too much velocity to abort the run. The Power Law ruled a spaceship's life; acceleration was constrained by gravity, and gravity weakened by the square of the distance. The farther away from the planet she got, the less she could affect her course. If the *Phoenix* had tried to call her back, she could have legitimately refused. Their own navcom would have told them she had no choice.

It was a dangerous gambit. If she had missed the node, the *Ulysses* would plunge helplessly into deep space, without any way to stop.

And the flip side of the coin was just as dangerous. If you came out of a node too fast and in the wrong direction, you might miss the planet. The mathematics of diminishing rates quickly added up to a death sentence, a long, cold journey into perpetual night. On a null-vector you couldn't even abandon ship. The landing craft was gravitics powered, too.

All you could do then was hope somebody with more money

than sense had a ship that was more fuel than anything else, a fusion engine that could make its own force without a planet nearby, and a willingness to come out and try and pick up your crew. Regulations called for all spaceports to have a fusion tug ready to launch within five minutes. But that tug would have its own point of no return, beyond which it could not reach.

The computer would digest it all, grind the numbers together, and spit out a vector calculation. Either it intersected your ship, or it didn't. If you miscalculated a node exit, you would know within minutes whether you were dead or not, no matter how many days or weeks your life support could keep you breathing.

You had to know going in how you would be coming out: which direction the planet was, and which direction the node pointed. Most nodes faced inward, aligned by the pull of the star. But not all did. And the planets might be on the opposite side of their orbits, too far away to use.

These chancy facts went a long way to explaining why most freight haulers stuck to the same ports of call. A popular, well-traveled route would have up-to-date information available at every stop, allowing traders to calculate how much cargo they could carry, down to the last kilo. Less frequently visited planets would have less accurate information, making them less profitable, which led to fewer visits and less information in a cruelly descending spiral. Nodes that were uninhabited were the worst; in the event of a cosmic catastrophe like a planetary collision or supernova, the inhabited nodes would at least generate a wave of refugees as a warning. The empty nodes, their tragic doom concealed from distant view by the merely ordinary speed of light, would lie in wait like an ant-lion at the bottom of its trap.

Unlikely events to be sure, but seasoned spacers did not settle for mere improbability.

Some ships were designed to handle the risks. Fusion-powered explorers and military boats, like the *Launceston*. It could creep through the node with virtually no velocity, relying on its atomic engine to accelerate to the next node or back into the one it had just left.

A ship like the *Ulysses*, though, couldn't afford to be caught "in irons," as the old Earth-saying had it, trapped in deep space without velocity or gravity to create velocity. A working ship like the *Ulysses* couldn't carry ninety percent of its mass in fuel. People making a living had to use the gravity of the last place to build up the speed that would get them to the next place, and carry enough cargo in between to pay the bills.

Now she worried about too much velocity. But the *Ulysses* was running light, its cargo no more than a slip of paper—the voucher to be cashed in at Altair. At worst, she would have to spiral around the planet several times to dock. That would earn her a ticket for unsafe navigation. Enough of those and they would take your ship away, for your own good.

Velocity was the porridge of commercial space travel. Too much or too little, and you got eaten by bears.

Her console sprang to life, in touch with the constant field of radio traffic that bathed every civilized star. No warning signals, no red lights here. Just a dozen offers for cargo transshipment, and one limited-time-only special on deck wax.

She touched the switch that made her part of that invisible web. If her orbital calculations were right, she had about three minutes to make a decision.

"Hail, Bruneis spaceport. This is the *Ulysses* hailing."

"Prudence? Is that you?"

A quick response for such a small port. They must be hovering over their consoles.

"Yes, Bruneis . . . Sharon?" She struggled to match the voice to a name. Garcia was so much better at that. "Listen, I have a problem . . ."

"Hang on, Prudence, the commodore wants to speak to you."

She hadn't asked for her favor yet, and the operator was already transferring her up the line. This was either good news, or very bad news.

"Captain Falling?" A more mature voice. Prudence had never had to deal with the head of Bruneis's space program before.

"Commodore, I would like to request permission for a flyby, to the Carnor node." It was a lot to ask. She wanted to streak through their system without stopping. That meant no inspection, which meant no cargo fees. Not very polite. "I'm running without cargo or passengers, and there's an emergency behind me. I have two minutes and eight seconds before I have to abort this course."

Despite the urgency, the voice hesitated before responding. Prudence gritted her teeth at the dramatics of power.

"On one condition, Captain Falling. You tell us what the hell is going on."

"Granted, Commodore." She relaxed in her chair. The course she wanted was already programmed, and the autopilot would make the minor corrections necessary. There were always corrections. Planets followed Newton's laws inflexibly, but there were so many factors that no simulation could be perfect. The subtle influence of other planets, moons, and even the waves of plasma on the face of the local star all added up. But she had been through here only a few weeks ago, so her navcom's data was up to date.

The commodore kept talking. "All we know, Captain Falling, is that the *Launceston* blew through here on a fusion burn. They didn't bother to ask for permission, either. And they didn't tell us jackson." Prudence grimaced in sympathy, but not too much. If the commodore thought she was aggravated at the imperiousness of Altair Fleet, Prudence could tell her a tale or two.

Which focused the issue neatly. How much could she tell them without compromising her invisibility? And how much could she keep from them without endangering them?

Bruneis was a dome world, rich in rare-earth elements but

barely habitable. Its population could not retreat to the forests to hide, because there were no plants of any kind. The Bruneisians wore nose-filters and oxygen feeds when they went outside. Other than being utterly devoid of oxygen, the atmosphere was quite pleasant, with a tang that reminded Prudence of baked cinnamon.

But a week without machinery or power would exterminate Bruneis.

"Kassa was attacked, Commodore. Bombed for days by an unknown force. I've been flying rescue missions since I got there. The *Launceston* is allegedly going to Altair to request more help." And, as she had expected, keeping mum as long as possible. "There's an Altair cruiser there now, the *Phoenix*. I don't know if they came through here, though." She hadn't seen the *Phoenix* arrive, and there were three nodes at Kassa.

"How bad is it?" The commodore was too distraught to even notice Prudence's subtle question about the *Phoenix*, let alone answer it.

"It's bad, Commodore. Perhaps twenty percent casualties." Ten thousand individual deaths, reduced to a statistic. "But there's nothing left standing—or moving—on the planet. They hit the infrastructure hard."

The commodore knew better than Prudence what that would mean for her own world.

"Who? Who did it?"

Prudence bit her lip. "I don't know." In a way it was true. "Nobody saw anything but bombs." Unless Prudence was demoting herself to the status of nobody, that wasn't true at all. "All I can give you are rumors and speculation, Commodore." Lies piled on top of lies. If deceit had mass, her ship would be dangerously overloaded.

"Then give them, Captain."

If she told them what she had seen, if she gave them details that could only have come from the wreck, then Altair Fleet would find out. And if there were a conspiracy here, then they would come after her. Kyle's last-minute rescue would be wasted.

Prudence said as much as she dared. "If something comes through the node, and it doesn't speak Terran standard ... start shooting."

Silence on the other end. Prudence kept talking. "That's just what I heard, Commodore. Nothing was taken; no one claimed sovereignty. They showed up, dropped bombs, and went away. For apparently no purpose that anybody can understand."

Another pause. Then the commodore responded. "I've asked my staff some questions about you. They assure me you do not play practical jokes. Nonetheless, I am going to ask you, under oath, to repeat that."

Prudence exhaled in relief. The commodore had given her a way out, an excuse to shut up.

"Not under oath, Commodore. If you want me to go on record, then all I can tell you are the facts. Kassa is in shambles, and no one knows who or why."

The commodore surprised her by swearing. "Bullshit. *Someone* knows why."

"Then they didn't choose to share it with me, Commodore. May I respectfully suggest you take whatever measures you can to protect yourself."

"How many were there? What kind of ships did they attack with? How can we organize a defense without knowing any of this?" The voice was angry, almost petulant. Prudence couldn't blame her, but it wasn't her fault.

"All I can tell you is they didn't land. They just dropped bombs—a lot of bombs. For several days. Kassa had virtually no defenses—only one patrol boat, and I honestly don't know if it was even armed."

"You can't tell me what I need to know—but you can spread

rumors of aliens." Bitterness overwhelmed the commodore's voice.

"I'm sorry, Commodore. But you can go and see for yourself. I'm sure Kassa would appreciate any assistance you can spare."

The appeal to humanity took the wind out of the commodore's sails. When the voice answered, it was apologetic. "Understood, Captain. We'll dispatch a rescue mission immediately. Can you tell us what they need most?"

"Yes," Prudence said with relief, "I can. Prepare for a data-dump." She pushed the button that logged her in to Bruneis's public network, and queued the transfer. Everything else would be automatic. The machines would talk now, without deceit or emotion, sparing Prudence and the commodore their artless fencing.

If only someone would invent a machine that lied for you.

"Pru?" Garcia on the intercom. "Did we exit the node yet?" The transition was undetectable by any sense human beings possessed. Short of looking out a window and noticing that the stars were points of white light instead of spectral streaks.

"We did, and as you may have noticed, we're still alive."

"For now."

She sighed. "We're on flyby to Carnor. From there it's one more hop to Altair, where we can cash in this voucher."

"Assuming Altair still exists." Garcia had been rattled for days. This was an uncomfortable experience for her. She'd seen him bet his life savings without a twitch, a dozen times.

"They didn't come through here, Garcia. So we have to be ahead of them."

The two of them had spent many hours poring over the local node-charts. A peculiar kind of map, it laid out all the popular nodes in terms of connections and travel times. The result bore no resemblance to the physical location of the stars. The star Prudence had been born around was actually visible from Altair, a bright neighbor in the spiral arm, even though it was more than a hundred hops away. Bruneis, on the other hand, was deep in the heart of the galaxy, where the stars were old and the planets were chock full of heavy metals. The nodes didn't care about linear distance, and after their first few hops, people stopped caring, too. A gulf of a hundred light-years was as impassable as a million. But a node was three to seven days, no matter how much space it covered. And no matter how fast your ship was.

"We're taking the shortest route to Altair," she repeated, a conversation days old now. She knew what came next.

"Unless they know a node we don't." Garcia lived by special exemptions, outs, and tricks. He always assumed other people did too.

It was extremely unlikely. Nodes were not particularly hard to find, with the right equipment. And a sophisticated planet like Altair would have swept their solar system out to a distance of billions of kilometers.

She had pointed all of this out to Garcia, but he refused to be comforted by reason and logic. Instead he'd combined drinking and praying. At least it left him conscious, unlike Melvin.

But consciousness meant more burdens, and the future demanded to be answered. Once they got to Altair, what next? Should they flee as far from Kassa as possible? Or join the resistance, enlist in Fleet, offer their strength to the war effort? The age-old dilemma, flight or fight. Each of her crew would have to make their own decision. Except for Jorgun. She would have to make one for both of them.

Running would be easy. The voucher would fill her hold with trade goods and fuel. And Prudence had spent her life leaving places.

But not to escape. She had been lured outward by a quest of her own choosing, not driven by fear. Other than that first good-bye. The distinction was important to her. She would not be defined by

her first act as an adult. She would make her own life, without re-
gard to what had been made for her. She would not run out of
habit.

But neither could she sign her life away to the oxymoronic
military mind. If she wanted to fight, she would have to find her
own way.

Bruneis spaceport staff were not the only ones hovering over
their comm stations. Within minutes of entering Altair system, her console lit up. Altair Traffic Control, of course, demanding that she confirm her identity and assigning her a docking bay.
That much she expected. Jorgun knew what buttons to push in
response, so she let him do it.

But he had barely acknowledged Control's message before she
had a half-dozen other calls. Independent freighter captains, some
of them friends, some of them strangers, and all of them com-
petitors.

She took a call from the *Starfarer*. Captain Welsing had bought
her a dozen shots of forty-year-old Scotch one night, sitting in a
high-class bar and trying to get her drunk. She'd poured most of
them into a container in her purse while he wasn't looking, but
pretended to get falling-down hammered, just to see what he was
up to. She was quite flattered to discover he was just trying to se-
duce her. He wasn't seeking trade tips or pricing information,
just sex.

She'd said no, of course. He wasn't really her type. Loud and
blustery, living the free-trader stereotype to the hilt. It probably
worked on civvies.

Later, Garcia had thanked her for the fine liquor, even though it
was in a plastic squeeze-bottle. He wasn't the type to stand on cer-
emony. She doubted he could tell the difference between the expensive stuff and the cheap hooch he normally drank, but she let
him pretend. Probably the most flavorful component in this case

was that the booze was free. That was something Garcia always appreciated.

"Captain Welsing. How can I help you?"

The comm beeped, but no one answered. It was an automated call. As she was reaching out to cut it off and select another one, a voice broke in.

"Prudence? Is that you?" Welsing sounded distracted. There were some odd rustling sounds in the background, and then a female voice, raised in complaint.

"Shut up, darling, this is business." Welsing had muffled the mike, probably covering it with his hand, but Prudence could still hear. "She's not another girl. She's a *starship captain*. Totally different!"

Welsing hadn't thought that when he was emptying credit sticks for her. But then, Welsing's definition of "girl" was remarkably plastic.

"Prudence, my sweet. How nice of you to call."

"You called me, Welsing. At least, your ship did."

"Right, right. I programmed it to contact anybody on my short list. Prudence, something's up. Something big. Altair Fleet went into high alert yesterday. They're canceling shore leaves, putting ships on active duty, and being real pricks about dockside inspections."

Just as she started thinking how nice it was that he had called to warn her, he went on.

"You wouldn't know anything about that, would you?"

"Now why do you think I would, Welsing?" She tried not to sound too exasperated. It was his nature, after all.

"Because you left out of here to Carnor, about two weeks ago. And whatever spooked Fleet came here from Carnor, on a patrol boat named the *Launceston*."

Damn. She'd passed through Altair with her shipment of threshing machines, now rusting in an abandoned Kassan wheat field. Since she had to log a flight plan with Fleet, her destination would be a matter of record. Fleet felt it was a public service to keep track of the free-traders, and to let everyone know what they were up to. Everyone but the free-traders probably appreciated it.

She was intending to broad-beam her news, anyway. No point in not telling Welsing. She sighed, not because she didn't enjoy talking to Welsing, but because she hated telling this story. "Wels, you better send the girl out."

"No can do, Pru, it's her room. Hang on a second." Screeching, the sound of something soft being thrown as violently as possible, and then the slam of a door.

Welsing came back on the line. "Okay, Pru, I'm standing in a hotel hallway with no pants on, but I'm alone. Spill." His voice started out aggravated, but by the end of his first sentence he had returned to his smoothest charm.

"Maybe later would be a better time?" she said, unable to resist teasing him.

"Nonsense. Now that I've been reminded of your stunning beauty, how could I possibly settle for that doxy? Just your voice is more sensuous than a dozen Vegas showgirls stark naked in a vat of butter."

She had to make a face at that. Jorgun laughed at her, although he couldn't hear what Welsing had said. Jorgun had his own headset on, and was watching something on his console. Probably the last few weeks of cartoons.

Normally he wouldn't notice anything outside of his cartoons. The atmosphere of tension must be getting to him, too.

"Real butter, Pru, not the synthetic stuff." Welsing was filling the silence. If she let him go on, he'd start describing the showgirls. "Vegas" wasn't a real place, just a slang term for high-class glitz and glamour, but she had no doubt his mind was full of very concrete images.

"It's not nice, Wels. But there's profit, if you're fearless. Kassa colony was bombed into the Stone Age. Thousands dead, no machinery, and winter coming on. They need stuff, a lot of stuff. I have a list."

The inevitable response. Swearing, then the question. "Earthfire! By who?"

"Nobody knows." The lie got harder every time she repeated it. "But . . . Fleet has plenty of reason to be on alert."

Welsing was a blowhard, but he wasn't stupid. "Why did you say 'fearless,' Pru?"

"If nobody knows why they came, nobody knows if they'll come back. I don't want you blaming me when a war-fleet drops out of the sky on your pizza delivery."

"Damn, Pru. Damn."

"Put me through to a data channel. I'll transmit the list. And Wels . . . don't keep this a secret. Tell everyone on your list. The long list. This is a humanitarian crisis, not a monopoly-profit opportunity."

She thought of something else that might be more motivational.

"There'll be plenty of profit for everyone. Especially if you're willing to take future-payment vouchers." Anybody who had the cash to lend could make a profit both on delivery and interest. Welsing was the kind of guy who always seemed to have a lot of cash.

"You don't want a window?" He was asking if she wanted him to sit on the information until she had time to cut a few deals.

"No, Wels. I don't think I'm going back there. It was . . ." It was too much to ask of Jorgun. "I've seen enough." It was too much to ask of her. Kyle might still be there, with his damnable papers and smoky black eyes. "I'm not giving you a window, either. I've got a dozen calls to answer, and I'll be handing out the list to everyone." The comm station had kept adding them while she had been talking to Welsing.

"Understood, Pru. I'll spread it around too. Humanitarian, like you said. Um, hate to chat and run, but I need to get some pants on. There's a bellboy at the end of the hall now, and he doesn't look amused."

Probably he just wanted to fill his hold with the prime cargos before the local vendors raised the prices. Welsing wasn't the kind of guy who worried about bellboys.

"Fair enough, Wels. Although I regret this comm was only audio."

"Honey, you have the taste to appreciate the unadorned human form. Not like these prudes on Altair. But call me later, we'll do something naked."

"Prudence out," she answered, rolling her eyes at his salaciousness. Constant repetition tended to rob it of effectiveness.

"Welsing out," and he was gone.

Sighing, she pushed another button at random.

EIGHT

Home

Kyle walked into his empty apartment and shut the door. Nothing greeted him, not even the apartment's computer. He'd programmed it to not announce his comings and goings.

Almost two weeks in the presence of the insufferably pompous Rassinger had flayed his patience to the bone. But he had learned things. He was certain, now, that Rassinger had expected to find the alien wreck. He was pretty sure that Rassinger had *not* expected to find Kyle.

What he didn't know was whether his tip had been a setup to get him killed, or a lead from a competing faction of the League. Or possibly even from an anti-League agent. And he didn't know *why* Rassinger was out there looking for alien spaceships.

After only one day, the *Phoenix* had loaded the wreck into its hold, and bolted for home. Kyle had begged a ride, partly to spy on the odious Rassinger, but also because he could accomplish nothing more on Kassa. The locals finally had enough government established that they resented his influence.

Rassinger had tried to hide the wreck from him, sealing off the cargo bay and posting armed guards. Kyle found it disturbing that the district leader trusted Fleet personnel more than he trusted a fellow League officer. One with a sterling reputation, no less. True to that reputation, he had not even tried to breach Rassinger's security cordon.

Instead, he'd bowed and scraped, flattered and obeyed. It was sickening.

Back on Altair, the *Phoenix* had vanished into the depths of a Fleet dock, discharging him like a bad sneeze along the way. He appreciated it. Security was tight, and the newsvid hounds had missed him. They found Rassinger and the captain of the *Phoenix*, through their various inside contacts, and ambushed the two officials with cameras and microphones. To little effect, since those two exalted individuals could cry "No comment" and push through the pack of slavering reporters with impunity. But a lowly functionary like Kyle would have found his private credit history accessed, and investigative snoops threatening to broadcast those indiscreet trips to the topless bar unless he gave them the scoop now.

Not that there were any such trips. He'd lived his cover twenty-four and seven. After the traffic stop incident, he hadn't really felt like a man, anyway. The urge had shriveled up and slunk away to hide.

It was back now, in full insatiated force. The cool, slim figure of Prudence Falling haunted his nights. Her ambiguous status only added fuel to the fire.

Was she a carefully placed operative or just a freelance captain in the wrong place at the wrong time? All he knew for sure was that she didn't like Rassinger. That made him like her, of course, but it wasn't quite enough. It didn't mean she was on his side.

If she was working for the League, and found out his true mission, she'd kill him without blinking. If she wasn't working for the League, then just the armband he wore would drive her as far away as star-flight could take her. Either way, Prudence Falling was going to be nothing but a memory for him.

Or possibly a lead. After checking his console for taps, snitches, and worms, he put out a few discreet inquiries. Starship travel schedules, sandwiched in between commodity prices. If anybody was watching, they'd think he was merely trying to profit off of his insider knowledge of the situation on Kassa.

Prudence's ship had left only a few hours before the *Phoenix* had dropped in-system. A wise move for her, and what he had expected, but he still felt the pang of disappointment.

She hadn't gone back to Kassa. The log showed her heading out another one of the twelve nodes that fed Altair. That wealth of connections combined with an innocuous ecosphere had quickly marked Altair out for local supremacy in this sector of nodes. Life had been easy and good for a hundred years.

Maybe too easy. Altair had stopped making hard choices a long time ago. The future looked like it was going to require some.

He corrected himself; she hadn't gone *directly* to Kassa. There were ways to get there other than the shortest route. Unwilling to trust the computer with such a sensitive inquiry, he printed out a node-chart and checked the routes by hand. She could still reach Kassa with seven extra hops.

So now he knew no more than when he had walked in the door.

The cupboard still had a few beers in it. Beer was old, old as Earth. Even on Earth it had been old. People liked that about it. They liked those little things that tied them to the past. People who couldn't spell "Earth" without blushing, people whose sense of history extended no deeper than last season's ball-game playoffs, would wax eloquent about the virtues of their favorite brand of beer, about how true its recipe was to the original, brewed by blind Tibetan monks in a stone castle a thousand years before electricity was invented.

Not that anybody even knew what a Tibetan monk was, really. Half the sources said they were religious zealots, and the other half said they were super-soldiers with magic powers. Whatever beliefs they had held, whatever principles they had lived and died for, were dust now. Dust on a planet no one even remembered how to find. All that was left of them was a name, a few stories, and beer.

Kyle popped the tab off the bottle, and waited the five seconds necessary for the contents to chill to the preset temperature. You could adjust it, if you wanted to, but Kyle left it at the factory default. It was his little homage to the wisdom of the monks. Presumably they knew what temperature beer tasted best at.

He told the house audio system to play something. It picked a recording at random, which just happened to perfectly match his mood. The guitar was a one-man instrument, played by skill and subtlety. More impressively, it was analog. Thus, no two performances could ever sound exactly the same. The iconography was irresistible.

Of course, his mood for the last five years had not changed. He was always alone, always in the dark, always brooding. Once he'd convinced the audio system to stop playing popular tunes delivered by advertising agencies, it had quickly learned to restrict itself to the solitary lament of classical guitar.

He had never heard a live guitar performance. He wasn't sure anybody on Altair even knew how to play one. The irony of appreciating an analog instrument, with its necessary unpredictability, through a digital recording, which was inflexibly unchanging, was not lost on him. It was just one of the many, many injustices he could do nothing about.

In the middle of the night, he was able to answer one of his numerous questions. When the bomb went off, blasting through the ceiling of his bedroom and incinerating his bed, he immediately understood that Rassinger had not expected to find him on Kassa *alive*.

The district leader was destined to be disappointed yet again.

Kyle had developed the habit of sleeping anywhere but his bedroom. Usually it was the couch, but he also had a polyfoam mattress in the study.

This was not as irrationally paranoid as it might seem. Kyle had his reasons, gleaned from a murder investigation several years ago. An assassin had rented the room below the victim's apartment, set a directed charge on a timer, and departed for parts unknown. By the time the bomb went off, the trail was already three months cold. The chances of catching a man in his bed at 3:00 A.M. were reasonably good. Not good enough for any normal assassin, who got paid only on a successful job, but good enough for an organization that had a very long-term view, plenty of money to spend, and a powerful need to be completely insulated from any taint of illegality.

An organization like the League, for instance.

Of course, they could have just blown out his whole apartment. But the chance of collateral damage was high, and that meant a bigger investigation. They could flood his rooms with a neurotoxin with a short half-life. But that level of sophistication pointed fingers of its own. A simple shaped charge, within the skill set of any amateur chemist, a dozen credits' worth of electronics, and a forged identity on a rental agreement were too generic to point anywhere.

Sometimes the most sophisticated method was the simplest. The League had precious few virtues, but a crude appreciation for effectiveness was one of them. This trick had been used enough times that the city government had considered imposing real-time identity checks for apartment rentals. Naturally, the legislation never made it past the "under consideration" stage.

Lying on his couch, watching the flames in his bedroom, he wondered what he should do. The internal fire control system was spritzing the blaze, and would eventually win its battle of chemistry. But police units had to be already en route.

Hopefully they would be loyal to the force, and not Rassinger's faction. Otherwise they might decide to finish the job before starting their investigation.

His comm unit started ringing. Struck by the sheer incongruity of it, he answered.

"Kyle? Are you okay?"

A friendly voice. Or rather, the voice of a friend. Sergeant Baumer was far too bald, thick, and beady-eyed to be friendly. But he was honest, clean, and still tolerated Kyle from the patrols they had shared before the League had taken over Kyle's career.

Flicking on the unit, Kyle answered. "Help me, Baumer. I'm badly burned . . . passing out. I've fallen and I can't get up." He tossed his comm unit into the bedroom, where the flames quickly devoured it.

It was a long shot. Baumer might or might not get the reference, and he might or might not be in a position to act on it. One of Kyle's first days on the job, Baumer had been tasked by the others to vet the new kid. A med comm call had come in, and Baumer had let his face sink into the most wretched seriousness. He'd driven like a maniac to the apartment building, a seedy retirement den, and sprinted out of the car with Kyle close behind. At the building's entrance he pulled Kyle away from the elevators.

"They can't be trusted, man, and it's a matter of life and death!"

After the first three flights of stairs, Baumer had collapsed, holding his ankle and cursing like a vid star. Kyle bounded up the next eight flights, his heart pounding, the fire in his lungs fueled by the desire to be a hero, the good cop, the man his father had expected. The locator led him to the apartment door, opened it for him, and he rushed inside.

Dolores McNabtree was ninety-seven years old, a little senile and a lot crabby. Lying on her kitchen floor, she hissed at him like a wounded cat.

"What took you so long? I've fallen and I can't get up. Don't just stand there, you young fool! Bring me my walker!"

He carried the aluminum walker the three feet from the wall to the old lady. Then he picked her up with one hand. It took him another fifteen minutes to escape her constant nattering. He finally had to fake another emergency call. By the time he got out of her apartment, the musty smell had rubbed off on his new uniform.

Baumer was sitting at the foot of the stairs, laughing his ass off. Dolores called in at least once a day. Sometimes three times a day, if her equally geriatric daughter failed to visit her.

"How do you know it's not a real emergency?" Kyle appreciated a good joke as much as the next man, but he wanted to learn.

The answer was simple. Whenever Dolores got bored and lonely, she would hold her breath until her medical monitor freaked out. Despite her age, she could hold her breath like a champion—the current record was three minutes and fifteen seconds. The way you knew it wasn't a real emergency was because of the unique combination of elements: a "not breathing" call, after two in the afternoon, from Dolores's med unit.

The lesson was that you had to learn your beat. You couldn't let a machine do it for you.

Kyle started packing a pillowcase with the things he might need. Papers, credit sticks, a change of underwear, that sort of thing. Not his service pistol. It had a GPS tracker in it. The police liked to know where all their people were. That was why he was using a pillowcase, too. All of his luggage had GPS trackers in them. So many ways to foil thieves; so many inconveniences when a man wanted to disappear.

The police were taking an unusually long time to appear. Kyle tossed his pistol into the smoking room—the fire was out now—and retreated to the study. Hiding in the shadows of his own apartment. If they came in with IR goggles, it wouldn't matter.

Finally the door swung open, unlocked by a police override. As he had hoped, Baumer stepped through it first.

"Kyle?" he called, softly.

Kyle made a softer sound, tapping the door he was half-hidden behind. Baumer flicked his eyes that direction, and then let in two more men.

Firefighters, not medics, which was odd. But they weren't wearing League armbands, which was a relief.

They closed the door behind them. The firefighters went straight for the ruined bedroom. Baumer let them go and then slipped over to Kyle.

"What on Earth is up, Kyle?" He kept his voice at a whisper.

That was a good question. But Kyle had one of his own. "Can you trust them?"

"Yeah. I told the ambulance team it was a potentially dangerous situation, and made them wait for the fire squad. Heck, it's even a fire. So I got my nephew in here. He'll play along, and so will his partner. But any second now those boys are gonna figure out there isn't a body in there."

"Sergeant Baumer," a voice called from the bedroom. "Could you give us a hand?"

Smooth kids. Aware that they might be being recorded, they chose their words with care.

Baumer looked at Kyle expectantly.

"I think the League is trying to kill me." "Think" wasn't really the right word, but it didn't matter. Baumer had never liked the League. He'd made plain his unhappiness over Kyle's involvement with it. That Kyle couldn't afford to tell him the truth was another crime for the ledger. "Cover for me, and I'll slip out behind you."

Baumer shook his head. "No way. What if they've got backup waiting out there? A rifle across the street. Or a car full of gunmen. You need an escort." He tugged Kyle's arm and led him into the bedroom.

"Looks like he's burned bad, boys." The kids were staring

oogly-eyed, but keeping quiet. "Put him on the stretcher and let's get him to the transporter."

The short one must be Baumer's nephew. He had the thick bull-frog look already developing.

"Gotta foam him, Sergeant. Or he won't survive the trip." They had the stretcher out by the time the kid finished talking. Kyle lay down on it, and the two young men started spraying him with medical foam.

Wonderful stuff. It came out like shaving cream, but quickly hardened to plastic. Porous enough to breathe through, it was waterproof and antibiotic. Within seconds Kyle was a white, lumpy mummy, covered from head to toe.

"Is it bad?" Baumer was saying. His nephew took the hint.

"Real bad, Sergeant. Hope he was having sweet dreams, 'cause he's never gonna wake up. A few days in the trauma tank, and then it's over. Burns like this, it's a waste to even try."

Kyle had gotten a glimpse of the bed before they sealed his eyes shut. If he'd really been sleeping in it, he would be a pile of ashes by now.

The sensation of being carried was more unpleasant than sitting on the deck of the *Launceston* under fusion power. In both cases he had to wait passively while someone else saved or lost his life.

He could feel nothing through the foam, so he didn't know when they went into the cold, open air. Only the sound of doors slamming told him he had made it to the transporter without catching a bullet. Either there was no backup, or the kids were putting on a great performance. If he was as good as dead, why complicate the inquest?

The transporter was gravitics powered. They had spent a lot of money making it small enough to fit in city streets, and it was still half the size of a bus. But it sailed over traffic and buildings smoothly, and carried medical berths for four patients.

More important, it would be almost impossible for anyone to

follow them. Only emergency vehicles were allowed in the air. Once the vehicle landed, Kyle would have a head start over any ground pursuit.

The nephew made it even better. "Hey, Jones, head for M7."

A voice responded through an intercom. "Navcom says Golden Hill is closer. And they have a great burn ward." That's where they would be waiting for him, then.

"Yeah but . . ." Baumer's nephew fished around for a reason. "I heard some dog on them, man. Their tank fluid's being recycled."

The intercom was disbelieving. "Are you serious? No way!"

"Earth, it's just what I heard. I dunno. But this guy hasn't got any skin left. I don't want him in a tank that somebody else might have to share. He's gonna die anyway, so what's the difference?"

A subtle shift in direction. The rumor was mightier than the computer.

The rest of the very short trip was in silence. The inside of the transporter was certainly under continual surveillance. Kyle revised his opinion of Baumer's nephew again, upward. Without the foam, the ruse would have been exposed immediately. The kid wasn't just reacting well, he was actively planning ahead.

Descent, followed by a gentle bump. The landing was smoother than being lifted out of the transporter. Kyle was helpless, his awareness of the outside world blocked by a layer of foam. He had to wait until the nephew told him when he could make a break for it.

More bumps—he must be on a gurney. Amazing that they spent so much money on a smooth ambulance ride, and then jostled him like a sack of potatoes for the last ten meters.

"Tell Kragen I've got a special for him." The nephew was speaking loudly—too loudly. Obviously half the message was for Kyle.

"Dr. Kragen is with another patient." A female voice, officious and bossy. "Take it up to the tank ward."

"Trust me, Kragen is gonna want to see this guy."

"Dr. Kragen doesn't specialize in burns, medic."

"Yeah, but this guy's a League member."

A brief silence.

"I'll page him." Then, mumbled, "Poor sap."

It challenged all of Kyle's newfound faith in the nephew not to panic at that.

More rolling, and then stillness.

It was only ten minutes. Kyle knew this because he counted his pulse. He didn't have anything else to do. After fifteen minutes he would assume he was alone, and try to escape. But he forced himself to wait, first. That was the most basic mistake the nefarious always made: not having enough patience.

Not enough prudence, even. The humor of the pun was quickly overwhelmed by the desire to share this warm, soft cocoon with her.

"Still alive, I see." A man's voice. Given that aura of authority, it had to be a doctor, which implied it was Kragen. "If you can hear me, try not to move. If you can't hear me, then don't worry about it." Graveyard humor. Not exactly what Kyle looked for in a doctor.

Something pressed on his chest. A monitor. The readings it would be giving off had to be most unexpected.

The monitor remained for a very brief moment. Then Kragen spoke in his ear.

"A curious chart. It says you're a badly burned League officer, in danger of dying at any minute. Given my public opposition to the League, one might think that you were sent in here to finish dying in my disinterested hands. The monitor, however, says you're perfectly healthy, and even a little bit aroused. But my sexual preference is a matter of public record, and in any case it's not my birthday."

A sharp edge brushed against Kyle's upper lip, pressure was removed, and then he could taste fresh air unfiltered through the antiseptic of the foam. Kyle was still catching up to Kragen's logic. The doctor was a fast thinker.

"My staff, expecting the possibility of my failing my Hippocratic oath, will automatically compensate by looping the vid recording, making it look like I spent five minutes in diagnosis instead of five seconds, thus covering up whatever criminal negligence they expect, or possibly hope, for me to commit. I suggest you keep your explanation terse."

It made sense. If the League was trying to kill him, why not take him to an anti-League doctor? Kyle was pretty sure it was only part of the League trying to kill him, though, and that meant that the anti-League might still view him as League, since their contacts in the League might still think of him as loyal. Unless those contacts happened to be undercover League anti-League agents. Like Kyle.

Okay, it didn't make sense.

Unable to meta-game so many layers of deception, Kyle settled for the truth. "I *am* in danger of dying. The League set my bed on fire."

"And I should care why?" Kragen was annoyingly direct.

"Because I'm undercover against the League." Kyle almost laughed. He had revealed his secret just like that, as easy as pie, to a complete stranger. The irony was that the only reason he could do so was because Kragen might believe him. And then he could claim to the League that he was pretending to switch sides, so Kragen would let him in the secret club, so he could bust them to the League. After all, why else would the League have arranged such an inept assassination, if not to get him a chance to infiltrate the opposition? It was such a compelling argument, Kyle almost half-believed it himself.

Kragen was still unimpressed, though. "What, exactly, am I supposed to do about your personal problems?"

"Get me out of here." Kyle didn't need much, just a few minutes' head start on the assassins. He'd calculated that it would take them at least twenty minutes to reach M7 by ground car. Assuming there was active pursuit, of course. But Kyle always assumed the worst.

"For the record, which won't exist since my staff is not recording this, I don't believe you. I am assisting you solely because you ordered me to, in your capacity as a League officer. I may hate and despise the League, and everything it stands for, but I am a loyal citizen. I will testify to this statement, should I be required to."

Kragen's capacity for double-dealing was awe-inspiring, even to Kyle. A whooshing sound, and then Kyle was covered in a layer of wetness as the foam melted away.

The doctor was hardly older than Baumer's nephew. Kyle hadn't realized people that young cared about politics.

"Thank you," Kyle said.

"I have a patient in another ward with terminal brain cancer. He is in a coma. It would be a simple matter for me to assign him to a different room, intercept his gurney along the way, cover him with foam, and switch charts. Robert Anton Wilson would leave a room, and Kyle Daspar would enter one. It would be days before anyone noticed the switch, and then I would explain I had been ordered to do so by a League officer, in an attempt to uncover a plot against the government."

"Thank you," Kyle said again, weakly. It was starting to sound inadequate.

Kragen agreed, and went on to explain just how inadequate it was. "It's ludicrous that a healer should be involved in such shenanigans. But it's ludicrous that a professional of my skill should still be assigned to the night shift of an emergency room. Either I have proven myself obedient to the League, in which case it must cease crippling my career, or I have aided an agent who will destroy the League and eventually achieve the same effect."

But now Kragen had said too much. He clearly wasn't that naïve. The League wouldn't stop harassing him just because he did what they asked. They wanted obeisance, not merely obedience. Which meant that he was telling Kyle he really was anti-League.

But only if Kyle was wise enough to understand it, which would imply that Kyle really was anti-League.

Kyle nodded in agreement. He couldn't think of anything to say that wouldn't make his head hurt.

"Naturally, I can't be held responsible for the theft of Mr. Wilson's identity cards from his room. That's a matter for the police to look into."

With that, Dr. Kragen threw a sheet over him and spoke a command. "Attendant . . . take this patient to room 715." And then the rolling journey again, as Kyle, protected only by cloth this time, waited yet again for someone else to take him somewhere else.

An elevator ride and several turns later, Kyle was left alone. Unable to remain passive any longer, he tore off the sheet.

The room was dark and empty, but he could hear voices coming. He hid behind the bathroom door, leaving it half-open so he could still see.

Two attendants rolled another gurney in, and spent a few minutes transferring a comatose old man to the bed. They puzzled over the second gurney for a moment, but unable to solve the mystery, settled for solving the problem. When they left, they wheeled both gurneys away.

Just as Kyle thought it was safe to come out into the open, Dr. Kragen strolled in.

With businesslike efficiency, he switched charts.

"Sorry about your grandfather, Mr. Wilson." Kragen spoke to Kyle without looking at him. "He'll be more comfortable here for the next two days. At most."

"Thank you," Kyle said again, but to Kragen's back as the doctor walked out of the room.

A brief fishing expedition through the hospital bag next to Mr. Wilson's bed yielded cards and papers. Kyle dropped them into his pillowcase.

Another elevator ride, this time under his own power, and he walked out the front door. It was amusing to think he might have passed some of the same people on the way down as he had on the way up, and they were completely unaware of it. Such were the dubious amusements of secret identities.

Outside, in the cool air, he thought about how Prudence and he had passed each other, buried under their own secrets. Dubious amusements, indeed.

NINE

Speculations

Zanzibar was a very fanciful name for such an unremarkable place. The spaceport was painted in bright colors that clashed, with tassels on overhanging awnings and faux crenellations on the shop fronts. But the colors were faded, the awnings threadbare, and even the stonework had holes and scrapes revealing the stucco underneath.

It was supposed to produce an exotic but personable impression, like an open-air market where travelers from faraway places mingled with friendly locals. A place where rules and regulations took a backseat to fun and adventure, and the import taxes were as lax as security.

The impression it always left on Prudence was that she should double-check the security settings on the *Ulysses* before leaving the ship unguarded.

"Are you going to let me find some real cargo?" Garcia was complaining, for good reason. He got paid a percentage of the profits. She'd left Altair with a full hold, but it had been merely contract shipments, the only thing he could arrange in eight hours. They paid a flat fee per tonne, barely enough to cover the cost of fuel. She couldn't really compete with the big freighters for economies of scale. Instead, she made her money speculating: buying goods outright and reselling them on other worlds. Garcia was generally very good at sniffing out deals and hawking wares.

And Zanzibar was the kind of place Garcia worked best in. Not because it lived up to its amusement-park hype of exotica, but because it was so disorganized that market inefficiencies abounded. Altair had huge computers listing every commodity and service imaginable, with inventory backlogs and appointment calendars updated continuously. Zanzibar was lucky to get the current temperature right.

"Sure, Garcia. Take your time." She'd already broadcast her news, from space, and now the sense of urgency was gone. She had spent the last two weeks running fast and hard, making four hops with no more than a day in between. At Altair she'd only delayed to re-fill her fuel tanks. Garcia had found them a contract shipment literally sitting on the docks.

She had cast her news out on placid worlds, like pebbles in a pond. Then she had fled before they could think to start asking hard questions. On Altair she hadn't even dared to inform the local spaceport authorities, just the dozens of free-trader captains that conglomerated there. Fleet already knew, and would tell the rest of Altair when they felt ready to. They wouldn't appreciate Prudence spoiling their surprise. And it didn't matter. She'd told the people that needed to know.

The news would spread like waves, as the independent freighters rushed to take advantage of it. Any day now she expected the overlapping splash, a fellow captain dropping out of a node and breathlessly telling her of the disaster on Kassa. Such was the nature of communications that had to be carried by hand. Radio didn't travel through nodes.

This had an unappreciated effect on social development. You could get anywhere on a planet in a few hours with a low-orbital flight. You could reach anywhere on a planet with vid comm in-stantly. People grew up that way, thinking of their whole world as one small place. That made the several-day trip through a node into a hurdle that most never bothered to leap. Unleapt, it was unthought-of. Nothing had done more to still-birth stellar empires than this reflexive laziness. Prudence had read stories of old Earth explorers, who had spent months or even years traveling just to make one journey, often under the most grueling circumstances. That spirit was dead, snuffed out by telecommunications and padded chairs.

It was an ironic fact that it could take longer to travel in-system from one planet to another than it did to travel through a node. But people didn't think of it that way. In-system, you were still in contact. An hour delay on radio chatter was not the same as absolute silence. So the frontier, the wilderness, was made up of other planets and moons, asteroid belts and periodic comets. The worlds on the other side of the nodes were not distant; they were imaginary.

Prudence had been to several hundred worlds. Every place she went, they asked her about her last port of call. But no one ever asked about her *first* port. No one ever dug deeper than the last hop, because one hop was indistinguishable from a thousand. They were all merely someplace else.

Melvin wandered past her, a glazed look on his face. She'd taken him to a dozen worlds, and he'd gotten stoned on all of them. Zanzibar was a good world for him, too.

"Keep your comm on," she called after him. He'd spent the last two weeks more incapacitated than usual. She was beginning to think about replacing him. He might be permanently broken.

"Can we go see the castle?" Jorgun liked Zanzibar too. He couldn't see through the illusion. To him, it was an exotic and mysterious bazaar.

Prudence finally confronted the fact that she was the only member of her crew that didn't like the place.

"Sure, Jor." It would probably take Garcia days to line up

something profitable, and Melvin at least that long to decompress. Prudence could stop running now, and let her crew catch their breath.

Herself included. Of all the local worlds, Zanzibar was the least likely to accede to an Altair extradition request. So it turned out she could find something attractive about Zanzibar's slipshod security, after all.

She made herself wait three whole days, until her news had been confirmed by other captains coming out of the node. Of course, all of them had originally gotten the news from her in the first place, but that didn't seem to occur to anyone.

Not directly from her. She saw a few ships she hadn't talked to. They must have gotten their information secondhand. Naturally they were the loudest, and the quickest to cry "alien." Ridiculous pictures were being passed around, claiming to be scientific projections leaked from government labs: the old standbys like skinny gray dwarves with bulging eyes and octopi-headed humanoids in flowing gowns, but also giant slavering spiders dripping venom and waving bulbous weapons in multiple legs.

But now that the subject had been publicly broached, she felt it was safe to start asking questions.

Mauree Cordial ran a dusty shop just off the spaceport grounds that catered to tourists and cranks. Real spacers who stumbled through the heavily barred doors invariably sniffed, laughed, or cursed before storming out. But plenty of them came back, late at night, to cut deals with Mauree. Maybe even in dark alleys and dank bars, as stereotypical as the fake glamour of Zanzibar. A bit of easy cash had a way of overcoming professional disgust.

Prudence squeezed her way through the aisles, looking for Mauree. The navigational difficulty was not from patrons—which, while numbering less than a dozen, nonetheless represented an occupancy record—but from the piles of junk precariously stacked to the ceiling. Mauree bought, collected, and occasionally sold alien artifacts. Since there were, in fact, no aliens, that meant Mauree's shop was stuffed with the random detritus of a hundred worlds, odd bits of useless crap from spacers' personal belongings, with histories culled from their imaginations, traded for a spot of drinking money or just a laugh.

Mauree bought it all, hook, line, and sinker. He'd never met a story he didn't believe, or a spacer he didn't trust. Prudence had first discovered the pleasant, crazy old man when she busted Garcia for selling him rocks at ten credits a kilo. Interesting rocks, smoothly rounded with a translucent sheen over assorted pungent colors, but just rocks. No, she had explained patiently, they won't hatch into lithids and start eating pollution, no matter how long you subject them to ultraviolet rays. She had offered to carry them outside, toss them in the Dumpster, and make Garcia refund his money.

Mauree had graciously declined. The rocks had stayed in one corner of the room, under an ultraviolet lamp, and remained there still. Out of sheer curiosity she had counted them on her last visit. Two had gone missing.

Prudence considered the hypothesis that they had indeed hatched and crawled off under their own power. Against this possibility she could set her personal observation of Garcia collecting them from a dome colony landfill, the waste products of some unknown and uninteresting manufacturing process. He had used them as ballast for a cargo of delicate hand-blown glass flowers. Since the petals and leaves were filled with vacuum, they tended to float entrancingly. Or inconveniently, given the context of the cargo hold. Multiple layers of bubble-wrap plastic proved insufficient, so Garcia had quite sensibly weighted the packages into stability, until the delivery was complete.

It was perhaps equally sensible to extract profit from the rocks themselves, instead of merely from their less substantial counterparts in travel, but not particularly ethical. Prudence had put a stop to it after the first dozen. Why he had only sold that few was still a mystery. Perhaps he wanted to inflate their value by artificially limiting their quantity. More likely he was just too lazy to carry any more than he had to. Having divined the depth of Mauree's pockets, Garcia had plumbed them for the easy pickings, and then told Jorgun to shovel the rest of the rocks into a dry gulch.

With so little evidence in favor of the reality of lithid eggs, Prudence was forced to conclude that Mauree had managed to sell two rocks for the posted price of fifty credits a kilo, despite the presence of a half-ton of identical rocks not a hundred meters from his front door.

Whether that made Garcia or Mauree the villain, and Mauree or the idiot tourist he had bilked the victim, was an ethical conundrum not worth solving.

What it did make clear was the futility of trying to sell Mauree the authentic alien artifact in her pocket, or even showing it to him. He would value it no more than he did Garcia's rocks. Open to all possibilities, he had blinded himself to genuine revelation.

But she hadn't come for money. She had come for information, information that Mauree might not even know he had. Mauree, like his shop, was a cornucopia of falsehoods and trivialities, but also of rumors, hints, and stray facts. Now that she knew what to look for, she might be able to sift a truth from the chaff.

She found him in the most unlikely place in the shop: at the register, recording a sale. Prudence always wondered about Mauree's customers. Superficially, they looked like normal people. This one, for instance, was a large, bearded man in casual clothes. He could be anything from a low-level accountant to a short-order cook. His purchase was a large chunk of rose quartz crystal. Curious, Prudence asked him what he was going to do with it.

"Good works, my dear, good works!" He blew out his cheeks fulsomely, a sheen of sweat glistening on his forehead. "These ordinary-seeming rocks contain alien souls, trapped millions of years ago under terrible circumstances. Innocent victims of violence—destroyed by atomic fire—blind and terrified—their essences took refuge in these entrancing crystals. We meditate over them, relieving their psychic anguish and releasing them from their prison, so that they may join the cosmic dance once again."

"A noble endeavor," Prudence agreed dryly. Such poetry from a man in a soup-stained cardigan suggested that he knew what it was like to be a vibrant soul trapped in a dull shell. "I'm surprised that Mauree is charging you twenty-seven credits for his participation. I would have expected at least a twenty-percent discount."

"Shipping costs," Mauree said gallantly. "It all adds up." Not a trace of defensiveness. That was what amazed her most about Mauree: he had no shame. Either he truly believed his own fantasies, or he was the most core-broken sociopath she had ever met.

"Just part of the cycle," the customer said. "Everyone who helps the spirits is rewarded. When their fear is assuaged, and their prison shattered, they grant luck and favors to those nearby. I can see by the subtle colors of this crystal that the soul within is both strong and eager to be released. A handful of credits to our dear Mauree and a few hours of meditation is a small price to pay for the gratitude of such an ancient and powerful being."

Why did the spiritual ones always turn out to be like Garcia? Long speeches about helping others, but always the inside deal, the percentage, the cut off the top. Nobility done for the basest of motives.

Prudence thought about the fat voucher she had cashed on Altair, and subdued her delusions of superiority.

"Often the pleasurable sensations of freedom at the moment of release are overwhelming," the chubby man continued. "The spirit broadcasts them willy-nilly, and rescuers have been known to be overcome by such exalted emotion. Occasionally even to the point of sensuality . . ." He smiled, aiming for inviting, knowing, sophisticated. He achieved leering.

At least Prudence hadn't flown two straight days of rescue hops merely to get laid.

On the other hand, sex was a healthy part of life. If that's what it took for Chubby to get in the game, who was she to complain? Just because he wasn't her type didn't mean he wasn't somebody's type.

"Sounds interesting," she said sweetly, "but that would conflict with my vow of chastity."

Chubby wasn't completely thick. He smiled sadly, achieving the expression perfectly this time—presumably he had plenty of practice with that one—and excused himself.

"Would you like a crystal of your own?" Mauree asked. "Perhaps you and your young man could do a cosmic good deed."

"Why would I have a young man?" she asked him. "I just said I had a vow of chastity."

Mauree looked over to where Jorgun was playing with some vaguely dinosaur-shaped toys, and shrugged genially. "I try not to judge."

Given that her relationship with Jorgun was both special and chaste, it was understandable that Mauree might think they were in some weird romantic entanglement. Mauree didn't necessarily know it was more like mother and son. Mauree wasn't trying to offend, and he wouldn't be offended, no matter what her relationship with Jorgun turned out to be. As always, she found his total acceptance of any arrangement, no matter how inherently unbalanced, to be itself a source of aggravation.

"No," she said, more shortly than she intended. "I'm here for something else. Something special, Mauree. Something . . . new."

"Battle tokens of the killer fleet that destroyed Kassa?" Mauree looked truly sad. "I don't have any. The shop's had more visitors in the last day than all of last week, but all anybody wants are Kassan souvenirs."

"Have you gotten any new curios in, Mauree? I mean in the last few months." If the ship had been planted, maybe they planted other evidence.

"Always, dear, always! Look at these Burgundian shamanistic feather-wands, still charged with power. And here are two ancient scrolls speaking of alien visitations, although sadly untranslatable by modern means. Or perhaps this vial of rare sea salt, said to restore youth and vigor . . . oh, you did say you were specifically not interested in that. Perhaps a chakratic notch filter? I understand it works off of an alien technology that enhances audio replay. A young fellow brought me some just a few weeks ago." Mauree started to wander down the corridor, peering at objects on the shelves, as if he were not entirely certain himself what a chakratic notch filter would look like.

She would have to steer him in the right direction. It should be safe to reveal facts to him that she had concealed from everyone else. No one was going to question Mauree, anything he said would be easy to deny, and in any case, he was unlikely to remember who had told him the facts in the first place.

"What about spiders, Mauree?"

"Eh?" he said, surprised. "No, I don't think so, dear. I had the exterminator in a month ago."

"Giant spiders, Mauree. Giant alien intelligent spiders with spaceships."

"Oh no, dear." His tone was authoritative and reassuring. "You don't need to worry about that. I'm sure this Kassan thing, however terrible it is, is just ordinary people misbehaving. There aren't any evil aliens in the great Out."

This answer was so utterly at odds with what she expected from Mauree the alien artifact dealer that her suspicion went into full thrust. If only she could figure out a plot that included Mauree in any capacity and still made a shred of sense.

He sensed her change of mood, and tried to comfort her. "My dear, the aliens mean us no harm. They're trying to help."

She remembered Kassa, smashed like a sand castle. She wanted to reach out and shake Mauree until his head cracked. She didn't, but she wanted to.

Mauree surprised her again, reading her emotional state. She had lied to smarter men than Mauree, deceived sharper vision than his rheumy old eyes. But now he could sense her pulling away from him, and he tried to bridge the gap.

"Let me tell you a secret, my dear." He lowered his voice, in conspiracy. Or perhaps just in shame. "All these artifacts are junk. They don't matter."

She followed him, to see where he would go. "Then why do you sell them?"

Mauree shrugged again, the same way he had at the register. "Because people need them. They need a focus for their work. But the artifacts are just signposts. The path is internal, my dear. We are the problem. Our own inner selves. Our own violent, petty human nature. They are watching us, you know, watching from other dimensions. They are waiting for us to cleanse ourselves, to outgrow our obsession with the physical and the material. To become like them spiritually, before we can join them."

She had to ask. "Who are They?"

He smiled at her. "The tech-ten, of course."

Prudence unconsciously fingered the medallion that hung around her neck. There was an obscure school of sociology that rated the technological capacity of various planets. The scale was logarithmic, from one to ten, and star-flight was set at seven, for unfathomable academic reasons. Level-one planets were in the Stone Age, capable only of making simple things that did not require tools. Prudence had never actually heard of a world that poor. Kassa had been classified as level two, producing biological goods like wood and grains. Altair was level seven, since it built starships. Level eight was the level of automatics, computers that anticipated your needs and ground cars that drove themselves.

According to the advertising industry on every planet Prudence had visited, this level was just around the corner. It had been just around the corner since mankind left Earth.

Level nine was true artificial intelligence: machines that were human. The robots of story and legend, the ones that pondered on their metaphysical condition and tried to take over the world.

And level ten was utopia, the pinnacle of achievement, the Highest Possible Level of Development. Genetic science that cured every illness, regenerated every deformed body into perfection. Ships that made their own nodes. Gravitics that fit into shoes, so man could fly as easily as walking. Nano-scale machinery that made wealth out of dirt. Free energy. Immortality.

"You're a starship captain," Mauree said earnestly. "You've been to many worlds. Some are behind and some are ahead. In all the many worlds of man, there must be one who has gone all the way ahead. Beyond technology, to spirituality." Mauree was citing the Doctrine of Transcendence, the mystical philosophy that claimed technology would eventually transform human beings into gods.

Consciously, she took her hand away from her throat, to argue. "Then why don't they do something? Why don't they share their knowledge? Altair conceals trade secrets for profit, but why would your angels care about profit?"

Mauree nodded. "Yes, why? Why indeed? But the answer is inside us. We are not ready for such power. We would destroy ourselves. Science brings knowledge to all, but wisdom must be cultivated in each individual. When our hearts are ready, then they will take us away from all this."

They would never take Jelly away. They would never do any good for the thousands that had died on Kassa. For the millions that had died in the flames that haunted her past. That Jelly's salvation should be denied because an aging con man was still struggling to purify himself was a cosmic injustice of unforgivable proportions.

Someday, when she found her mother's world, the place that made the nanosharp knife that hung around her neck, she intended to demand an explanation.

For now, she confronted Mauree with her own doubts.

"What if tech-ten isn't transcendence? What if it's not *perfect*, just *better*?" What if people were still people, even though they could fly? What if utopia offered no improvement on the human soul, no protection from evils that ordinary men and women could give birth to when driven by greed, fear, selfishness, and indifference?

Mauree shrugged, undefeatable. "Then tech-eleven. It doesn't matter what the number is, you see. All that matters is that everything can be fixed, even people. And if it can be fixed, then surely it must have been. Humanity is less than a million years old. The galaxy is billions. Some alien race must have already evolved to the end, already solved everything. We don't need to struggle to develop new technology, my dear. We only need to develop ourselves, our own inner lights."

Prudence imagined a two-meter-wide spider biting off Mauree's head and looking for an inner light. Petty, yes, but it put things into perspective.

"I don't think it's that simple, Mauree." She settled for dry exasperation. It was the only compromise between rage and grief that let her speak.

"Of course you don't. You're too successful. You have your own starship, the respect and admiration of your fellows. You have too much attachment to this world. But you must not let your imagination be stifled, or you'll turn out like that poor fool Rama Jandi." Mauree was trying to remain noble, but the flush of animosity crept through.

"Who's that?" she pressed. Prudence was currently not very sympathetic to Mauree's feelings.

With the tortured sigh of the persecuted genius, Mauree

launched into an answer. "An academic, of great stature and honors, but cold and dead inside. He has taken his hope and imagination and killed it. Now he lashes out at anyone who dares to reveal a true human soul."

All she had to do was quirk an eyebrow, and Mauree was happy enough to dish out more slander. Perhaps he needed to spend more time meditating over his crystals.

"He had me thrown off Altair, can you believe it? Hounded out by threat of prosecution. Me! For doing no more than selling hope. A few paltry artifacts to the university museum, a pathetic handful of credits, and he cried bloody murder. Said he could prove they were not really alien. Said he could prove I knew it. Called me a fraud!"

Since Mauree had just confessed that everything in his shop was junk, Prudence found his outrage remarkably misplaced. She didn't remark on it, though. "He sounds like a terror. Altair, you said?"

"I used to run my shop there. It seemed like a nice place, but what kind of intolerant planet would let retired professors ruin businessmen?" At least Mauree didn't describe himself as an honest businessman.

"Is he aligned with the League?"

Now it was Mauree's turn to ask. "The who?"

If Mauree thought Altair had been intolerant before the League, he would be in for a terrible surprise now. However, it was a good sign for Prudence. If this Jandi person predated the League, he might not be in on their plot. If there was a plot.

She'd gotten all the help out of Mauree she could hope for. If Jandi was in the business of examining alien artifacts, then that was the lead she should follow. Even if it meant risking a return to Altair.

Speaking of risks, she should repay the favor, and try to return a little guidance. "Mauree, promise me something. Promise me you won't try to sell any Kassan souvenirs. Or buy any. Just stay out of it, okay?"

He looked at her curiously.

"Trust me on this, Mauree. The violence was terrible; people's reactions are going to be dangerous." If there was a plot, and Mauree got on the wrong side of it, they would destroy him without hesitation. And if Mauree got involved in any way, it was inevitable that he would wind up on the wrong side. Even without a plot, he could only suffer from their attention. Prudence had gotten angry enough to want to clobber him over his eccentric philosophy. The League would consider him an active traitor to their triune god of Progress, Development, and Security.

She needn't have worried. Mauree's instincts were sound. "I don't think the energy coming out of Kassa is conducive to my program of gentle development," he agreed. "It's exactly the kind of negative tech I'm trying to rise above."

Prudence remembered the image of the alien warship in the snow. Negative tech, indeed.

TEN

Crumbs

He was Robert Anton Wilson for less than an hour. Most of that was in a cab.

Going to the spaceport was a risk, but it was the only place in the city that rented rooms without asking for ID. People in spaceports didn't necessarily have Altair-recognized identification.

The cabbie didn't ask. The scanner at the spaceport gate was automatic, recording his name but not checking the picture on the card against the man carrying it. The hotel clerk was bored and didn't care.

Kyle spent less than thirty seconds in the room. He ruffled the bedsheets, programmed the computer to hold all calls, and flushed the toilet. Then he left, checking that the door was locked behind him.

Spaceports were interesting places. Kyle had only been to a few, and none of them compared with Altair's. Soaring glass and concrete towers, gently lit in pastel colors, pronounced Altair's wealth and sophistication, but that wasn't what made it impressive. The way you could tell that Altair was an important planet was that its spaceport was always busy. Even in the middle of the night.

Ships came out of the nodes at all hours, and their occupants could be at any point in their daily schedule. Thus, you could buy breakfast, dinner, or a night of heavy drinking at any time of day in the spaceport. Often in the same establishment. The handful of people in the city who worked unusual schedules, like ambulance drivers and such, tended to come to the spaceport to socialize. As did hip young people, quirky retirees, and pretty much everyone who didn't fit seamlessly into Altair's social net.

Including, of course, those up to no good.

That was the thing about being an undercover cop. You learned how people got along, undercover. Under the radar, off the grid, behind the shed door, or whatever metaphor you wanted to use. And it wasn't as simple as snitching somebody's ID card. It took planning, money, or sheer desperation. Fortunately, he had all of those covered.

Five minutes of walking brought him to an automated storage locker. This was the most dangerous moment of his journey. The storage locker itself was harmless. It didn't even ask for ID, just a password. It didn't check what you stored, as long as it fit into a single cubic meter. And you could pay for the space as much as ten years in advance, using anonymous credit sticks issued by any of a dozen planetary banks.

This made it the ideal place to store illegal things, like drugs, weapons, or even inconvenient bodies. Kyle had busted plenty of thugs doing exactly that, as had almost every detective on the force. If there were any cops actively staking out the spaceport, they'd be here. The danger was that one of them might personally recognize Kyle.

The place was also under automatic surveillance, but that wasn't important, either to Kyle or the hoodlums. People's ability to outwit cameras was an evolved response, always one step ahead of automation and authority. Kyle didn't even try. He didn't care about leaving a record. It would be days before anybody checked the files, and by then it wouldn't matter.

He called up his cube and waited patiently for it to be delivered.

This was the kind of job that automation was good for. Everything was in its place, nothing changed, so there were no judgment calls. A task like driving a ground car was an insurmountable nightmare, from a robot's point of view. Anything could happen. Kids and dogs in the road; ice, gravel, or glass; mechanical failures of the vehicle; or just lousy weather. But the storage system was sealed. Nobody could get in or out, so nothing unexpected could ever be in the way.

Come to think of it, it sounded a lot like how the League thought the rest of the city should be.

His cube contained a briefcase. The briefcase contained a change of clothes, a handful of credit sticks, a very expensive fake ID, and a gun.

The gun bothered him. It was unregistered, completely illegal, and he'd stolen it from a crime scene. The League had asked him to, of course. Some low-level blackmailer had gotten popped on a contraband charge. The League had made sure he was on the first team of detectives into the guy's apartment, so he could remove the weapon before it was entered into evidence.

He had almost blown his cover then. No amount of investigation could justify destroying evidence related to any kind of crime that involved a gun. Even as he stood at the door, waiting for the building super to unlock it, he had considered doing the opposite— making sure the gun was found and not lost by some other League stooge on the team.

But inside it had become obvious the contraband was a plant. Kyle figured the gun had to be a plant, too. They were just testing him again.

So he kept his mouth shut. The unlucky blackmailer plea-bargained a deal, sparing Kyle the need to perjure himself in a trial. Kyle rationalized his participation in the frame-up. The amount of time the guy got for the contraband was a lot less than he would have gotten for blackmailing. The government didn't have a strong moral stance against people poisoning themselves. But blackmail, that was different. That tended to piss *important* people off.

Now he tucked the gun inside his jacket. A nasty little thing, made off-world. His service pistol could fire a variety of ammunition, including stunners and narcos. A thousand-volt discharge or a quick-acting drug could solve a lot of problems, usually without killing people. But this gun only fired one kind of round. Shredders. Horrible little projectiles that came apart when they hit something soft. They turned people into hamburger.

Walking back to the hotel district, he checked in to the one across the street. An equally bored clerk gave him a room that overlooked his last room. If a security team swooped down on Robert Anton Wilson, Kyle Daspar wanted to know.

Having set his snare, he settled down to wait again. This was where he would be smarter than the fugitives he routinely caught. He had the patience of a stone.

Sitting in his room, he thought about loneliness. He had been insulated from the feeling. Staying in the same apartment, seeing the same faces at work, he had not noticed. There was a vase in his living room, a present from a woman he had dated a few times. It was a nice vase, although it didn't really go with the rest of the room, and he never put anything in it. The vase was three years old.

No one had moved it, replaced it, or even commented on it. For years he had buried himself in his work, both his day job and his secret job. Wary of every person he met, assuming any woman who showed interest in him was a League spy, treating every man as either a League stooge or a League victim, he had ceased to be human. He wasn't much better than the robot at the automated storage locker. Everything was in its place, nothing changed, and no one could get inside.

———

He woke up with a start. It was midmorning.

If a security team had come looking for Wilson, they must have been remarkably discreet. Flashing lights and door-breakers should have woken him up. So either the doctor was on the level and really covering for him, or the League had sent an assassin to silence him on the sly. In that case, the assassin would still be out there, waiting for him.

The ghost of the possibility that they might have sent Prudence made his heart thud. Her perfect cover act hinted at hidden skills. She would be incalculably more dangerous than a common thug.

His mission was bigger than arresting assassins. He checked out and left the building by a back entrance, avoiding visual contact with the other hotel.

The first thing he had to do was find out if the League was against him, or if it was just Rassinger's faction. Paradoxically, the best place to get accurate information about the League was his network of anti-League agents. People in the League were either too stupid or too fearful to do any fact-checking.

He tossed the gun in a trash can before queuing up at the spaceport exit. There was no way he could sneak it past the sensors. It had served its purpose, bought him a night of security. Now the tool had become a liability, and he discarded it without sentiment.

It was a hideous tool, anyway.

Choosing a credit stick from a different off-world bank than the one he had paid for the room with, he rented a ground car. Too far away from the spaceport, he might draw attention using non-Altair credits. He didn't have a whole lot of those in the anonymous variety.

As prime minister, Dejae had introduced a government plan to reimburse people for stolen credit sticks. Of course, this meant they would have to register their sticks first, thus allowing the government to track every purchase, exchange, and transaction.

Civil libertarians howled and authoritarians cheered, as they always did, every time this subject came up throughout history and the *okimune*. And, as always, the issue was decided by the same factor: human laziness. Registering every single transaction was a pain in the ass. Anonymous sticks owed their birth to the lawyers, but they owed their continued existence to the fact that they were just easier to use. There were always some floating around, and there always would be.

As a young cop, Kyle had sided with the government in trying to outlaw anonymous sticks. As a League opponent, he had trembled in fear of the power such a move would give them. As a fugitive, he was immensely grateful the efforts had failed. The innate sloth that allowed the League to advance was, in this case, its most effective resistance.

A man not on the run for his life might have reflected on the irony. Kyle filed the thought away for another day, when hopefully he would be such a man.

Standing around outside the skyscraper, he waited for lunchtime. It wasn't really a skyscraper. It was anchored to the ground. The original Altair charter, in a fit of nostalgic superstition, had forbidden the use of grav-plating in constructing residences. The rule had stuck, and Altair society had spread out over the ground instead of clumping up in the sky. The biosphere of the planet consisted of thoroughly harmless moss and algae that produced a pleasantly breathable atmosphere. There was nowhere you couldn't build a house, if you wanted to.

But people like living in groups, so towns and cities formed naturally. You could still go out to the marshes and build yourself a cabin on a plain of flat rock covered in dull green moss, next to a silent sea with nothing but dull green algae in it, but who would want to do that? Kyle had adapted to a life of isolation, but not so much that he found such a prospect palatable.

Kyle preferred the orderly arrangement of civilization. Even while he was plotting to prevent the *too* orderly arrangement of civilization. Moderation was the key. That's why he was wearing a fake beard, absurdly hip clothes from three years ago, and waiting on a fellow plotter.

Ricarada Baston. Slim, dapper, officious-looking. Probably drank fruity drinks when he went out to the bars, which would be only on holidays. His clothes weren't hip, but they weren't out of date, either. He strode purposefully across the plaza, carrying on a one-sided conversation over a headset.

Kyle tailed him to a nearby fish-and-chips shop. The cheapest of the cheap; vat-grown meat and vegetable material deep-fried in synthetic oil. Rica made plenty of money as a government prosecutor. He could eat lunch anywhere, even at those fancy restaurants that grew actual fish in tanks and real plants in hydroponic chambers. Kyle had never figured out if Rica ate junk food because he was cheap, making a political statement about solidarity with the poor, or merely oblivious to the difference.

Getting in line behind him, Kyle ordered the wasabi tuna. He didn't know what a tuna was supposed to be, but it was bland enough to make the burning spice tolerable. Right now he needed something to make him feel concrete sensations, something to anchor his emotions in this new reality.

"Is the fettuccini good?" he asked Rica, a random stranger striking up a meaningless conversation. Except that fettuccini wasn't on the menu.

"Not here," Rica replied, and moved on, ignoring him.

Kyle sat by himself in the corner, where he could watch every entrance. Rica only finished half his meal, then abruptly walked out.

The anti-League conspiracy didn't have a lot of protocols. Kyle wasn't sure what the signal meant, but the tuna was bad enough that he didn't care. They hadn't changed the frying oil in days. Resisting the urge to write somebody a health-code ticket, he tossed the food into the garbage and left.

Rica was waiting for him outside, at a bus stop. Kyle sat down next to him on the bench. The noise of the street would make long-range eavesdropping difficult, assuming anybody was watching. Rica must assume no one was, or he wouldn't dare to be here.

"Somebody set my bed on fire," Kyle said. He leaned forward and rested his head in his hands, looking down at the clean, white concrete.

Rica was having a subdued conversation on his headset. "Did they make you?" He said it so naturally it took Kyle a minute to realize Rica was talking to him.

"I don't think so." If they had suspected him, they wouldn't have sent him out to Kassa in the first place. "I think somebody upstairs just doesn't give a rat's ass about whether I live or die."

"Why do housecleaning, unless you're expecting company?" Rica was being really cryptic with his codes, and Kyle was annoyed by it. He was still tired. Not just from having his sleep disturbed last night, but from all of it. The trip home in close confines with Rassinger, the cloak-and-dagger games with Prudence, the whole disaster on Kassa. The last five years.

Then it occurred to him that Rica's obtuseness was a code in itself. The danger level must be high.

"Yes," Kyle said, "we're expecting company. But not the in-laws."

"I don't put a lot of stock in rumors." Meaning that Rica must have already heard some.

Kyle didn't know how to communicate the full impact of his message in code, so he said it outright. "They're not rumors. I saw." A curious choice of pronouns. Why was he still trying to protect Prudence and her crew?

Rica scanned the streets for a moment. A pointless gesture. If they were under surveillance, Rica wouldn't be able to detect it. All he would accomplish by looking for watchers would be to alert them that he was about to say something important. You'd expect a prosecutor to know these things.

"Tell me."

"I got to Kassa after it happened. But they left some nasty surprises for me. Then I found a real surprise. A ship, fighter-craft sized, lying in the snow. I don't think I was supposed to find that. It's not human, Rica."

Rica pursed his lips in disapproval. "Fleet headquarters is sealed up tight. No news in or out. Leaves are canceled. The prime minister will be making a speech tonight."

Kyle understood his disappointment. Everything was happening exactly as it should. Rica wasn't the kind of man who appreciated it when his opponent made no mistakes.

But they had made one. "They sent me there *before*, Rica. The League dispatched me to Kassa days before the attack happened. And then Rassinger showed up, right on schedule." He and Prudence had orbited the planet many times, looking for radio signals from survivors. They hadn't seen the distress beacon from the fighter ship until hours before Rassinger arrived. And it was a strong signal—the *Phoenix* had found it with no trouble.

"Why send you at all?"

It was a good question. The answer couldn't be just to kill him. Patrol boats were not cheap.

"They almost vaporized the rest of the *Launceston* along with me. Maybe they wanted to kill several birds with one stone?" Maybe Captain Stanton did more than just turn his nose up at League armbands. Maybe the man was part of the secret resistance. It was about the level of irony Kyle had come to expect.

"We don't have a mutual defense treaty with Kassa," Rica pointed out. "Legally, we don't have a *casus belli*. An attack on one of our vessels would give us justification."

That was insanity. "There are ten thousand corpses on Kassa, killed by *aliens*. Did they really think they'd need a *law* to start a war?"

Rica smiled, a sad little smile of disappointment. "Our friends often seem to underestimate emotional reactions. I used to think they were just arrogant."

In all this time, Kyle had never considered the possibility that the League was working *for* the aliens. It was simply too incredible.

"I've met the prime minister, Rica. He's a human being. He can't be working for aliens. Nobody would sell out their own *species*."

"When did you meet him?" Rica was surprised, as he should be. Detectives didn't usually keep company with prime ministers.

"About five years ago, when he was just the mayor. Stopped him for a minor traffic violation. I didn't ticket him, not even a warning. He told me to let it go, and I did. Shortly after that, my career took off." And his life had gone into the toilet.

Rica looked at him quizzically. "You let him go? But why?"

Kyle felt his face flush. "Because I knew he would kill me if I didn't. He had something to hide; something worth killing for. I've spent five years looking for it, investigating every crime committed on that day, from missing person reports to shoplifting charges."

"Exactly what day was that?" Rica asked, out of professional habit. Whenever a crime was brought up, the prosecutors asked the same questions: when was it, where were you, did anybody see you there?

Usually, people could barely remember what they had for breakfast the previous day, but this date was stamped into Kyle's memory, indelible as an acid burn.

"The second of August, 785."

"Well, I can alibi the prime minister then." They both smiled at the irony. "From two until four, he was giving a speech to the attorney's office. I specifically remember making a notation in my daily journal: *this is the end of my career advancement.* I should have gone into private practice then, but I couldn't bear to let the thugs win that easily."

"What?" The vision was clear in Kyle's mind. Checking his watch just before he stepped out of the patrol car, so he'd know what time to put on the incident report. The data tablet had a clock on it, of course, but he'd learned his lesson by then. You don't let a machine do your job.

"I thought I could do more to protect civil liberties from the inside. So I stayed at my desk, even while—"

Kyle interrupted him. "What time did you say the speech was?"

"From two until four. With a social hour afterwards. Why, what time did you stop him?"

The glowing green digits of his watch hovered before Kyle's memory.

"Three forty-eight. In the afternoon."

Frowning, Rica tapped at his comm unit and showed the results to Kyle. On the tiny display, there was his personal planner entry for that date: *PM Speech, 2–4. Notes: WTE!!! end of cr advnce!*

"One of us must be mistaken."

Kyle had spent years investigating the events of that day, checking for crimes that could have been committed in the hours before he had stopped Dejae. He had assumed Dejae was running from somewhere he shouldn't have been. It had never occurred to him to search for where Dejae was *supposed* to be.

"I was in fear for my life, Rica. I remember what time it was."

"When you eliminate the impossible, whatever remains must be the truth, however improbable." Rica grimaced. "There must be two Veram Dejaes. One was bad enough."

Kyle shook his head in dismay. "A twin brother? How much does anyone know about Dejae's past?"

"Not as much as we should." Rica shrugged. "He only came on-planet ten years ago. He was wealthy then, and he got wealthier fast. That buys a lot of secrets."

"Why bother to hide something like that?" Since when was having a twin brother worthy of state secrecy?

"A good question, Lieutenant. One of many I have never seen a satisfactory answer to. We've sent investigations to his previous planet of residence, Baharain, but they came back with nothing suspicious. Whether they were bought, fooled, or League agents from the beginning, I can't say. It didn't seem important. Altair politics are extremely public, with well-crafted checks and balances. One man can't corrupt the system, not even the prime minister."

"Unless we let him," Kyle said, thinking about how Captain Stanton had knuckled under to a piece of paper. Even Prudence had.

"What could compel the people of Altair to turn their political security over to a man they hardly know, one that isn't even a native? What kind of threat could make us give up our clumsy, slow, ineffective, but extremely democratic system?"

It was Rica's favorite kind of question—rhetorical. They both knew the answer.

An alien invasion. The threat of annihilation at the hands—or legs, or claws, or whatever you called spider appendages—of inhuman monsters.

"He'll ask for emergency powers," Rica said. "He'll get them. Then he'll simply never release them. As long as the threat of alien attack remains, we'll go along with it, until we can't remember how things used to be different."

Kyle had seen Kassa firsthand. If the choice was between that and Dejae's absolute rule, even Kyle would choose Dejae.

"The aliens are real," he warned Rica. "They must be in some kind of collusion with the League, but they're real. Kassa was bombed by lots of ships, too many to not be accounted for. Not even the League can be hiding a private fleet."

"Stipulated, Lieutenant. But now we know Veram Dejae is not real—or at least, not what he seems." Rica reached into his pocket, pulled out several credit sticks, and dropped them into Kyle's hand. "You need to go to Baharain and find out why there are two Veram Dejaes. That's our only lead."

Rica didn't know about the blue data pod. Kyle didn't have it on him; he'd stashed the thing in case he got caught trying to connect with Rica. It was too late to bring it up now. But there was something he could ask about.

"There's a ship involved. The *Ulysses*, captained by a woman named Prudence Falling. I can't tell if she's an agent or a hapless civilian in the wrong place at the wrong time."

Tapping at his comm unit again, Rica shook his head in warning. "Fleet records say she claims to be from a place called Strattenburg. That's an impossible one hundred hops Out. A rather obvious fake identity. The League is getting sloppy."

Kyle nodded in agreement. It was the same conclusion he had reached. He understood he would never see her again, except to kill or be killed. Asking Rica about her had been a sentimental weakness, a childish hope that she might be what he wanted her to be. What she had been when her voice had come out of the vacuum of space and saved his life.

On his side.

"Not so sloppy they can't kill you, Lieutenant. Be careful. But don't contact me again. It's too dangerous."

Nobody was ever really on your side. Life was something you went through on your own. Kyle walked away from the bus stop, alone, as always.

ELEVEN

Slivers

Going back to Altair felt like a very bad idea. Prudence did it anyway.

Garcia had filled the *Ulysses* with anise seeds. Zanzibar made fantastic spices but lousy packaging. The whole ship stunk of sickly-sweet licorice. Garcia had spent the entire four days in node-space trying to convince her to spread the rumor that Zanzibar had been bombed, and this would be the last shipment of anise Altair would ever get.

She told him to spread it himself. But of course no one would believe Garcia. He couldn't spread butter on toast without people checking their pockets to see if they had been robbed.

There were hailed the instant they came out of the node. Normally it took a few minutes for the signal to travel out to the node from Altair. For the call to come so quickly, it had to be local. Somewhere out there in the dark hovered Fleet. Running silent, invisible to her sensors. Prudence muttered a futile prayer of commiseration for them. A terrible duty, sitting quietly in a ship full of anxious, edgy spacers, waiting for death to fall out of a hole and eat you. She wondered how much they had been told. Did spiders haunt their nightmares now?

The *Ulysses* answered automatically, identifying itself, keeping a twitchy gunner from firing—this time. It was only a matter of probability before some comm glitch got an innocent ship vaporized.

Her news was now two weeks old. Catching up on the political broadcasts, she was surprised at how calm things were. But independent verification still hadn't come back. It would be another week before the first wave of free-traders from Altair could return, bringing with them pictures and eyewitnesses and casualty lists.

Altair spaceport gave her an entry vector and a landing berth assignment without any trouble. She'd been half-expecting a seizure order. On a whim, she typed in a news-search for the dreaded Lieutenant Kyle Daspar. Was he enjoying his fifteen minutes of fame as a heroic rescuer?

A single headline appeared.

League Officer Assassinated by Terrorists.

A picture of a smoking building. A vid interview with the ambulance tech, talking about how the body had been burned beyond recognition. An official statement from the League, lamenting the loss of a good man and darkly hinting that Something Must Be Done. She clicked off the monitor and looked away.

She told herself the numbness she felt was because of the danger. The League had killed Kyle because of the alien ship. And that meant they would kill her, too, if they knew what she knew. How could she trust that he had not given her up before he died? Why wouldn't he?

She remembered his eyes, pleading with her to not reveal their secrets to the *Phoenix.*

The alien threat was the least of her worries. There wouldn't be any arrest warrants waiting for her when she landed. The League was playing for keeps. They would send an assassin to come at her in the middle of the night, with a needle that would make it look like natural causes. Or maybe they'd let her load a cargo and leave, with a bomb planted in the shipment. A fiery bomb, like the one they had killed Kyle with.

In her nightmares the fire always followed her, consuming guilty and innocent alike, burning in her footsteps as fast as she ran.

A rational part of her mind tried to argue. *One dead man out of thousands on Kassa, and you didn't even like him.* He was working for the enemy, anyway. One less League officer should be a cause for celebration.

But she could not escape the recollection of his voice, demanding justice for the Kassans he had never met.

"*No. It's not good enough,*" he had said, and she had agreed with him.

Whatever twisted rationalizations had kept him in the League had not destroyed him completely as a man. So the League had finished the job. She was not fooled by the babble about terrorists. The only resistance to the League she had ever seen on Altair was talk.

Not that it mattered. If there was an anti-League, by the time it bombed its way to the top, it would be indistinguishable from the League. When the political process was carried out by daggers hidden under cloaks, it didn't matter who won. The end was always the same.

A crematorium for the Other. The enemies of the state. The losers. The nightmare returned, all the worse for being a waking memory.

She concentrated on breathing. This was not Strattenburg. This planet was not choking in overpopulation. The only infection here was fascism, not eugenic madness. Power and empire were their goals, not a pogrom against those the State named *undesirables*. There was no reason to think otherwise.

But as she watched the green planet sparkle below, she could not shake the specter of death.

Be careful." She tried to warn her crew, but it was futile. Melvin was stoned into near-unconsciousness, Jorgun could not understand, and Garcia could not obey. He took risks automatically, like a fish breathes water. Her advice was wasted.

And hypocritical, given her intentions. If the League was at the stage where they simply killed the people that threatened them, then visiting Rama Jandi would put both their lives in danger. She was going to do it, anyway.

"Can I come with you?" Jorgun asked. All she had accomplished with her warnings was to scare him. Normally Altair was one of the few ports of call she could let him roam freely. In idle moments she had considered writing a spacer's guide to planets, rating them according to how many hours you could let a simpleton walk around unescorted before he would stumble into trouble. Altair had been the top of her list. Kassa had been second only because a person could get lost in those ridiculous forests.

Having that sense of safety taken away hurt physically, like a punch to the kidneys.

"Sure," she answered. The fear of entangling him deeper was overridden by the recognition that she would be more worried every second he was out of her sight.

Walking out of the spaceport in broad daylight, in the middle of crowds, she nonetheless found herself instinctively hiding in his shadow. Circling around him, using him like a shield against the sniper she imagined on every rooftop. Cold, but not cruel. She had to be their first target. They would know that shooting him would only alert her. Surely they understood she was the dangerous one.

If they killed her first, Jorgun would stand dumbly over her body while they reloaded.

The people in the crowd didn't know that. They gave way to Jorgun's size unconsciously, flowing around the rock instead of trying to move it. With his shades on, he looked intimidating. He looked like a bodyguard. Could she trust that the League had done its homework?

"Can we go see a cartoon?" her protector asked.

"In a bit," she muttered. Standing in front of a public net console, she tried to stop dodging invisible bullets and focus on typing. She hadn't wanted to search for Jandi from her ship's computer, in case they were watching. But the public console was anonymous. Not that the locals used it. Virtually every person on Altair had a comm unit in their pocket. She vaguely remembered some government program that distributed them to the financially disadvantaged. And yet they still provided free public consoles.

It was ironic that the only time she had ever used one was when she wanted to avoid precisely the government that had made them possible.

The first search result was a recorded appearance speech by Jandi, on some daytime babble-fest vid channel. The host, Willy Billy, looked like his normal topic of conversation was which celebrity was snubbing who, but for this broadcast he'd put on his Serious Face.

"*You're saying, Dr. Jandi, that the aliens aren't dangerous?*"

Jandi was an old man, small, stooped, and wreathed in a great white mane.

"*I'm saying there aren't any aliens. I've studied nonterrestrial biology for sixty years. We have no evidence of any other intelligent life, let alone space-faring bug-eyed monsters.*"

"*Are you serious, Dr. Jandi? No monsters? Then what do you call this?*" Willy rolled his eyes as the camera cut to an inserted shot, and his audience duly laughed.

The screen displayed one of the less absurd mock-ups of a huge spider, a 3-D model allegedly derived from forensic reconstruction. The picture had a government label on it; they were now pretending to confirm their pretend leaks. At least this one didn't have a half-naked woman struggling in its grasp.

Jandi was unperturbed. "*I call it an artist's rendering, which is what the government lab that released that picture called it. The overactive imagination of an underpaid academic is not evidence.*"

Prudence shook her head in dismay. The old man was talking above his audience. All they would remember was the picture.

He was billed as Altair's resident specialist on alienology, but there were no more public appearances on record. Mauree had described him as being retired years ago. Either he was too old and out of touch to be of concern to the League, or they had already silenced him. The news reports showed there were plenty of working scientists willing to endorse their arachnophobic vision.

With a little prodding, the console yielded a contact code. When she used it, an automated response filled the screen, a cartoon of a little green man in a plumed helmet.

In a squeaky voice, it said, "Oh drat these computers, they're so naughty and so complex, I could pinch them!"

Then it waited patiently for her response.

"Dr. Jandi," Prudence said, "I got your name from a mutual friend." She stopped, wondering how much she should give away. "Mauree sends his . . . cordial greetings. If you have some time, I'd like to meet with you."

The screen dissolved into Jandi's lined face. "Time, my dear, is something I have remarkably little of remaining. But what better way to spend it than in the company of a lovely young woman?" The old rogue was still dangerously charming; Welsing would have melted with envy.

"Is today convenient for you?" she asked.

"If you are not opposed to vat-grown vegetable protein, then you may join me for lunch. This sad diet is a punishment from my doctors, and misery does love company." He did something on his end, and an address appeared on the screen in front of her, spelled out underneath his chin. With an arched eyebrow he glanced past her. "Shall I cook enough for your massive young man lurking in the background, as well?"

Age had not dulled Jandi's perceptual abilities. Poor Mauree must have been as transparent as glass.

"Yes, please." Remarkable that he would invite two strangers into his home. Especially given that he knew she was an off-worlder. He would not have bothered to ask an Altairian if they objected to vat-grown food. Even the wealthy elite ate the stuff for breakfast.

"I'll be expecting you at noon." Jandi smiled what was probably meant to be a friendly smile, but came off as a college professor assigning a particularly wayward student a trip to his office after class. The screen went blank.

"You want to go for a ride?" she asked Jorgun.

"To see a cartoon?" Ever hopeful, he was.

Prudence hailed a cab, a ground car. Part of Altair's fetish for growing out, not up. Grav vehicles were restricted to emergency and military use. Prudence didn't particularly like ground cars. The sensation of speed was magnified when you were that close to the ground, and she always wondered how they avoided running into each other. On the tight, narrow strips of concrete the little cars were often less than a meter apart.

In the sky, there was plenty of room. Vehicles kept a safe buffer around themselves, never coming closer than a hundred meters for anything the size of a starship. That struck her as a much more sensible arrangement.

"Do you have a vid?" she asked the driver.

"Yes, lady." He was an off-worlder too, with an accent from several hops away. The cab drivers were always foreigners. It made no sense to Prudence. Surely the locals knew their way around better. "The latest news on now. Alien spiders!" The cabbie grinned at her. An incongruous reaction, she thought.

Inside the cab, she gave the driver an address on the opposite side of the city from Jandi's house. She had time to waste, and she wanted to see if she was being followed. Jorgun set himself to the vid controls and found a cartoon channel by the time the cab started moving.

"Aren't you worried about the spiders?" She instantly regretted starting a conversation with the cabbie. He hardly seemed to be paying attention to the traffic as it was.

"Yes, of course, lady. But it is good news for me. Immigration is hard. I want to bring my cousins to Altair; the work is easy and the air does not stink. But that whoreson of a dog stopped the immigration. Now, with the aliens, they will have to start it again."

She hazarded a guess. "You mean the prime minister?"

"Yes, yes," he said, as if it were obvious. "The whoreson of a dog. That one. He is an immigrant himself, but does that matter? Not to a dog that eats his own vomit."

She hadn't known that about the prime minister. Or about dogs, either, but that part might just be color commentary.

"Why do you think the alien problem will restore immigration?"

The cabbie grinned at her in the mirror. "It already has. Fleet is recruiting. Anyone in Fleet can become a citizen. Many other foreigners are joining Fleet, to become citizens. And who will drive the cabs then? My cousins."

A remarkably provincial view of the threat of alien invasion. The inability to credibly project the future was an intractable flaw in the human design.

But if the cabbie could project the future she remembered, he would be paralyzed by horror. Maybe it wasn't a design flaw. Maybe ignorance was the only thing that kept people going.

An hour in the cab left her with motion sickness. It wasn't the rapid changes in velocity that did it, but the constant rush of objects past the window. In space, the stars did not move. The background was always still.

She had wanted to close her eyes and ignore it all, but she had to watch for surveillance. After a handful of false destinations, she had directed the cabbie to Jandi's house. Now they were parked outside, while she tried to decide if it was safe to go in.

"We were not followed." The cabbie was grinning conspiratorially again. It seemed to be his only expression. He'd used it even when he was insulting the prime minister. "I drive like a madman. And the government, it cannot put secret cameras in the cab. It is not allowed."

Yet, she thought, but kept it to herself. "What makes you think I was worried about being followed?"

"Pretty girls are all the time taking long cab rides with young men. I won't tell your rich husband, lady. If I were a rich man and my wife cheated on me, it would be my fault, for not making her feel like a queen."

"Don't they usually end up at hotels?"

"Yes, lady." He grinned even wider. "That you come to such a fine house means your husband must be very rich indeed."

She tipped him well. He deserved it. Then, gratefully, she put her feet on unmoving ground, and dragged Jorgun after her.

Jandi's house was indeed "fine." Not a mansion, but large enough to be stately, and on a private lot. The entire neighborhood was like that, the street lined with tall, majestic trees. On Kassa trees were cut down as a nuisance. On Altair, they smelled of age, stability, and money.

On the door screen, the same little green man glared silently at her, holding up a small box with a button in one hand. When she reached to push it, he moved it away.

She tapped on the center of the screen, ignoring the antics of the little figure. It squeaked at her in annoyance, but she could hear a door chime sounding inside the house.

"Come in, come in!" The door opened as Jandi hauled on it from the other side. The door was two meters tall and made out of a single piece of wood. Altair must pay their professors quite well.

"Do you like my door? It's an import. Something I picked up on a field trip. All of my colleagues thought I was insane to pay the freight charges to bring it home. All of my neighbors are insanely jealous, and think I paid a dozen times what I did."

The trader in her couldn't resist asking. "Why didn't you import a dozen more?"

Jandi smiled at her, crinkling the bulk of his face into an impish grin. "The value of the door as a stanchion of perspective was greater to me than a fistful of credit sticks."

"I like the cartoon on the front," Jorgun said.

Jandi bowed his head in respect. "A discriminating taste you have, young man. That is also an import—said to be an image from Earth itself. Do pardon my speech, I beg you; I am an old man and politeness is such an imposition on my time. I have what is reputed to be a digital copy of the original sequence: the little man, an alien, engages in a comic battle with a Terrestrial rabbit. Would you like to watch it?"

Jorgun nodded eagerly. Probably the only thing he got out of the speech was the swear word and the idea of watching a possibly naughty cartoon. It was enough, for Jorgun.

Snapping his fingers, Jandi led them into a large den, where a wall-mounted vid sprang to life. He rattled off some commands and the vid began displaying a cartoon, complete with the strangest music Prudence had ever heard. Its age was undeniable; the graphics were primitive beyond belief. Yet despite their crudeness, they had an innate power, like cave paintings of men hunting deer.

Prudence had only seen pictures of cave paintings in history books. She wondered what it would be like to see one for real. To view an artifact that had been made by human hands before the exodus. All she had ever seen were digital reproductions of digital recordings.

"Make yourself comfortable, lad." Jandi waved at the various couches sprawling about the room. "My dear, if you would help me in the kitchen?"

She followed him through the house, feeling the need to reassert some control. "We can talk in front of him. He's not simple enough to babble to strangers."

"I did not doubt his valor," Jandi responded politely. "But I thought you would not want to disturb him with your speech. I presume you did not really come out here to discuss Mauree Cordial. How is the old rogue, by the way?"

"He seems happy enough. Zanzibar suits him."

"Yes, it would," Jandi agreed. "Flavor over substance. And none too picky about the cleanliness of the plate it's served on." That did describe the planet succinctly, to Prudence's mind. "But now that we've established your bona fides, we can stop sparring. Why did you come? Surely not just for the free meal. I am vain, yes, but not about my cooking." They had reached the kitchen, and he lifted a pot lid, stirring the contents. Cubes of various vegetable proteins, boiling in a thick broth. Stew, soup, mush, gruel, whatever you wanted to call it. It had a thousand names and flavors on a hundred worlds. Prudence had stopped counting long ago. Jandi's version at least smelled palatable.

"I watched you on the Willy Billy show." She took the bowl he was offering, held it while he spooned soup into it. "I wanted to tell you that you're wrong."

"You believe in space-faring aliens?" He raised his bushy white eyebrows, like snowy caterpillars on parade.

"I saw the evidence myself. A ship, crashed in the snow. A single-pilot fighter, but not built for humans."

Calmly Jandi snapped on the vid screen over the stove, flipped past the cooking channels, and called up a picture.

The alien fighter craft. Photographed in a warehouse, lit by floodlights. Jandi paged through a dozen shots from different angles.

"Fleet has been handing out these pictures to their friends. I still have friends at the university, so I've received an unofficial copy. I've seen the pictures, and I'm still not convinced. Ships are made by men."

Prudence fished a plastic bag out of her pocket. Inside was the precious sliver, stained in blue. She offered it to Jandi silently.

Taking it gently, he held it up to the light. "A nice touch, making it blue. Any idiot can tell it's not human that way. But why bring this to me instead of the government?"

"What government? All I've seen is the League. There was a League officer on my ship when I found the alien vessel. Then a League officer showed up and claimed the prize."

"And you don't like the League?"

"I was born on Strattenburg." She didn't know if that would mean anything to him, but it meant a lot to her.

He looked at her sadly. "Are the rumors true?" He was an academic, a member of a university, the one social institution that lived longer than governments. They were the only entities that tried to keep any kind of contact between the far-flung driblets of the *okimune*. He had at least heard rumors.

"No. The truth is worse."

"You fear it could happen here? The situation does not seem analogous." He spoke about tragedy in scientific terms. She had to remind herself that he couldn't help it. He was an academic.

"All I know is what I feel. And the League scares me."

Jandi nodded in acceptance. "I can analyze this without going through official channels. But it will take time. Yes, I know, you are in a hurry. Young people always are. I am in a hurry, too, my dear. My doctors are terrible liars. Take some soup to your young fellow. Enjoy the cartoon. I will contact you as soon as I can."

She left her berth number at the spaceport, and went to find Jorgun. He ate his soup without comment, watching the end of the cartoon. Prudence waited with him, wondering if the police were on their way now, wondering if Jandi had betrayed them.

"That was funny. But they said the dirty word a lot."

"It's a grown-up cartoon, Jor," she reassured him. "They're allowed."

Jandi's voice came over the house intercom.

"My apologies for being such a poor host. But I have so little time left, and this puzzle needs solving. Please show yourselves out—I've already summoned a cab. Do not despair, my brave young captain. I will not fail thee in thy hour of need."

"He has a puzzle? Can we play with it?" Jorgun was phenomenally good with jigsaw puzzles. Prudence wasn't sure why he enjoyed them. All he did was take the pieces out of the box, one at a time, and put them where they belonged. Once she had chastised him for tossing a piece into the trash when he was halfway through a puzzle. Contrite, he had fished it out again, and placed it on top of the duplicate piece already on the table. After that, she had let him do the puzzles his own way.

"It's not that kind of puzzle, Jor. But we can go get you one from the store."

Outside, they waited for the cab. The cab would take them to her ship, where she would wait some more. Prudence tried to pretend that she was in a node. Those days of enforced waiting never bothered her. They were like vacations from the world. There was nothing that could touch you, and nothing you could do about it. The node was safe.

Kyle Daspar's death had proved that Altair wasn't.

TWELVE

Miners

Baharain was an ugly planet. No wonder Dejae had left it.

The atmosphere was toxic. Not merely oxygen-free, but actually poisonous. The gravity was heavy, the days were short, and the solar radiation was carcinogenic. As if to celebrate these ugly features, the domed cities were smelly, squat, and dark.

The planet was rich in heavy metals and closely placed to a node. A hundred thousand people made a living out of these two slightly less ugly features. If you could call artificial light, air, and gravity a living.

Next to metals, immigrants were Baharain's chief exports. People came to work, saved their credits, and left as soon as they could. A suitcase full of gold or palladium would fund retirement on any planet.

Kyle sank into this stream of economic adventurers without a splash. Asking questions and getting answers proved to be more difficult. People here were suspicious of everyone and everything, and with good reason. Kyle had learned that at least one planet used Baharain as its penal system. Crimes were punished by fines measured in kilos of metal, which amounted to years of servitude. The offenders were shipped off to Baharain to earn their redemption, die, or give up and accept permanent banishment. While Kyle could see the advantages for the locals, it was rather an impolite way to treat the rest of the galaxy. Sweeping your trash into your neighbor's yard wasn't very neighborly, even if it was historically commonplace.

Suffering under the peeling, drab dome, watching men and women trudge from their hovels to their pits, Kyle wasn't sure how many of the men he'd sent to prison on Altair would switch places with these poor drudges. Prison was just another society. Some men took to it, and some didn't. Some were better once they got out, and some weren't.

It was hard to think of Prudence as one of those eternal wanderers, floating without connection from place to place. Was she a criminal, banished from her home? Or had she sent herself into exile, fleeing guilt or shame or simple dissatisfaction? It hardly mattered if she were really from a distant world or not. Star-farer or secret agent, she was cut off from her past just as irrevocably. She could never return to the life she had left. He wondered if she remembered that old life, the way he sometimes remembered his life before the League.

The wretches on Baharain didn't think about their past lives. They barely remembered their own names. None of them remembered Veram Dejae. He crawled through the restaurants and bars, looking for a crack in the wall of ignorance and disinterest. He hadn't bothered with official channels. That had been done before, with no result. Rica had given Kyle a copy of the previous investigator's reports. What passed for a government on Baharain was a collection of corporations, and they were not interested in discussing where Veram Dejae had come from.

But he certainly hadn't come from here. Only the poorest or most negligent parents would try to raise a child on this sorry excuse for a planet. Dejae was too healthy, too smart, too tall to have grown up in this stultifying environment.

There were no clues to be found in the nooks and crannies of these domes. But Kyle had learned how Dejae worked. The secret would be in plain sight.

The first step was to find out how Dejae's money got delivered. Baharain had its own credit system, but nobody took their sticks off-world. They took sticks of precious metals instead. Barbaric, but effective, and harder to trace than even Altair's anonymous credit sticks.

He spent three days in dirty clothes and week-old stubble trawling the spaceport. The ships that wouldn't offer him passage at any price had to be the ones carrying cash payments. The one going to Altair—a beefy freighter three times the size of Prudence's little ship—had to be Dejae's. Even Kyle's Altairian accent couldn't get him on that ship.

There was no hope of finding out what or who had loaded the ship, of course. Merely asking could prove to be dangerous. Instead, Kyle watched who came to *unload* it.

The majority of the cargo seemed to be machine parts. Altair's highly skilled workforce and advanced technological infrastructure made plenty of those, and a world like Baharain would need them. The bulk of the parts went to a mining corporation called Radii Development Corp.

One area the local government did pay attention to was corporate filings. For good reason—they charged companies to file them, fined companies for not filing them, and collected a fee from anyone who wanted to look at them. Kyle paid without complaint. It seemed morally less objectionable than bribing an official to give him the information on the sly, like he would have had to do on any other world.

What he learned was the same thing he'd heard on the street. RDC was an interstellar conglomerate, like all the major players on Baharain, but about fifteen years ago it had started pulling ahead of the competition.

Scouring years of business records reminded Kyle of why he

had never been able to stomach forensic accounting. At least the street criminals were living people, however broken. Corporate lawyers were like zombies. They said as little as possible, took as long as they could to do it, and lied without even realizing it. Kyle began to hate them more than he hated juicers. At least the juicers had *fun* while eating their own souls.

Eventually he managed to find out why RDC was winning the game. They had adopted a policy of automation, replacing more and more workers with automated equipment. An unobvious choice, given how cheaply human beings could be hired. The business vids debated the wisdom of RDC's course, suggesting that the cost of development and maintenance of the machinery would eat into their profit margin more than their increased production would grow it.

The records seemed to indicate they were right. RDC was taking market share, but not making any more money. Yet RDC went on deploying automation, year after year. This was exactly the kind of uninteresting mystery Kyle was looking for.

The other fact that he learned from the government database was a detail too old and trivial to filter up from street gossip. Fifteen years ago RDC had acquired a new chief executive officer, from off-world.

Kyle couldn't find any pictures of the man, but he didn't need one. He already knew what the chief executive officer of RDC looked like, because he'd already met him once. Five years ago, on Altair. In a sporty ground car. Making an illegal turn.

A shower, a shave, and a fresh suit later, Kyle went to renew that acquaintance.

RDC's corporate headquarters were more impregnable than the Fleet War Room on Altair. Kyle didn't make it past the secretaries.

Personnel made him fill out forms and said they'd get back to

him, but generally they didn't hire security officers without a rec-
ommendation. Investor Relations wouldn't talk to him until after
he purchased at least a thousand shares. Public Relations was willing to talk, but after two hours he knew less than when he'd walked
in the door. The only thing he got out of the day was an offer to
work as a miner, for about two-thirds the going rate.

He took it. He was running low on leads and credits. And it had
another advantage.

The job involved leaving the domes, which meant stepping off
the grav-plating while wearing a chem suit. He would be exposed
to the native environment of Baharain, protected by only a few
millimeters of expensive plastic. It didn't sound fun and it was certainly dangerous, but the company would provide training and
equipment. Those were both necessary to fulfill his sudden desire
to go sightseeing outdoors.

This desire sprung from a casual fact he had gleaned while in-
terviewing for jobs. The management of RDC maintained a series
of private domes for executives and their families.

Dejae's twin would live in one of those. Kyle would never get
past security to access them normally, but all he needed was a
single photograph. The public domes were transparent on most
optical wavelengths, filtering out only the dangerous rays. Letting
the local sunshine in was cheaper and more naturally satisfying
than purely artificial light. No doubt the executive domes were the
same. They would, at the very least, be transparent during the
night. Everyone liked to look at the stars. Everyone stared up into
the great void from time to time, wondering which insignificant
sparkle was the light of ancient Earth. A still-living Earth: humanity had left only centuries ago, and they had traveled thousands of
light-years through the nodes. The light from that ancient Earth, if
it could be resolved into pictures, would show a shining blue ball
painted with strokes of green and white. Oceans teeming with
schools of fish. Forests whose branches were alive with troops of

monkeys and flocks of birds. Plains where herds of animals thundered in glorious freedom.

The visions of Heaven were out there, if only a man could stare hard enough to see it. No one could, of course. It was optically, mathematically impossible. But that didn't stop people from trying.

The domes would be transparent at night, and Kyle would get his picture. Then he could go home again.

The foreman was scarred, ugly, and one-eyed, but that eye was keen. He barked out corrections and derisions with uncanny accuracy. Kyle wondered why boot camp always felt the same, no matter what boot you were learning to wear.

"Nobody dies on my watch." The foreman was adjusting Kyle's suit. "It detracts from my bonus. Your helmet's too small, man. Get another one."

"Yes, sir." Kyle shuffled over to the equipment table and found a helmet with a larger number printed on the collar ring. When he got back to his place in line, the foreman was waiting for him.

"Don't sir me. This ain't Fleet. You're just an idiot on the wrong end of a shovel, and I'm the guy handing out shovels. That makes me smarter than you, but it don't make me a sir."

"Fair enough," Kyle said with a grin.

"Yeah, yeah, yuck it up. They all do, the first day. We'll see how much you're laughing at the end of the shift, when just raising your nose to sneer at me feels like lifting a two-ton hopper. No, you idiot, the other way." The foreman reached out to twist Kyle's helmet into the locking ring.

"Sorry . . . I'm not used to space suits." On Kassa they had only worn them for warmth.

"I can see that, man. And I can see you ain't Fleet, either. I don't care. You ain't from here, you ain't staying here, and you got a sob story an hour long. And I don't care. All I care about is that you're clocking out in six hours with all your parts attached." He raised his voice, shouting so the rest of the workers could not fail to hear him even through their suits. "That goes for all of you. Stop thinking you can do this. You've been in sims—I hope, and if not, it's too late to tell me now—but real heavy G ain't like a sim. It don't go away after half an hour. It tugs at you all the time, drags at every fiber of your being, sucks you down like the dying pull of Earth herself. It is your enemy. Forget that for one microsecond and you'll be a debit in my paycheck. So stop thinking you can do this job. And start focusing on *surviving* it."

It was only seventeen percent over Terran standard. Kyle had tried the sim, doing deep knee bends in a gravity-enhanced chamber, and while it felt ridiculously uncomfortable, he had passed the medical exams.

"Every step you take is a fifth harder. Every drop you fall is a fifth longer. Everything you pick up is a fifth heavier. All them fifths add up fast, in ways your idiot brains didn't evolve to handle. You can't operate by instinct out there. Every single action has to be consciously evaluated before you do it. You will burn calories you didn't know you had. You will strain muscles they ain't even named in the medical vids. If you try to act like you're in normal G, your suit's air-cracker will not be able to keep up oxygen production, and you will pass out. This is for your own good. An unconscious idiot is cheaper than a dead one. We can fix your air, but we can't fix your heart if it bursts a chamber."

The idea that he could die of heartbreak struck Kyle as unlikely. If that were possible, then walking off the *Ulysses* for the last time should have killed him.

"Now get your arses into the air lock. We're gonna shut the door and flood it with kelamine. If you start throwing up in your suit, that's 'cause you didn't seal it properly. You can thank us for saving your life after you clean out your suit."

The suits were different from Prudence's. Heavy opaque rubber instead of the clear thin plastic he had expected. He didn't know if that was because they needed to be stronger, or if the rubber was just cheaper. The suit was impregnated with heavy salts to block radiation, but so was the glass faceplate of the helmet, and it was transparent. On the other hand, there wasn't much value in being able to see through these suits. They didn't contain slender dark-haired girls with intense black eyes.

The air lock cycled, lights going from green to yellow. Nobody threw up, which Kyle took as a good beginning. Then the lights went red, and the outer door creaked open.

Climbing down a short set of stairs, he took each step carefully. The foreman was standing to the side, watching the new recruits critically. Kyle stepped out of line to join him.

"Why kelamine?" he asked.

"We used to just use a stinker, but one day we got a jackass with anosomia. Couldn't smell a thing, and didn't think to mention it until it was too late. The kelamine means we don't gotta rely on you idiots to tell us something's wrong. Plus, it washes off the suits easier."

Kyle debated asking if it was cheaper, too, but decided not to.

"See that one?" The foreman pointed to a young man who had taken the last two steps in one go. "That jackass is gonna get somebody killed. Go ride his arse and keep him in line. Can you do that?"

"Sure," Kyle agreed. The foreman had an impressive sense of judgment. He seemed to already know what every member of his team was capable of.

Kyle shuffled over to join up with the young stallion. "Hey, slow down a second. Give an old man a break."

The kid turned and stared at him through his glass bubble, trying to see if Kyle was ribbing him.

"The foreman teamed us up," Kyle explained. "This is my first time out here. How about you?"

"Yeah," the kid agreed. "But I did a lot of time in the sims. I'll be okay."

Kyle hadn't asked. The kid must be pretty nervous to volunteer so much information. People always led with what they were trying to hide.

They climbed onto an open-bed truck with the rest of the squad. The foreman came by to make sure everyone was hanging on to a safety strap. Then he shouted to the driver, and the truck rolled forward, jiggling heavily over every bump. Kyle watched the alien landscape bouncing by for as long as he could stand it. The rocks were almost all the same dull gray, with only the occasional streak of brown or black. Wind had shaped the landscape, carving out pillars and valleys, smoothing craters and building drifts, but after the first five minutes it was just a bunch of rocks.

The truck descended into a valley, rock walls rising up and spreading away.

"Why don't they use grav-cars?" he asked his young companion.

"Cost. The extra Gs makes them burn too much fuel." The kid had done his homework.

"Where are you from?" Kyle regretted asking it immediately. On Baharain, people didn't like to talk about their past, and Kyle had no particular desire to discuss his own. But he liked this kid.

The kid hesitated, but talked anyway. He would learn some expensive lessons about trust, if he stayed in this cesspit long enough. Hopefully the lessons wouldn't be fatal.

"Kassa. We got attacked. I used to cut trees, but my dad said we'd need hard currency to make it through winter."

The effluent of war. Refugees.

"I heard about that," Kyle said, feeling like a heel for lying. "But you'll pull through."

"If they don't come back. Dad says why would they, but nobody knows why they came in the first place."

"Is anybody sending help?" His news was a few weeks out of date.

"Altair Fleet is there, but they don't do much. Just hang around in deep space, looking for secret nodes. Other planets have sent food and stuff, but we don't need that. We need a fleet of our own."

That surely couldn't be what the League wanted to hear. They wanted the worlds cowering under their thumb, not arming themselves for resistance.

"Fleets are expensive," Kyle said. It was a perennial political football on Altair. Fleet never seemed to provide anything except prestige. Not everyone felt that was worth paying for. Kyle's experience as a cop had convinced him that the reason Fleet had nothing to do was because it existed. Just like detectives had a lot less to do when there were regular patrols by beat cops. If Fleet didn't exist, then Altair would pretty quickly find out why they needed it.

He imagined there was a lot of crowing and finger-pointing going on right now, back on Altair. The people who voted for Fleet would be bragging about their prescience. He wasn't ready to join them, though. Not until he was sure Fleet could actually help.

Not until he was sure whose side Fleet was really on.

The truck rattled around a corner, exposing a vast but shallow crater. The road crept along a lip of the crater. Men and machines labored below. Kyle goggled at them, stunned by the improbable sight.

"What are *those*?"

His knowledgeable young guide answered. "Crawlers. The company's secret weapon."

The crawlers were large, compared to men, but small on the scale of starships and earth-moving equipment. The other companies used massive bulldozers and ore transports the size of houses, or sometimes the size of entire apartment buildings. These machines seemed almost delicate in comparison. Only five meters high and ten wide, they looked like animated bowls carrying ore from place to place. What shocked Kyle was how they moved.

On eight legs. Like insects, stepping gingerly from place to place, moving in unnatural gaits with their own sense of purpose.

The wheel was as old as Earth, tried and tested by the ages. Improved by tracks and rails, it could go anywhere. The only technology that had superseded the wheel was gravitics. Wings, hovercrafts, and jet propulsion had all fallen by the wayside. Not every planet had an atmosphere suitable to aerodynamics. Not every planet had an atmosphere.

But they all had gravity, and they all had surfaces. Gravitics and the wheel had carried man to the farthest reaches of the galaxy. Why change?

"How are you supposed to drive one of those things?" Kyle had mastered several versions of the ground car, with various numbers of wheels from two to twelve. He couldn't imagine what kind of controls would be needed for legs.

"That's the trick," his companion said. "You don't. They drive themselves. They're robotic. That's why they can justify paying us less. No human can operate those bloody machines, so they don't have to pay for skilled labor."

No human could *design* those bloody machines.

The image of the spinning disk flashed through Kyle's mind.

Eight resting places. Eight kickplates. Eight legs.

Would anybody else make the connection? Would anyone on Altair think of this distant mining camp and its eight-legged robots? Probably not, because no one on Altair had any reason to. They were thinking about hairy monsters from the dark, not technological beings who made machines in their own image. But that might change when they found out their prime minister had a twin who played with spiders' toys.

The foreman was right. After five hours of heavy G, Kyle could feel the weight of his eyebrows pulling on his face. The thought of lying down and taking a nap wasn't refreshing. He knew that his ears would try to stretch to the ground, his lips would slide off his teeth and into his jowls, his tongue would fall back into his throat and suffocate him, if the effort of lifting his chest with every breath didn't. Lying down would just be giving in to the gravity.

Instead, he pointed his laser at a gleaming patch on the ground. Human brains were good for something. In a matter of minutes he had learned to distinguish between dross and value, with an accuracy the dumb robots could never match. One color of laser for inert material that needed to be hauled away to the dump, and another for ore to be fed into the refinery. That was tiring enough. He couldn't imagine wielding a real shovel in this environment.

The mechanical spider that towered over him waltzed to his signal, lowering itself over the spot and biting into the earth with black iron jaws. Fangs of shining steel jackhammered from its lips, cracking the ground into rubble, while knobby teeth chewed and swallowed. When the beast was full, it waltzed off to the appropriate destination while he sought out the next target.

So many legs in motion could not be described any other way than waltzing. The contrast between the elegant dance and the slavering feast sickened Kyle. He was tired of contrasts. He wanted something in his life to be pure and simple, without silver linings or feet of clay. He wanted something to be straightforward, without hidden depths or secret angles.

The spider-machine stood, began its waltz. Two steps and it faltered, like a dancer losing the beat. Years of paranoia moved Kyle before he was conscious of the danger. His puny biological brain, so adept at recognizing patterns, sent him stumbling backward on a tangential line for no logical reason.

He collided with an iron post. The leg of another spider, too close behind. His own machine put down legs at random, confused, while the choreographed waltz transformed into senseless flailing. The machine toppled under its momentum, falling with unnatural acceleration.

The side of the beast slammed into the ground where Kyle had been standing. Ore spilled from the top, flowing over him, knocking him to the ground under its weight.

He rolled with the blow. Better to be crushed under weight than to tear his suit trying to escape. Broken limbs could be healed, but the atmosphere would poison him in minutes.

Voices yelling. Hands at his suit, digging him out.

"Is your suit still sealed?" The foreman held Kyle's helmet between his hands, shouting at him, demanding attention.

Kyle focused his eyes on the virtual display projected onto his faceplate. Warning beacons flashed in red. Belatedly, an alarm began to beep. Underneath it he could hear a rushing hiss. The air felt heavy and dense in his face. The foreman must have seen the answer in his face.

"Earth-fire! Can you stand?" The foreman wasn't panicking, so Kyle didn't either. He stood up, shocked that nothing was broken. From his left shin white vapor spewed forth. Kyle stared at it stupidly, but the foreman was already kneeling, swatting at the plume of precious air.

The hissing stopped. A few seconds later the alarm bell shut off. The air still felt dense and confining.

"What's your pressure say now?"

Kyle tore his attention away from the patch on his shin, and looked at the display. "A hundred and twenty-seven percent."

"Okay, good. Can you walk? Don't worry about the patch. It's stronger than the suit. But you gotta move, show us if there are any other ruptures about to blow. Do it while you still have over-pressure. The blowback will keep the atmosphere out. You'll be fine."

Kyle took an experimental step. Nothing bad happened. He could see men crowding around the wreckage. He could see his young companion, paralyzed by horror, standing next to the offending spider.

His spider. The kid had steered his beast too close, and Kyle's had become confused and lost its footing.

"Earth-damned model sevens." The foreman gave in to swearing, which meant the danger must be past. "These bastards get in each other's way. Only happens when they're trying to stand up. I know they have an upgrade module. Heard it went through quality testing. Ought to have all these units retrofitted. Take another step, man. Tell me where it hurts."

"I'm fine," Kyle said. Bruised and battered, but not broken. He could still wiggle his fingers and toes.

The foreman walked around him, visually checking for damage to the suit. "Okay, go ahead and vent your over-pressure. I'll plug in another emergency canister, just in case. Take these patches. If anything starts spurting, slap one on it."

Kyle wasn't sure he was in a state to be slapping anything, but he took the patches. They felt comforting in his hand. He spoke the command word and a jet of vapor shot out of the side of his neck.

His face no longer felt like invisible hands were pressing on it.

"You okay?" The foreman was asking about his mental state this time.

"Yeah, I'm good." Kyle forced himself to breathe through his nose. "I'm okay. But my spider's down."

The foreman shrugged. "Forget that piece of shit. Go back to the truck and sit down. The shift's almost over, anyway. If you get woozy or anything, trip the alarm. Don't let yourself go to sleep, though. That will trip the alarm too. I've got your suit's vital sensors jacked to mine, so just kick back and take it easy. Can you do that?"

"Sure," Kyle agreed. That was pretty much all he was capable of at the moment.

"I'm sorry." The kid had come over, close enough that Kyle could see his blush. Kyle wondered how the vid industry was managing, since apparently the League had hired all the best actors and turned them into assassins.

But that was paranoia talking. The kid wasn't necessarily trying to kill him. The accident could have been caused by someone else, remotely messing with the spider's programming. Really, any of a number of people here could be trying to kill him.

It was even conceivable that it had merely been bad luck.

He waved the kid off, unable to deal with the turmoil of suspicion. Stumbling to the truck, he thought about how the puzzle pieces fit together. From the too-early tip, to the twin prime minister, to Radii Development Corp. The stray threads kept popping up all over the place, and when he tugged on them, things exploded, caught on fire, or fell on his head.

Maybe the only puzzle, then, was why he kept tugging.

But when he closed his eyes, all he could see were visions of Altair in ruins, its beautiful cities shattered and lifeless like the smoking husks of towns on Kassa.

THIRTEEN

Party Shoes

Jandi only made her wait three days. By then, early vid recordings from Kassa were all over the network. Garcia was frantic, wailing about the opportunities they were missing all day, and drinking himself into a coma every night. But Prudence didn't have a destination yet.

Or a complete crew. Melvin was missing. She hadn't heard from him since they landed.

"Captain Falling? If you could attend for dinner, I would be delighted." Jandi's smiling face was strained and haggard through the vid screen.

"Of course, Dr. Jandi."

Pretending it was part of her disguise, she dressed for a dinner party. Girly clothes instead of jumpsuits. A silk frock, deep royal blue, purchased in a moment of weakness years ago and never worn.

It didn't exactly go with work boots. Even the cabbie complained.

"The restaurant won't let you in," he announced. "Not in those shoes."

"I'm not going to a restaurant."

"Then your friends will make fun of you, and your young man." Jorgun was wearing his best jumpsuit, spacer-gray and slightly worn. "I will take you to the shops. They will fix it, cheap. You will see."

She let him have his way. It would give her more time to check for surveillance.

The shopping mall was the most extravagant structure she had seen on Altair. Glowing signs stretched a hundred meters into the sky, and there was at least one building up there that had to be grav-supported. Chattering people thronged the walkways, sitting on the grass in little groups and socializing. The cabbie led her through the crowds to a storefront.

"Here, you see. Ten minutes. I come back for you." He strode off in a different direction. Altairian cabbies were worse than Virtue police. The police at least were prepared for the prospect of disobedience.

She almost did disobey. The store was full of teenage girls. Not the kind of place she fit into. But before she could walk away, a pretty young clerk approached her and Jorgun.

"A spacer party? You don't want to go as a deckhand. Why not go as an admiral?" She pointed to a wall hung with costumes. Deep blue and soft gray uniforms with gold braid sprouting from them like shrubbery. "We have a special on." She smiled at Jorgun. "Because of the spiders. Fleet outfits are very popular."

"Can I be a captain?" Jorgun asked Prudence, like a child asking for something he knew he wasn't allowed. She didn't think the clerk noticed. The girl was too busy admiring him.

"Sure." What difference did it make?

Jorgun grinned stupidly and started walking toward the wrong section—the children's section, with outfits from his cartoon shows. The clerk attached herself to his arm and gently redirected him.

"Can we help you, too, ma'am?" Another young female clerk swooped down on Prudence.

Restraining a grimace at the terrible word, Prudence shook her head. "I think I'm good."

"We have some very nice temporaries. The cost is extremely reasonable, considering what you get. Take a look at these shoes—they would really set off your dress so much better."

The girl was like a gravity field. Subtle, constant, and too much effort to escape. Prudence let herself be led to a different display counter.

"How about these, for instance?" The clerk pointed to a beautiful pair of white strapped sandals with an arched heel. They were stunningly elegant and sparkling with clear gemstones. Prudence couldn't believe the price.

"The tag must be wrong."

The clerk grinned. "Not at all. Yes, they look just like Sammon Steps, because they are. A perfect replica of his latest, most fashionable design. A real pair would cost over five thousand credits, but you can wear these tonight for only twenty."

"You're renting them?" The shoes were brand-new, clearly unworn.

"Not the shoes, the design. They're time-stamped. Eight hours after you put them on, they will melt into a nontoxic, perfectly safe lump of plastic. But until then—you'll look like a millionaire."

It was the stupidest marketing scheme she had ever heard of. Even Zanzibar wasn't that shallow. But the shoes really were lovely.

While she was still justifying the expense, the other clerk brought Jorgun back.

The uniform would have looked silly on a smaller man. On Jorgun, the tangles of braid were tamed by his blond hair and massive frame. White and gold were not normally what Prudence thought of as a match, but the cloth of the uniform had a pearly, holographic sheen that reflected subtle colors as the light shifted. It wasn't an official Fleet uniform, of course. It was much too flashy for that. With his glasses on, Jorgun didn't quite look like an admiral. He looked like a vid star pretending to be an admiral.

On Altair, that was probably better than being a real admiral.

The clerk let go of him, reluctantly, and handed Prudence a bill. "We hope you enjoyed your shopping experience at Cinderella's, but we know you'll enjoy your party experience tonight! Come back soon."

Prudence touched her credit stick to the bill, handed it back to the girl. Then she put her arm through Jorgun's and led him away. The clerk watched them go, wistfully.

Was that part of the act? Any normal man would have been puffed up by so much attention. Maybe the girls did it on purpose.

Except that plenty of girls were watching Jorgun now. Teenagers, she thought, until she looked more closely. Most of the girls weren't really much younger than Prudence. They just acted like children.

Jorgun, who really was a child, didn't notice them at all.

"I wanted to be a Space-Wolf, but she said you would like this one better."

"It's wonderful, Jor. You look great." She hadn't expected to be able to say that so truthfully.

The cabbie pounced on them, his mouth and hands full of an aromatic treat from one of the vendor carts that dotted the pathway. "You see? You see, yes?"

"Yes, I see. But we're going to be late now."

He shrugged. "All the best people are late to parties. You will see."

Standing outside Jandi's door, she tried not to be nervous. The house was dark and quiet.

The little green man still guarded the door. Perversely, when Jorgun reached out to press the animated button on the little box he held, the cartoon figure didn't move it out of the way. A doorbell chimed in the house. Eventually the door creaked open.

"Angels!" Jandi cried in mock horror, staring at them. "Am I already that far gone? But I haven't even tasted the fish yet. Come in, come in, my glorious friends."

He led them to the dining room, the smell of fine cooking growing stronger with every step. The room was gently lit by candles hanging from a chandelier. Real candles, burning with the pleasant scent of sandalwood.

Silver dishes sat on the table, maintaining the temperature of the food. Jandi began whipping off covers, revealing a feast of real fruits and vegetables, steamed to a perfect consistency. The biggest dish contained an entire salmon, missing only the head and tail.

"You shouldn't have," she admonished him. "Especially for only three people." There were no other guests.

"But I wanted to. Even my doctors admit it no longer makes any difference. Their only complaint is that I'm spending my money on something besides them."

"Is that rice?" she asked. Real rice, in tiny, fluffy grains, not cultured rice-protein. You could tell the difference because the fake stuff melted into a gluey mess when you cooked it.

"It's imported. Real broth, too, from an animal."

Prudence frowned.

"Indulge an old man. Decadence is all I have left. You can nurture your morals when I'm gone."

She could hardly object while she was wearing those ridiculous shoes. "Don't explain it to Jor."

Jandi took the lid off of another dish. Formed, pressed protein cakes, fried in synthetic oil, still in the instamatic wrapper. Junk food for kids.

"I thought he might prefer this."

He did. There was something comical about an admiral eating star-shaped crunchies with his fingers. No, Prudence decided, not comical. Sweet.

A strange family gathering, between the old man and the boy. Prudence wasn't sure whether she was supposed to be mother, daughter, or sister. But she had learned to take her family where she found it.

"Ah, that we could eat like this every day." Jandi was immensely satisfied with his feast.

"On Kassa, they did." Kassa grew their grain outside. Prudence had always been confused by that. Surely washing the contaminants off had to be harder than just growing food in a vat. "I didn't notice that they were any happier."

"Altair grows happiness in vats, too. Not as enjoyable as the real thing, but cheap enough for everyone. It's the secret of our success."

She cut into her fish, waiting for him to satiate his love of being cryptic.

"Seriously, my dear. Though I've not been to as many planets as you, I've been to many, and Altair is the blandest of the bland. That blandness is the source of our wealth. Nothing particularly succeeds on Altair, but nothing ever fails. On this blank canvas we can project whatever we want. We might as well grow people in vats. Altair is like one giant people-vat."

Jorgun laughed.

"Most would say that's a good thing," Prudence commented.

"And so do I. So do I, my dear. Still, I enjoy the fish. How do you find it?"

"Marvelous." It melted in her mouth, leaving an exotic tang she could not identify. So many times today she had said nice things that were true.

"It's a rare planet that does not force man to adapt to it in some way. And we all struggle against that current. Like salmon, we refuse to spawn in any other stream than our own. Change is universally recognized as bad, and so evolution is dead, killed by our technological prowess and cultural stubbornness. On Altair, we didn't have to fight that battle, because there's nothing here to fight against. Instead, we built a society that mimicked our fantasies of home. People flocked to it, and here we are. An empire of nondescription."

"An empire under attack."

"Indeed," he said. "Kassa is a muddy little world. If our spidery friends wanted it, they could have bought it for less than the cost of their bombs. No, they must have a larger goal, and that goal is Altair. For the same reason we chose it: its blandness will support the spider's dreams as easily as it supports the monkey's."

"So you accept that the alien threat is real?"

"Not at all," he said, and stuffed his mouth with salmon.

She had to wait until he was finished.

"The *aliens* are real, yes. The blood you gave me does not match any genotype in our catalogs. Of course, we can't unwrap the genetic code and reconstruct the creature, despite what the popular vids would have you think. Genes express over time and through environment, and we have no clue what gene does what. Or, for that matter, which bits are actually genes. The blood sample could be from a brainless mite or a philosophically inclined walrus. All we can say for sure at this point is that it is verifiably alien, which tells us nothing new."

"But . . ." because she knew there was one coming.

"But the *alien threat* is not." He grinned, at this moment happier than she had imagined that tired old face was capable of. This must have been what he looked like when he was tearing poor Mauree to shreds, or when he was thrashing out some scientific conundrum in a hall full of academics. He had found an anomaly and battled it, man to mystery, in mortal combat. Now he was as proud as a warrior who had killed the enemy captain with his bare hands.

"They always screw up the little things. It's hard making a really good fake, because it's hard making anything good. To be fair, they could not have expected you to bring me that little sliver. Nor would they have expected me to test *the glass*. But I did, because I am an obsessive. I want to know everything. What I found out in this case is that anti-radiation materials work off a common physical principle. Salts are impregnated in the substance. The energetic particles strike these heavy molecules, transforming themselves into harmless heat instead of deadly penetration. A necessary technology to a star-faring race, naturally."

He refilled his wineglass.

"Like anything good, these salts are not easy to manufacture. They require stellar furnaces. It is much cheaper to simply mine them from planets in the old parts of the galaxy, where nova after supernova has poisoned the worlds with heavy metals. But stars are not factories. They are not vats, controlled for purity. They contaminate everything they make with their own private signature, their own particular concentrations of trace elements. From an analysis of these traces, we can conclusively state that the shattered glass of your little alien ship was first formed on an industrial planet not too far from here, by the name of Baharain."

An unpleasant place. Prudence had visited it once, but couldn't afford to buy a trader's license. A few large fleets had a monopoly on the traffic, and the local government seemed content with the situation. "What does that mean?"

"It means that someone on Baharain is equipping the enemy. It means I was right. There may be aliens, but the only threat is people. As always. And, as always, I already know who those people are. Or at least, one of them."

How could he get all that from a sliver of glass?

"Did you know our prime minister is an immigrant from offworld?" Jandi asked, as if it were relevant.

"I heard as much," she said, thinking of the cabbie's rant.

"I'll give you exactly one guess which planet he's from." Jandi smiled, a sad, crinkled comment on the relentless duplicity of mankind.

Prudence put down her wineglass. "Who do we tell?"

"We?" Jandi raised his eyebrows. "You don't tell anyone. They will kill you, Prudence. They will kill me, too, but that hardly matters now. I will go public with your splinter, pretending that I received it from one of the scientists studying the wreck. They will disavow everything, of course, calling me a foolish old man merely seeking attention, and trot out their own experts to contradict me. The leak will justify increased security, leading to a purge of anyone not wholly in their pocket. Eventually they will replace the glass in the wreck so they can release public samples, thus proving that radicals like me can't be trusted. And of course, at some point in these events I will have an unhappy accident."

Jandi's catalog of futility was impressive.

"Then why try?"

"Because, my dear, it's what I must do. Having to discount me will cost them credibility. Purging their staff will cost them competence. Releasing a public sample will set a precedent. That is the problem with these people. They have no principles to guide them, merely a destination. They will paint themselves into a corner, eventually, and then the rest of the world will have one chance to fully see their destination is a dead end. Historically speaking, the people are unlikely to utilize that opportunity to protect their freedom, but that's not my problem. I'll be dead by then, even without the League's helping hand."

"Unlikely, but not impossible." She needed to believe that.

He smiled at her again, repeating his earlier sadness at self-deception, but his voice was gentle. "Have you joined the Cult of Transcendence, too? Do you think that somewhere out there, human beings have finally found a technological fix for human nature?"

She had never shared the hidden nature of her medallion with anyone. Her father had passed it to her as a sacred trust, a secret he had kept for sixteen years. Sometimes she hated him for that. If he had sold the damn thing, he might have been rich enough to escape before the cataclysm devoured his world. But once it came, no amount of money was enough. In a sea of madness, even hard cash sunk without a trace. The medallion, unable to change reality, had become merely a symbol that a better world was possible.

Now she needed help in believing the dream.

"I know they've found something, Jandi." She opened the wire locket, taking the medallion in her hand. Professionally interested, he watched her with eyes like microscopes.

Pressing on the medallion, she extended the blade. Gently she moved it across her ceramic plate. The dish did not change, still holding a puddle of carrot juice. Only a thin line through the white pottery testified that she had done anything at all.

Jandi reached out and gently tapped one half of the plate. Disturbed, it jiggled, the crack widening into reality, no longer watertight. Bright orange juice dribbled onto the table.

Heedless of the mess, dumping food onto his tabletop, he picked up the plate and critically examined the cut.

"Don't touch it," she warned. "It could be sharp." The molecular edge of her knife made even ordinary objects dangerous.

He dragged a napkin across the edge. The cloth fell in two pieces. But when he repeated the experiment, nothing happened.

"I'm afraid I've just polished my atomic evidence out of existence." Picking up the other half of the plate, he did the same. "Let me get you another plate, dear. Don't bother to clean it up, just move to a new chair." The table was large enough to seat a dozen people. "Remarkable," he said, when he came back from the kitchen with a clean plate. "All those years I wasted flying around in space to find alien artifacts, and the only one I'll ever see walks through my front door."

"It's not alien," she said defensively. "I got it from my mother."

"Did she say where she obtained it?"

Prudence bit her lip. "I never met her. She died when I was an infant."

"May I?" he asked. Prudence put the medallion in his open palm. "Can you show me?"

She touched it delicately, with one finger. "Here, here, and here. Not anywhere else. It's very hard to do, though."

Jandi fumbled with the medallion for a moment, and then the blade slid out. Prudence caught her breath in surprise.

"A misspent youth," he grinned. "I used to hustle vid games in bars, when I was a boy. I've kept up the dexterity through constant practice. On the odd chance I could win a bet, or impress a pretty girl. But I agree: it is not alien. It is too perfectly designed for the human hand. So somewhere out there a world is making nano-tech pocket knives. And your mother . . . ?"

"I don't know. My father was a baker. He never went more than fifty kilometers from the apartment block he was born in. She was a traveler . . ."

She had been a spacer, a wanderer, a free spirit that flitted unanchored through the galaxy, working her passage on an endless succession of stray freighters and liners. Something about Prudence's father had caught her, and she had fallen for the last time into the gravity well of a planet, to bud and seed like a tumbleweed taken to root.

Within a year she was dead.

Prudence had been the only thing her father had left of his beautiful star-crossed bride. He had married again, because that is what people do. He had loved his new wife, and the children they made; he had been a dutiful husband, a loving father, a good man. He had built a normal life. When he tried to tell Prudence the stories her mother had told him, the places she had been and the sights she had seen, it was as if he was relating a fairy tale that he had read in a book. Only when he had shown her the medallion had it become real to her. Only then had she seen the memory of grief in his eyes.

A few stories, a medallion, and the legal status as half off-worlder were all the inheritance he could pass on to Prudence. The thing she envied the most, the time that he had spent with that wonderfully exotic person, could never be shared.

When his homeworld of Strattenburg had burst into self-immolation, Prudence had fled in helpless despair. Only her status as half off-worlder had let her escape the clutches of a mad bureaucracy. Only the invisible beacon of her mother's world had given her direction, kept her moving on an uncharted course instead of drifting aimlessly.

"You found Baharain, from a sliver of glass. Can you find her world from this?" Prudence didn't dare hope, but she had to ask.

"No," Jandi said. He put a data cube on the table. "I was going to trade you this, for your sliver. It is a copy of the university's star compendium; every fact, observation, and rumor we've collected over the last hundred years. To buy it would cost a fortune, and undoubtedly break a law in the process. So I thought it would be a fair trade, but now I am in your debt again. The most I can tell you is that nothing vaguely like your artifact is described in that cube. I cannot guess how the medallion came to you, yet no other technology followed."

Prudence had thought long and hard on the problem. "Maybe a node failed. Maybe we're cut off now, the *okimune* split in half. Or still connected, but by a roundabout way, and it's just taking this long for knowledge and tech to work its way through node-space."

Jandi shook his head sadly. "There are a thousand maybes, Prudence. War, disease, stellar collapse, or even aliens could have nipped this flowering in the bud. Or maybe they just don't care. Maybe the gods are jealous. Prometheus is still bound to his rock; perhaps no other chose to join him."

"I thought Hercules set him free."

A twinkle of dark humor in Jandi's eyes. "You believe in heroes? But of course. You are full of hope, as the young should be. Even a tired old man like myself can look at the edge of your knife and see possibilities. Take this cube, Prudence, and continue your quest. I lay only this charge upon you. When you find another university that has not heard of Altair, share the contents of the cube with them, even if they refuse to share theirs with you. We academics have learned to overlook petty stumbles in the march of knowledge. When you're so far away from here you can't gain any profit from it, then give it away, as I gave it to you."

Prudence probably couldn't gain any profit from it now. She already had a database of the local stars, and it was undoubtedly more up-to-date on current commercial issues. Kassa's sudden change in buying patterns, for example.

But for a person intent on traveling beyond common knowledge, it might be of considerable value.

"Thank you," she said. "I will."

"If you can bear it," he added softly, "you might update the entry on Strattenburg. We chose not to slander based on rumors. But you know the truth."

She would have to think before she made that promise. Carrying his data cube like pollen to a distant flower was one thing. Bleeding her heart into it to make it richer was something else.

"I'm going to update the entry on Baharain first. By going there."

"I advise differently, my dear. I advise you to run without looking back. You cannot materially affect the collapse of this world, and why should you try? Your fate does not lie with us, child. We strangers cannot ask this of you."

Coming from a man who had just announced his intention to commit state-sponsored suicide, this paean to self-interest was unconvincing.

"It's what I must do," she parroted at him. "For my own sake, Jandi. I can't flee without at least trying to help."

He sighed. "You should. You would serve us better as a pollinating bee, not a warring wasp. One sting more or less will not matter to the bear who raids our honeyed chambers. At least promise me you won't surrender completely to vainglory, to the point of thinking your *death* will matter. I know mine won't; I offer it only because it is already so immediate. The advantages of decrepitude—one has nothing left to lose."

More lies. It was obvious that Jandi would have picked a fight with the League at any age. Courage was as integral to his character as the sharp eyes and deft fingers.

But would he have endangered a wife and children? Would he have stood up to the authorities if he had a family that depended on him, children who needed him, innocents they could threaten with destruction?

There was a reason the heroes of legend were never married. There was a reason so many people on Altair stood by silently and did nothing. It was the same reason that so many on Strattenburg had done nothing, until it was too late. Only the people without attachments could afford to risk everything. And if they weren't attached to the world, why would they care what happened in it? Prudence had kept herself free of attachments since the day Strattenburg had burned them all. Or tried to; people kept creeping inside her defenses, like Jorgun and Jelly and Kyle and now Jandi. She had been running away out of self-protection, but now she found herself too detached to fear and too attached to flee.

Jandi pushed the cube into her hands. "I can give you two days' head start. Go and see, but don't touch. And don't come back! The danger that they linked us together will be too great. On that cube is a list of scholars you can trust. Send them the results of your investigation by parcel post, and then abandon us to our fate. It is no more than we deserve."

She left that night. No point in trying to find a cargo. Altair had stopped all outgoing shipping. The planet had become a black hole of commerce. Goods poured in, but the only thing that could escape the pull of the government's gravity was that mass-less, ephemeral substance known as debt. Theoretically it was self-regulating. The physicist Hawking had proven that the virtual particles that leaked out of the event horizon of a black hole would eventually evaporate it. But physicists were not known for their financial acumen.

She had to kick a dent in Garcia's door to wake him. He was too drunk to understand the dangerous course she was setting, but he refused to leave the ship. It was a choice, of sorts. As much as she could give him at the moment.

Melvin's network contact was now listed as "unregistered." When she went to his stateroom, intending to pack his belongings into storage at the spaceport, she discovered it was already empty.

"Yeah," Garcia mumbled, when she confronted him again. "I forgot. Melvin bailed on us. Bastard didn't have the guts to face you. He waited for days for you to leave the ship so he could clean out his locker. Don't know why. He won't need any of those surfer clothes now."

"Why not?" she asked, wondering what terrible fate she had consigned her crewman to when she had chosen to land on Kassa, instead of running away.

"He enlisted. Can you believe it? Fleet took him. Him! Earthfire, he even tried to get me to enlist."

This war was sucking her clean. Credits, crew, cargo—everything she had that wasn't nailed to the deck. They only left her with the broken bits, the simpleminded Jorgun and the incurably dishonest Garcia.

No, she thought, not even the broken were hers to keep. Kyle Daspar had been something she might have repaired, an old cracked vase that she might have found value in, but the League had taken him too.

In the early hours of the morning, when Fleet finally gave her clearance to approach the node, she felt something warm on her feet. The shoes had melted, turning dull gray and soft. They were no longer pretty.

FOURTEEN

Stakeout

He exploited the kid shamelessly.

The company gave Kyle a few days off to recover. He spent the time hatching a plan. To get outside the dome, you needed official documents. To do anything on this cursed planet required documents, because then they could charge a fee for it. Kyle began to miss simple bribery. At least it generated less paperwork.

The only open ticket for wandering around the planet's surface was a prospector's license. Money wasn't enough, though: you had to pass exams to qualify. Kyle's employment card got him past the pressure-suit exam, and his Altair documents let him waive the driving test for an explorer buggy, but there was no way he was going to learn enough about mining in the next few days to get a prospector's license.

That's where the kid came in.

The day after the accident, Kyle ambushed him after work, falling in step beside him outside the RDC complex.

"You coming back soon?" the kid asked hopefully, clearly still blaming himself. That made Kyle feel guilty for what he was about to do, but he reminded himself he was doing it for Kassa, too. If he could tell the truth about what was going on, the kid would volunteer anyway. So really, it wasn't trickery, just basic security procedure—"need to know" and all that.

"I got a better idea," Kyle answered. "Here, let me buy you a beer."

Three drinks later, Kyle had him convinced. Now that they were partners, Kyle decided he should start thinking of the kid by name, instead of as that gangly young idiot.

"Bobby, right? My friends call me Kyle. It's a nickname." Kyle was still using his fake identification from the storage locker, but he felt Bobby deserved to know his real name.

They shook hands and agreed to meet tomorrow. Then the kid went home to study some more. Kyle spent the rest of the evening trying not to feel dirty. Since everything on Baharain was perpetually dirty, he failed.

Bobby was waiting for him when he got to the examination office. Kyle had come early; Bobby had come even earlier. He looked nervous.

"Worried about passing?" Kyle was. He needed this kid's help.

"Nah," Bobby said. "I can do it."

Kyle shrugged questioningly.

"I didn't tell my parents. Sent a letter last night, but I didn't tell them." Bobby was morose. At the end of the week there wouldn't be a paycheck to forward to them.

Kyle forced himself to grin. "Don't worry, it takes days for a letter to get there and back. By the time they can ask, we'll be staking our own claim."

"Sure," Bobby said, but he still looked green.

Kyle took him inside and paid the fee. It cost half the credits he had left. Then he went to spend the rest of his money renting equipment.

---

ou didn't get a plasma torch?"

Kyle pointed at the camera in the cargo bay of the buggy. "I figured we'd just take pictures, for our first trip."

Bobby shook his head. The prospecting license had stiffened his backbone. Now that he had a piece of paper, he seemed to think he was in charge.

"We need a plasma torch, too. Look, there's a rental store right next to vehicle air lock twenty-seven. We can stop on the way out."

Bobby hadn't questioned why they were leaving for a field trip in the middle of the afternoon. The kid was too eager to get his new career started. Kyle pulled over when they got to the equipment store, and shelled out some more credits. For now, he needed to keep Bobby fooled.

They swiped their papers and the air lock let them through. Once you got your documents, the government seemed to lose interest. Probably because there weren't any more fees to be paid.

Outside, in the harsh light, Kyle accelerated, putting distance between themselves and the dome. Not giving the kid a chance to get cold feet.

Bobby spoke first, shouting over the noise of the buggy and the rattle of equipment. He wasn't using a radio link. "We're not really prospecting for metals, are we." It wasn't a question.

"No," Kyle admitted. "I'm after something else. But I needed you to get me out here. Look, you can go back to work in a few days. They'll still need you."

"How do I know you aren't bringing me out here to kill me?"

Kyle laughed, a short bark that was more anger than humor. "A little late to worry about that, isn't it?"

"That's why I made you get the plasma torch."

Kyle noticed that Bobby had the fuel tank on the floor between his knees. His right hand rose up out of concealment, holding the nozzle.

"If I wanted you dead," Kyle explained, "I wouldn't have left in the same vehicle through the same air lock."

"Maybe you were gonna fake an accident. You know, some kind of karmic revenge."

"Then all I had to do was leave you alone. A kid as stupid as you, somebody is going to clean you out sooner or later. You told me your life story before you knew my name."

Bobby was silent for a minute.

"Well . . . I'm learning." He hefted the plasma nozzle again.

Kyle grinned. "Yes, you are. Now put that thing down before a bump in the road fries us both."

"It woulda looked suspicious going out prospecting without one, you know. We had to get one anyway." Bobby dropped the nozzle and put his foot on the fuel tank, to stop it from bouncing around.

"Good call. Okay, here's the plan. We're going to mess around until nightfall. Then I go into sector E-3. You'll wait outside in the buggy. I'll come back for you, and if I don't, then you take the buggy and go on home. If they ask you questions, tell them I lied to you."

"Why?"

The less he knew, the better off he was, but Kyle needed to build some trust. If Bobby thought he was out here to plant a bomb or perform an assassination, he might abandon Kyle the first chance he got.

"I want to take some pictures of the chief executive officer of RDC."

"Blackmail . . . I bet that pays better than prospecting."

The kid wasn't so innocent after all.

"No, Bobby. I won't be asking him for money. I'll be taking the pictures back to Altair, and asking them to arrest him."

Bobby stared at him.

"I think he had something to do with Kassa," Kyle said.

They rode in silence for a while, anger radiating from Bobby's gangly frame.

"I'm going with you," the kid said. Not arguing, not asking, not whining. Just a statement.

War made people grow up fast. Too fast. Kyle almost turned the buggy around and took the kid home, but he knew it was too late. The young man had a right to strike back at the people who had destroyed his home. There was a war on, and Kyle had made his first recruit.

The sun finally approached the horizon, and their suits started cooling off. As hot and uncomfortable as it had been, it was about to become even worse. The heat you could at least shade yourself from, but the cold would reach you no matter where you hid.

"They don't even allow flybys over this sector." Bobby knew way too much about Baharain security, and he kept telling Kyle why their mission was impossible. "What if they have guards?"

"I looked, but I didn't see any ads for external security staff. If they had outdoor guards, they would have to hire new ones on a regular basis. Nobody could do this job long term without quitting." Running security patrols in a place where the greatest danger was the air around you was the definition of a dead-end job.

"Cameras?"

"That's why we're going over at twilight. The rapidly changing contrasts should confuse any automated surveillance. I doubt they have people watching the entire border."

They didn't even have a fence. What they did have was a bright orange post stuck in the ground, with a warning sign. The sign was so old it was illegible. Kyle could see another post a hundred meters to the left, and assumed there would be one to the right somewhere.

The buggy's navcom lit up, telling them they were on the edge of a restricted area. Kyle told it to shut up. He'd already cut off the buggy's communications with the dome. Although the vehicle was equipped with satellite tracking, it was only for the driver's convenience. It didn't automatically report their location to some central headquarters. The government respected the typical prospector's paranoia about being followed by their competition.

Kyle drove past the signpost and tried not to flinch. This would be a good place for anti-vehicle mines, but he didn't really expect any. The insurance liability would be too great for a corporation to stomach. Only governments could leave a piece of ground fatally armed for decades. That was one of the weaknesses of government, in Kyle's view.

They crept through the growing dark, sticking to the valleys and low-lying patches. There was no vegetation to shield them, but the rock formations were complex and jumbled. In the fading light, they almost looked like trees or houses.

A glow from ahead told him they were getting close. The reflected light from the domes hovered like a halo in the sky.

He stopped the buggy at the foot of a small hill.

"I'm going up on foot to see if I can get a clear line of vision. You wait here and cover our line of retreat. You can drive the buggy, can't you?" he asked as an afterthought, cursing himself for forgetting to check that detail.

Bobby shrugged. "Sure," he said. He was a terrible liar.

Lugging the camera and its telescopic lens, Kyle clambered up the steep slope. The hill was treacherous, carved with pits and sinkholes. It resembled a coral reef more than a lump of rock.

Creeping over the top, he saw the valley spread out below. The various domes in the complex glowed invitingly, gentle warm yellow leaking through their transparent tops. Kyle had planned his route to bring him to the backside of the one place in the sector the corporate recruiting literature didn't brag about. He knew all about the suites and recreational facilities of the rest of the complex. By the process of elimination he had figured out this one undescribed patch had to be where the bigwigs lived.

A distant shadow to the right caught his eye, but when he stared that direction, he saw nothing. The twilight was affecting his vision, too. Aiming the camera at the dome below him, he scanned it, looking for clues, hints, or just an uncurtained window.

Stakeouts were a matter of patience. Typically one waited days for something interesting to happen. Kyle had rented the equipment for a week. But when he saw a person standing in an observation deck, looking up at the stars, he accepted his good luck. He felt he was owed some.

The man was the right height and weight for a twin of Dejae. Clicking the zoom factors up, Kyle narrowed in on the face, running the vid recorder at maximum resolution. And blinked. The man was wearing a mask, an extravagant tribal affair with feathers and glittering gems. He appeared to be having a conversation, but a few minutes of observation convinced Kyle that the man was alone in the room, talking to a comm unit.

Was he getting ready for a party? Maybe life in the executive dome was one wearying masked ball after another.

The man turned, as if interrupted, facing a closed door on the other side of the room. The man crossed the room to open the door, his back to Kyle, and as he walked, he took off the mask and hid it behind his back.

A servant was on the other side of the door. She handed him a drink from a silver tray, curtsied, and left. He closed the door. Before he turned around, he put the mask back on.

Kyle was dumbfounded. There was clearly no one else in the room. The conversation on the comm unit was over; the man relaxed on a divan, alone, sipping his drink.

While wearing a mask.

Kyle recorded the whole insane performance, the masked man finishing his drink, setting down the glass, and wandering out of

Kyle's view. A second later the room went dark. Without backlighting, Kyle couldn't see through the reflectivity of the dome.

He popped the data chit out of the camera and stuffed it in his suit pocket. Slotting in another chit, he prepared himself for a long wait. His luck hadn't changed, after all.

Why would someone wear a mask, alone in their own house? His futile speculation was cut short by a sound that was not the wind.

Immediately Kyle began slithering down, trying to escape the view of the dome complex, while looking frantically for the source of the harsh click. To his left a monstrous shape appeared, blotting out the horizon. Kyle jumped, heedless of where he would land, and the hulking brute landed where Kyle had been a heartbeat ago.

Sparks flew from the ground as stone chipped and sprayed outward. In the momentary illumination Kyle could see glittering fangs, bristly hair, and legs. Too many legs. A spider twice the size of a man, with faceted eyes that revealed no humanity.

Kyle crashed back to earth, halfway down the hill. The spider gathered itself, a giant barrel sprouting hideous limbs. A meter wide at the body, with legs twice as long. Its claws clattered on the stone, and when it hissed at him, he could see the faint reflection of silver. Its fangs and claws were capped in metal. He could imagine it in the cockpit of the deadly little fighter-craft on Kassa, searching for targets, seeking out men and women to kill.

And now it was coming for him.

Kyle had faced many weapons, thugs with guns and knives, and once, a jar of acid. He had stared into the eyes of men who wanted to hurt him, to make him suffer and die. But he had never feared being *eaten* before.

The terror was atavistic. Scrambling madly, Kyle plummeted down the hill, seeking escape or just a place to hide, every step in the heavy gravity like wading through a nightmare. He threw himself into the first narrow crevice he found.

The monster pounced again, sealing Kyle in his tomb. Its fangs gnawed at the narrow lips of stone. It was trying to stick its horrible maw in to bite him, instead of just fishing him out with its legs.

The radio whispered in his ear.

"What on Earth is that?" Bobby was on the edge of panic, his voice trembling and wet. Paradoxically, his terror rallied Kyle.

"GO!" Kyle hissed over the radio. "Get the fuck out of here! While it's still occupied with me—I don't think it can catch the buggy. Go, damn you!"

The creature began flaying the stone with its claws. It was going to dig him out.

"Is that what attacked my world?" Bobby was asking intelligent questions, and it was pissing Kyle off.

"Get the fuck out of here! Go get help!" Kyle didn't have a weapon. He didn't have room to fight, even if he could get his heart to stop pounding long enough to think about fighting. He couldn't see anything except the dark bulk of the monster, blotting out the sky.

It stopped, freezing perfectly still. Its motion had been unnatural, inhuman, alien; now it was almost comical. One leg stretched out, claw-first, reaching down to him. It had finally figured out that all that was required was a single puncture of Kyle's suit.

A flare of light. Sobbing in fear over the radio, Bobby unleashed the plasma torch on the creature, having crawled up the hill unnoticed. Instantly the monster reverted to mindless spider, and sprung on him. The two of them rolled down the hill, disappearing from Kyle's sight.

He kicked his way out of the crevice. He was too late.

On the plain below him, the spider straddled Bobby, pinning him with half its legs, rising up on the other half. Futilely Bobby cradled the plasma tank for protection, trying to hide behind it. The fangs descended like a jackhammer while Kyle cried out in helpless rage.

Sparks of metal on metal, and then the tank exploded.

The flare was blinding. For a moment Kyle could not tell ground from sky. When contrast returned, all he could see was the horizon, a cardboard cutout standing against a starry background. On his hands and knees he slipped and slid down the hill, every bump rising up to punish him, every hole trying to suck him down.

He collided with something that was not rock. A leg. Groping, he found another. Scraping his helmet on the ground, he tried to bring the scene into the horizon. Above the legs was nothing. Sparkles slowly began to appear. Parts of bodies were burning, but Kyle's vision could not identify them.

His hearing returned, and he realized the clicking sound was not part of the ringing deafness in his ears. Somewhere out there the creature still moved, trying to stand. That it was severely injured was deducible only by the fact that Kyle was not yet dead.

Crawling on the ground, he picked out the silhouette of the buggy. As much as he wanted to, he could not stand and run, because then he would lose sight of the buggy. As if he could run blind across broken ground, anyway.

The shadow from before, from on top of the hill, flashed through his mind. It had been to the right. This creature had come from the left. There was another one out there, still stalking him.

Scrabbling on all fours, dipping his head to keep the buggy in sight, he battered his hands and knees without mercy. It was the longest seven meters of his life.

Crawling into the buggy, he flicked on the exterior headlights. They would give away his position, yes, but without them he simply could not drive. On their brightest setting they revealed only outlines. He could avoid boulders, but crevices would be invisible to him. He would be lucky to survive the first kilometer.

He was still owed some luck. But he wasn't sure he deserved it.

————

After five minutes he stopped and turned out the lights. Closing his eyes was unbearably hard. Forcing himself to count to one hundred was the most terrifying thing he had ever done.

When he opened them again, he could almost see. If he drove slowly enough, he would not need the lights. The lights would kill him. Driving too slowly would kill him. Wrecking the buggy would kill him.

There were a lot of ways to die out here, but all of them were the same, in the end. A spider standing over you with shining fangs. Kyle thought about what spiders did with things they caught.

Bobby might have been the lucky one.

But he wasn't. Kyle's damned luck held out. Gradually he drove faster as his vision returned, and nothing sprang out of the darkness on him. He found a road, and picked a direction at random. After a kilometer he thought to turn the buggy's navcom back on. It told him he had chosen correctly. It even warned him about upcoming curves and rough spots.

Damned luck.

Pulling up to the same air lock he and Bobby had left, he was too tired to be worried. The authorities wouldn't give him any trouble. Dejae-2 couldn't afford to let people know he had killer spider guards. Instead, he would send an assassin, somebody who had to work outside the system. That meant Kyle had a little time.

It also meant that he had to ditch the fake persona he had been living under. He didn't think he could even risk going back to his hotel. His documents opened the air lock, but they also marked his presence outside the dome, and every person who returned after the spider died would surely be investigated by Dejae's agents. He drove in, waited for the scrubbers to cycle the air, and drove out the other side. At least he didn't have to present a credit stick to pay a fee. All the air locks let you in for free, a reasonable safety precaution. That just meant they charged you double to get out.

Parking the buggy behind a rowdy bar, he left the keys in it. Maybe someone would do him a favor and steal it. He dropped his old documents into a curbside trash disintegrator, and shoved his pressure suit in after it. The machine choked on it, but after a few well-placed kicks it fired up again and shredded the suit. Kyle idly reflected that you could probably shove a body down the damn thing.

All he had left were the clothes on his back, two credit sticks, his original Altair ID papers, and the data chit in his pocket. Bobby had died so Kyle could get a vid of a man in a mask.

Kyle consoled himself with the fact that he would probably die over the same useless vid. Then he found a cheap, cheap hotel room and gave up one of his credit sticks.

Seven hours in the heavy G had drained him, leaving him brittle like a rag wrung dry and left in the sun to parch. He should have collapsed into unconsciousness as soon as his head hit the disposable foam pillow. But the memory of the young man struggling under the spider would not leave him. That should have been him; would have been, if not for Bobby's heroics. In the grand scheme of things it was just another casualty of the Kassan war, but this one had been on Kyle's watch. He had never lost a member of his squad before. He didn't understand how to deal with it.

Only the inescapable fact that escaping from this planet would be impossible, and therefore he would soon join Bobby in death, let him finally sink into sleep.

In the morning he did the only thing he could. It would be what they expected, of course. But he didn't have a choice. Five minutes in a convenience store and he was deep brown, staining his face with some cheap cosmetic intended to preserve skin in the harsh recycled air, but undoubtedly chemically inert and useless. Then he went down to the docks, to try and find a ride home. A tramp freighter would be his only hope. They would search the passenger liners, like the one he had come on. Not that he could afford a luxury ticket, anyway.

There didn't seem to be a lot of tramp freighters on Baharain. He wasn't sure why, and he didn't dare consult an official registry or government information kiosk to find out. Instead, he went from bay to bay, looking through the windows to see if there was a ship outside. He was tired, anxious, and angry. That's how they caught him by surprise.

He heard a voice behind him. Soft and yet hard, familiar and yet exotic. Fear bit into his belly like the spider, his stomach muscles contracting involuntarily. He spun, knowing what he would see.

The perfect operative. Always right behind him. Prudence eyed him suspiciously, something glittering in her right hand, while her massive soldier reached out to grab Kyle's shoulder.

Kyle struck, sinking his fist into Jorgun's gut. The man was huge, but Kyle would not die without a fight. Jorgun fell like a tree to the ground.

The giant stared up at him in anguish, and burst into tears.

FIFTEEN

Revelations

She nearly killed him.

Stepping deftly forward, the mordant knife shielded behind her body, she was already in motion. The name came to her from ancient fairy tales. *Wight.* A dead man, returned from the grave to seek vengeance. He looked the part, disheveled and haggard, his eyes dull and flat. His face was the wrong color, his hair untrimmed.

He couldn't be a supernatural undead monster, of course. He was just an ordinary, living monster, sent here by the League to intercept her. Covering their bases. She had stumbled too deep into the web, and now they had caught her.

But not without a fight. Not without cost to themselves. With her left hand extended, covering her approach, she moved into killing range.

"I'm sorry," Kyle said to Jorgun.

"Why did you hit me?" Jorgun whimpered through childlike sobs.

Kyle's face was a mask of confusion. Unconsciously Prudence stopped, waiting for the answer.

"I thought you were someone else," Kyle said, shrugging helplessly.

She tapped him on the chest with her left hand. She could have used her right hand, delivered the fatal blow. She could have gutted him from sternum to throat in one smooth, easy sweep. But she didn't.

What kind of wight apologized? What kind of assassin attacked bare-handed?

"Who are you?" she demanded.

"Kyle Daspar. The real one." He grinned lopsidedly at some private joke. "Who the hell are you?"

"That's an idiotic question."

"And yours wasn't?" He swayed a little, as if he were dizzy.

"When I left Altair, you were dead. Burned in your bed. So, no, my question was not idiotic."

"They missed me. Bungled it, like they always do. And now here you are, to finish the job."

On the edge of her vision, two men approached. Wearing uniforms of gray and blue. Station security.

She let the knife collapse into a harmless medallion.

"Are you done?" she said loudly. Bending over, she picked up Jorgun's sunglasses and put them on his face, hiding his red-lined eyes.

"What's the trouble here?" The thick security guard was the first to speak, his voice challenging, like a dog daring you to pet it.

"No trouble, officer." She tried to smile sweetly, but under the circumstances, she didn't think it came off very well. "Just a crew dispute. I don't allow violence on my ship, so they had to wait for port to settle it."

"We don't allow violence here, either, spacer." The thick one wanted a fight.

The skinny one just wanted to make fun of someone. "Why's the big guy crying like that?"

"He's ribbing me," Kyle answered. "Said I punched like a girl, so he might as well cry like one."

The skinny guard guffawed, satisfied with a target of scorn. Kyle reached down and offered his hand to Jorgun. With the glasses on, Jorgun looked like a grown-up. He took Kyle's hand and stood up, grinning weakly.

"That was funny," Jorgun said.

"Sure it was." Kyle clapped him on the back. "Just a couple of tough guys, we are. Sorry, officer, it won't happen again."

"Show me your IDs. All of you." Chubby was angry at being disappointed.

Kyle reached into his back pocket, pulled out a card, and handed it to the officer. Prudence stood perfectly still, waiting to see what would happen when he ran it through his scanner.

The officer glared at Kyle.

"There isn't a date of arrival for you. Why don't you have a date of arrival stamped in your file?"

Kyle shrugged and looked over his shoulder, at the hatch that led to the ship.

"Guess the system hasn't updated yet. I mean, come on, I just walked through that door."

The guard grunted and handed the card back. He turned to Prudence, took the card she extended.

"I'm logging a complaint on your file, Captain. Any more of this crap and you'll be fined."

"Yes, officer." She'd started out disliking this planet. Five minutes on the ground had brought that to a full boil of hatred.

The three of them waited, doing nothing, while the security team wandered off.

"Back to the ship," she ordered.

"I can't check out." Kyle objected. "They monitor every person in and out. You'll have to sneak me out in a cargo container."

As a smuggler, the man was a complete failure.

"Come here." She grabbed his arm and dragged him through the hatch.

Inside the tube-way she banged on the comm panel until the screen lit up.

"Hey," she said, before the tired-looking girl on the other end could speak. "You didn't register my crewman. He just disembarked, walked through the hatch with us, but your damn machine didn't take his ID swipe."

"Ma'am, the machines don't—"

"He's right here. Look, here's his ID." She held his arm up so the camera could see the card in his hand. "There's a fine for this crap. I'm gonna make sure you pay it, unless you fix this right now."

Prudence's conscience twinged when she saw the girl was too tired to even complain.

"Swipe it again, sir."

Kyle obeyed, playing the part of slack-jawed hayseed to perfection.

"Okay, you're clear now. Sorry for the trouble, Captain."

Prudence wanted to thank her, but she couldn't break character. If the girl knew that Prudence had just got what she wanted, she might become suspicious.

"Stupid machines," she grumbled. It was the closest she could come to an apology.

The screen clicked off.

"Damn, Pru," Garcia said from the ship's hatch. "I thought that dude was dead."

If Garcia had spoken seven seconds earlier, they would have all gone to jail. But it wasn't luck. Garcia was naturally adept at conspiracy.

"So did I." She stared at Kyle.

"He hit me," Jorgun offered helpfully. "But then he said he was sorry."

"Maybe we should, you know, set the record straight." Garcia brought his right hand out from behind his body, revealing the splattergun he was holding. "It's not like anybody is gonna be look-ing for the corpse."

"Put that away, Garcia," Prudence demanded. With this angle of fire, he was as likely to kill her and Jorgun as he was to hit Kyle.

"I thought we were against the League." That was a surprise, coming from Garcia. She hadn't realized he cared one way or an-other.

Kyle laughed. "Then why are you volunteering to finish their job? You won't even get paid for it." He was arguing for his life, but he didn't seem to be trying very hard.

"Nobody's going to kill anyone," Prudence said. Kyle had stopped fighting when Jorgun had started crying. That earned him a chance to explain. "Kyle is going to take a shower. Garcia, you're going to take Jorgun into the city and buy him a puzzle. Then you'll start looking for a cargo."

"We can't transport out of here." Garcia knew they didn't have a license.

"Pretend you don't know that. Act like you're here for a legiti-mate reason, for crying out loud. Act normal."

"What are you going to do, Pru?" Jorgun asked her.

"I'm going to get a stateroom ready for Kyle." One with a drop-bar on the outside sounded like a good idea.

She and Kyle swiped their IDs again, indicating that they were returning to the ship. Stupid machines.

While he showered, she went through his pockets.

Only two items looked interesting. The blue pod from Kassa, and a data chip. She plugged the chip in, but it was encrypted.

"What's the keyword?" she asked him as soon as he stepped out of the washroom. He was wearing only a towel around his waist. She could see bruises on his chest, and a nasty scrape on his shin.

She could also see the breadth of his shoulders, the tight mus-cles of his belly, the bulge of his thighs. He was solid. Dense, even.

He was definitely her type.

She stood up from the screen, stepped away from it, making room for him to type in the key. Keeping her orbit at a safe distance.

"The password is 'twin.' I only encoded it because the camera made me." He tapped the keyboard, and the screen blossomed with a vid. "I don't have any secrets left, Prudence. I'm out of money and time. I'm out of secrets."

She didn't believe him. People had secrets they didn't know they had. No one ever ran out of them.

"What are we looking at?" He had paused it on a man in an artistic, tribal mask. It was as dull as a tourist's home vid.

"Not much, I'm afraid. I thought it would be a picture of Veram Dejae."

The man in the photo looked about the right size and shape for that.

"Why on Earth would the prime minister of Altair wear a mask like that?"

Kyle grinned lopsidedly. "I didn't say it was a picture of the prime minister. I said it was a picture of Dejae . . . one of him, anyway."

She glared at him from across the room.

"There's two," he explained. "Five years ago I almost arrested one for making a wrong turn, while the other one was making a public speech on the other side of the city. Now I'm trying to figure out why Dejae needs to hide his twin brother."

"The twin is on Baharain?"

Kyle tapped the screen, and the vid zoomed back to the beginning. A glassy dome set in wind-shaped rocks. "He's head of RDC, the largest and most productive mining concern on the planet. He also has a hobby. A nasty, vicious hobby." His face was bitter and hard.

"What?" Prudence asked, unsure of what to expect. Had Dejae inflicted those bruises?

"He keeps pets. Spiders, to be exact. Two-meter-tall spiders that kill people that get too close to his dome."

A shudder of dismay ran through her spine. Jandi had prepared her for double-dealing, some criminal smuggling of tech and weapons. But Kyle was describing a partnership. How could a man turn against his own species? She grimaced in disgust.

"You don't look very surprised," Kyle said.

"The spider-ship we found—it was made on Baharain. Or at least, the cockpit glass was. I stole a piece, had it analyzed." Distressingly, Kyle didn't look surprised at that. With effort she returned her attention to the screen. "Why is Dejae wearing a mask? Was this at a party or something?" It looked like the kind of extravagance Cinderella's would love to sell.

"No, he was home alone. When a servant came to the door, he took the mask *off*."

"Wearing a mask while alone?" That sparked her memory. She'd spent the three hops from Altair reading through the cube Jandi had given her, out of idle curiosity. Now she tapped at the screen, trying to pull the data up.

"Damn." The cube was in her stateroom, on a private hookup. "I need to check something in my cabin."

Kyle eyed his pile of filthy clothes. "Where's your washer?"

She waved at the back of the hall distractedly. Was he going to walk around in that towel all day?

"Maybe you could get some pants from Garcia's locker."

"Are you serious?" Kyle shook his head. "Have you seen the clothes that guy wears?"

Prudence felt that rather missed the point that he wore clothes, instead of bathroom accessories. But Kyle was already stuffing his into the machine next to the shower.

"Let's go," he said.

Apparently he didn't see anything wrong with walking into her private stateroom while practically naked. Where was the stand-offish, proper gentleman that had stalked off her ship on Kassa?

His face was still gray with fatigue, but the light was back in his eyes. There was something else, something odd about his mouth. Prudence finally realized he was trying to repress a smile.

She had to find out why. "What did you mean, in the port? Who did you think I was?"

He looked at her with those black eyes, a gaze so intent she could feel it on her face. "From the instant I came out of the node at Kassa, people have been trying to kill me, in a variety of unusual ways. I thought you were one of those people. An operative; an agent. But Jorgun . . . he's not faking it. It's not an act. And that means you can't be acting, either."

"But you were." He had been lies and contradictions from the moment she saw him. No, before that, when he was just a voice on the *Launceston*.

"Yes. I am a double agent. I've been one for five years, so long I thought I had forgotten how to be anything else."

"If you don't work for the League, then who do you work for?"

He shrugged. "We don't have a name. We're just people that don't like the League. I didn't even know there were any others, when I started. I didn't know there were people like you."

"I'm just a tramp freighter captain," she said, feeling defensive. Jandi's lecture about heroism echoed in her head. "That's all."

"I know," he answered, and now he could not hold back the smile. "You're exactly what you appear to be."

It had been a long time since a nearly naked man had smiled so openly at her. And she still had her clothes on.

Going into her stateroom, she left the door open.

"Dejae obviously isn't quite what he appears." She tried to steer her thoughts back to the topic at hand. "I was told he came from Baharain, but I don't believe that."

"He's only been here about fifteen years. He's been on Altair about ten. I mean, the other one . . . you know what I mean. But yes, both of them are from somewhere else."

She tapped through the cube, searching. The cube was dense, packed with academic information, and not particularly user-friendly. But "private masks" yielded up a single entry.

"Monterey."

Kyle shrugged. "Never heard of it."

"Neither have I . . ." She skimmed through the entry. "A dome world, unknown population, but estimated to be small. Very private . . . it was originally a religious retreat, funded by a wealthy industrialist. Founded about two hundred years ago."

"What does that have to do with spiders?"

She started paging through node charts.

"It's only three hops from Kassa. And they're dead ones, so no traffic." A dead hop was a system without a colony, a lifeless and uninhabited star. People tended to avoid those for the same reasons you avoided dark alleys. There was no one there who could help you if you got into trouble, and if there was anyone there, they were probably the source of your trouble in the first place.

"Could the spiders be using Monterey as a base?"

She linked her screen into the ships' network, and through that to Baharain Traffic Control.

"There's a liner listing Monterey as part of its itinerary, within the last two weeks. Monterey is only two hops from here, through a large colony called Solistar. I can't imagine the spiders are squatting on a system right next to a heavily populated world, and nobody has noticed."

"There are bloody spiders squatting on *this* world, and apparently nobody has noticed." Kyle's face was black with anger.

She waited, letting him unload the burden at his own pace.

"I got a kid killed." He sighed, biting his lip in shame. "He survived the attack on Kassa, came all the way out here to make a paycheck for his family, and I went and fed him to the Earth-damned spiders anyway."

It must have happened while he was taking those pictures.

"Should we go after them?" Jandi would die of shock if she brought him a whole alien, rather than a mere artifact. Actually, he probably would have a heart attack. Maybe she would just show him a leg or two.

"No," Kyle said. "I don't know how many there are, but it doesn't matter. We can't poke Dejae's security net again and expect to leave this planet alive. I'm not sure we can get out of here as it is. And it's no use going back to Altair. These pictures aren't enough." His lips tightened in pain, the jaw underneath set in mulish anger. Those pictures had come at a high cost.

"Then . . ." But she already knew the answer.

"We're going to Monterey."

Garcia had gone straight to a bar and started drinking. Prudence could hardly complain. She'd told him to act normal.

"Buy a bottle of whiskey from the bartender," she instructed Jorgun over the comm link. "Tell Garcia he can have it when he gets back on the ship. Don't let him trick it away from you, Jor. Just hold it high in the air, where he can't reach it."

She was still trying to get clearance to launch when her pied piper came on board dragging his rat. Garcia was cursing savagely, but he pulled himself together when he walked past the open door to Prudence's cabin. Kyle was in there, still hunched over the data console.

"You don't have any pants on, man." Garcia seemed to be asking for confirmation. He must have been drinking hard.

Kyle looked up from the screen in surprise.

"Oh. Right." He ducked out of the room and headed aft to the shower.

"That man didn't have any pants on," Garcia shouted down the passageway to the bridge. "I leave you for one lousy minute and you get naked with the League!"

"Jor, give him the bottle," Prudence shouted back.

Kyle came onto the bridge, finally dressed. He was going to be a problem that couldn't be solved with a bottle of free liquor.

"So how long will it take?" He sounded like a man in a hurry.

"It's a three-day hop from here to Solistar, and another five to Monterey. That doesn't count in-system travel time. And we'll have to dock at Solistar. We need fuel and cargo. If we show up at Monterey with an empty hold, they'll be suspicious. So make yourself comfortable, Lieutenant. It's a long trip."

"Call me Kyle. I don't think dead men have ranks."

"You can call me Captain," she said. In case he might be getting silly ideas.

"Of course, Captain." He said it with an exaggeration of his bureaucratic obsequiousness. She was surprised how much it hurt to hear that tone again.

Jorgun made a mockery of her formality anyway. "Do you want me to look at the cargo lists, Pru?" He was trying to do his job, the one thing he was good at.

"I'm sorry, Jor, but we don't have any." Normally he would examine all the destinations, fees, and expected returns, and put the stops in the best order. It was called the "Traveling Salesman" problem. Computers could solve it, of course, but it was a pain to enter all the parameters and assign the right weightings. Jorgun could do it instantly, and besides, he enjoyed it.

"Garcia said if we didn't get a cargo soon, we'd be landed." Jorgun probably didn't know what landed meant, but he was upset anyway.

"Garcia is drunk," Prudence pointed out. "Don't worry about it, Jor. We've got a lot of money from—" She stopped, not wanting to mention Kassa. "We still have lots of money." Now she was telling outright lies. "We have enough."

"Enough to get us back to Altair?" Kyle wasn't so easily fooled.

"Us? You can take a commercial liner back." Landing on Altair with the renegade dead League officer-turned-betrayer as her cargo would be equivalent to suicide.

He didn't argue. "Just get me in and out of Monterey. I'll take care of the rest. It's not your problem, Prudence. But I appreciate the help. Altair appreciates it."

"I'm not doing it for Altair." She bit her lip. Why did she have to keep reacting to him?

"Nonetheless, we appreciate it." He couldn't seem to stop smiling. It was so very different from the last time he had stood on her bridge. "Dejae went through a lot of trouble to hide his planet of origin. That means there's a good chance they kicked him off. If he left enemies on Monterey, we might find some friends."

"And if not?"

Kyle's smile turned wry. "Everybody has enemies." That was closer to the man she remembered.

She tried to keep that man in mind over the next three days. She wanted to remember that Kyle could be false. He'd demonstrated the ability to lie convincingly, wearing a cover persona for years at a time. He was a dangerous man. Not just because he was strong and trained in combat by the police force, but because he was emotionally capable of extreme dedication. She had been mistaken in thinking he was not as hard as a soldier. He was stronger than that. The years of obedience had not left him dulled and useless. They had not killed his passion.

Right now he seemed passionate for justice. That was a goal she could identify with, despite the attendant danger. Justice was never free, and sometimes it could be quite expensive. If Kyle had to sacrifice her and her crew for the sake of Altair, he would do it. But she was prepared to run that risk.

What she was afraid of was what came after. Once he had

achieved his goal—or figured out it was unachievable—what would he do then? What direction would all that pent-up passion take? A man like that, with so much energy, so much life to recapture, might do almost anything.

What he did for now was to fit seamlessly into her crew. He played cards with Garcia and vid games with Jorgun. He took his turn in the galley, without being asked, making a credible casserole out of the random contents of their freezer.

And he kept his distance from her, never pushing, never crowding. But sometimes, when he didn't think she noticed, she caught him staring at her.

Jorgun was happy with their new crew member. She was a little surprised to see him playing his favorite vid game, Starfighter, with Kyle. It was one of the things Jorgun and she shared. Garcia had no interest in any activity that didn't result in exchanges of wealth, and Melvin had been unable to take the game seriously. He'd get stoned and fly around in spirals grooving on the pretty lights instead of shooting the targets.

"I like playing with him," Jorgun explained, when she asked him about it in private. "He doesn't have to let me win."

She had developed a careful habit of losing approximately every other game when she played with Jorgun. The game was too similar to the sims she ran to practice her flying skills, so her reflexes were completely dominating if she didn't rein them in. But she hadn't realized Jorgun could tell. All those years she had fought to get others to not underestimate him, and she'd being doing it herself.

The shame mixed with the jealousy to form a biting hole in her stomach, much like Garcia's absurd chili recipes always did.

"I'm sorry, Jor. I just thought it would be more fun that way."

"You always ask me who won the last one, and if I say you did, then I win."

Stupid of her. Of course he had detected the pattern.

"But Kyle is funny to play with. Sometimes he flies into things by accident. I keep telling him not to fly so fast, but he always forgets. And he doesn't get mad when he loses, like Garcia does."

The litany of Kyle's perfections exasperated her. She wanted to pretend that she was angry at him for ingratiating himself with the simpleminded member of her crew, worming his way into her affairs through the weakest link, but down the passageway she could hear Garcia laughing with him over one of his stupid police stories.

She took three steps in their direction before she realized what she was doing. Annoyed, she turned around and went to the bridge instead.

There she could drown her tiny fears in oceans of dread, staring at the node-charts for hours and trying to guess where the spiders came from. Where they would go next. Where they might be, even now, descending on some helpless world trapped in their web.

SIXTEEN

Fire

It was impossible to fear the sparkling blue and white jewel that slowly filled the vid screen on the bridge. Solistar was a beautiful planet, and if it hadn't been for the star's unfortunate tendency to belch out random storms of radiation, it would have been a friendly one.

As it was, the planetary network warned them never to go outside without heavy rad-protective clothing, and then made sure they understood by displaying twenty-seven commercials in a row for various forms of it. Kyle had never considered the merits of designer rad-suits, and now that he was exposed to them, he found himself severely underwhelmed.

"At least it's safe," Garcia grumbled. "Not even the spiders would want this place."

"We don't know that," Prudence countered. "It has a breathable atmosphere. That's worth something." The source of that air, single-cell life-forms in the oceans, had evolved immunity to the occasional bursts of silent, invisible death, by the virtue of being absurdly simple. But complex, multicellular creatures like human beings fell apart in an astounding variety of creative ways after one or two exposures.

"Do we know what the spiders breathe?" Kyle asked. On Baharain they hadn't cared about the toxic atmosphere.

"No," Prudence conceded. "But it has to be oxygen. Everything breathes oxygen."

"Baharain doesn't have oxygen. And the spider I saw wasn't wearing breathing equipment." Between the darkness, the terror, and the flash of the plasma explosion he hadn't gotten a very good look, but he distinctly remembered seeing the creature's fangs. "I saw its teeth."

"Spiders don't breathe through their mouth." Prudence could be amazingly contrary when she wanted to. "Maybe it had oxy feeders plugged into its trachea."

In Kyle's opinion, she had spent way too much time studying spider anatomy over the last few days. She kept leaving pictures of various horrible eight-legged monsters on the data screens, and it was creeping everyone out.

"They're not actually spiders, Prudence. They just look like them. They have eight legs and fangs. Other than that, we don't know much."

"Except that they're immune to tetrodotoxin." Prudence had looked up the name of the stuff that made Baharain poisonous. You didn't even have to breathe it—just getting it on your skin could be fatal. "And we can assume they are more resistant to radiation than we are. That fighter-craft wasn't shielded very well."

"Then how do we kill them?" Garcia was exasperated. "You've ruled out air, poison, radiation . . . what's left?"

"A plasma bomb works pretty well."

Kyle hadn't meant to sound so bitter.

Garcia matched his bitterness, and raised him by a gallon of bile. "Maybe we have some, then. I'll just check the cargo manifest . . . oh, look. We don't have a cargo manifest. Because we don't have cargo." The man seemed less concerned about the fate of millions than he did about the percentages he wasn't making.

But Kyle knew it was an act. Everybody wore a persona like a space suit, designed to insulate them from the cold emptiness of life. Most people lived in that suit so long they forgot it was on, like Garcia had. Mercenary profiteering was the only way Garcia knew how to deal with the world.

"We don't have plasma bombs," Jorgun said, confused. "I don't remember those being on any cargo list."

Kyle had to revise his cynical conclusion. Not everyone wore a fake persona.

"We disguised them as cuckoo clocks," Garcia said. His voice was laden with withering scorn, but Jorgun was as oblivious to that as he was to sarcasm.

"I don't remember any cuckoo clocks."

Garcia lashed out. "Do you even know what a cuckoo clock is, you big dummy?"

"Garcia!" Prudence barked at him, and Garcia bit back whatever comment he was about to add.

"No, but I know it was never on the cargo list." Jorgun knew something was wrong, but he stuck to his guns. The kid—because it was impossible to think of him any other way than as a child—was brave.

"There weren't any clocks, Jorgun." Kyle couldn't stop himself from playing the protector. "Garcia's just upset. He's afraid of the spiders, and he doesn't know what to do."

"Garcia is upset because he's made one commission in eight hops. Garcia is upset because instead of carrying cargo, we're carrying a criminal who can't even pay his own fare. Garcia is upset because that flaming planet is probably crawling with spiders, and we're flying straight towards it." Talking about himself in the third person robbed Garcia's rant of vitriol. Jorgun was smiling again by the end of it.

"You can get us a transport for Monterey," Prudence said. "No passengers, though. And try to get something low on mass. We need to be nimble."

"Can I ask the brain trust here a question?"

"Sure, Garcia," Prudence said. Kyle was amazed at her patience.

"If we don't find spiders on Solistar, why are we going to go looking for them on Monterey? Isn't the point to *avoid* being eaten by spiders?"

Prudence answered before Kyle could.

"Can you guess how much Fleet would pay to know where the spiders' base is?"

It wasn't the answer he would have given.

"Information is the best cargo, Garcia." Prudence smiled at the angry man. Kyle felt like getting angry himself. He wanted her to smile at him like that. "Its mass-to-value ratio is infinite."

"There's no profit in being dead," Garcia grumbled, but he deflated like a balloon with a pinhole in it. Kyle had seen the trick done once. You stuck a piece of clear tape on the balloon, and then you could poke it with a needle and it would slowly shrink, instead of popping. Prudence was a magician, and her crew were her props. Spending days trapped in a bubble of unreal space on a tiny, fragile habitat made management a survival skill. Fleet accomplished it with discipline; corporate liners relied on the promise of money; but the captain of a free-trader had only her wits to work with.

Garcia left the bridge, grumbling, and Kyle followed after him. He needed to get out of Prudence's presence before he said something stupid.

"Tell me the rules again, dummy." Garcia was blocking Jorgun from leaving the ship.

"I can't take off my hat." Jorgun, like the rest of them, was wearing a rented rad-suit, topped off with a beekeeper's bonnet. Multiple strips of clear plastic hung down from the broad rim, creating a bubble around the wearer's head. It was a cosmic irony that air could penetrate the shifting, porous material, but gamma radiation could not.

"That's right, because if you do, that stupid star will burp, and then you'll be ugly as well as dumb. And I'm ugly enough for both of us."

"I'm dumb enough for both of us." Jorgun was grinning, but it made Kyle wince to hear him talk like that.

Prudence issued orders. "Kyle and I are going to look around. You two go find us a cargo. And a new puzzle for Jorgun. Do you hear me, Garcia? No bars. Puzzle stores. Got it?" She sounded less like a boss than like a mother talking to rowdy children.

"Yes, *mein capitan*." Garcia was as insouciant as a twelve-year-old.

Kyle shook his head in dismay, watching the two of them walk off. He was too young to be playing the role of father.

"It's better than the alternative."

She must think he was still upset over Jorgun's comment. He shrugged it off, but she kept talking.

"Jor *is* dumb. He needs to remember that. He needs to tell other people that, so they don't have an excuse when I make them pay for taking advantage of him."

"Okay," Kyle agreed. "But Garcia doesn't need to be an asshole about it."

"He is what he is." Now she shrugged. "He won't sell Jor for a bag of magic beans. He fears me enough to not be that careless."

Kyle smiled wryly, but kept his comments to himself. It wasn't fear that made Garcia obey her. How she could manipulate the man so well and yet not understand the source of her power was remarkable.

Garcia, like every other man that spent more than ten minutes in Prudence's presence, was in love with her. Thankfully, she was blind to the effect she had on men. Otherwise things would have been even more difficult for Kyle than they already were.

Time to change the subject. "So what are we looking for?"

"Information on Monterey. Jandi's data cube had very little, and it was last updated twenty years ago. The first stop is the public Traffic Control board. I didn't want to check the registry from the ship, in case they were watching to see who's looking."

"And you're bringing me along because you need a strong man to back you up? Or because you don't trust me enough to let me out of your sight?"

She tried to deflate him. "If I wanted strong, I would have brought Jor." But it didn't work. Kyle was just happy to be with her, whatever the reason.

They met up with the other half of their crew on the patio of a busy restaurant, just after the sun went down. All around them people were shedding their rad-suits, revealing fashionable eveningwear and attractive gowns, like butterflies emerging from cocoons. Their waiter offered to take their suits, explaining that the rental company had a drop box there for tourists, and that they would deliver a fresh suit tomorrow morning before sunrise.

Kyle and Jorgun handed over their suits gratefully. Garcia had already forgotten about his suit, in the fifteen seconds since he'd had it off. He just waved in the general direction of where he had left it, and went back to trying to puzzle out which of the drinks on the menu would get him drunk quickest. Only Prudence hesitated, unwilling to give up her protective clothing.

"He's a waiter, Prudence. Not a stranger in an alley. If the suits never make it back to the company, the restaurant will be liable." Kyle felt odd trying to convince her to act like a civilized person. He was used to thinking of her as the sophisticated one.

"We'll have to be home before midnight," she said. "Or risk turning into pumpkins."

"It will be safe until morning, Prudence." Kyle wondered what a pumpkin was.

"But not after. If Garcia gets drunk in an alley, he could wake up in trouble."

Obviously she wasn't worried about that. The buildings were all safe, with steel roofs and thick rad-glass windows. It would be illegal to deny someone shelter, and the suit company made deliveries. Garcia would be fine.

If they were on the run from agents of the League, however, those niceties might not apply. Kyle looked wistfully after the disappearing suits, but it was too late.

"Are you buying, Pru?" Garcia was focused on more immediate matters. Much more immediate.

"Food, yes. Booze, no."

Garcia frowned, and went back to studying the menu, obviously trying to factor in the constraint of cost against alcoholic effectiveness.

"I take it you didn't find a particularly profitable cargo," Prudence said wryly.

"No," Garcia mumbled, distracted by the menu. "Contract shipments. Sealed, no less. The skanky bastiches don't allow speculation. You fly in with a prepackaged load or not at all. And you're not even allowed to know what you're carrying."

"Unfriendly skies," Prudence muttered, shaking her head.

Kyle didn't know much about interstellar commerce, but he could recognize a racket when he saw one. "Every planet around here seems to have its node traffic tied up pretty tight. Isn't that kind of unusual?"

"It's not very attractive to free trade," Prudence agreed. "Most places want new faces to stay in port for a day or so, to make sure there isn't a warrant on their tail. But Baharain and Solistar don't seem to want honest independents. They don't seem to want independents at all."

"If they tried an outright ban on unregistered ships, there would be quite a fuss, wouldn't there?" Freedom of travel was one of the universal rights, inherited from the ancient fear of being trapped on a dying world. Baharain required a license to trade, but they couldn't stop ships from just visiting. "But by making things unprofitable, they've made the independents think avoiding this sector was their own idea."

Prudence narrowed her eyes. "So the thicker the web, the closer we are to the center."

"You should have been a cop." Kyle wondered why she was glaring at him, until he realized he'd said that thought out loud. "I mean, if Monterey is even more restricted, we'll know we're getting warmer."

"Great, then we can go home now." Garcia looked up from his menu. "Because Monterey is as tight as a bar tab at closing time. I've been talking to people while you two were sightseeing. This sealed-cargo crap has been going on so long nobody's even curious about it anymore. There isn't a stray credit to be made out of that node. And since Monterey doesn't connect to any other nodes, it has to be the end of the line."

"That's not quite true," Prudence corrected him. "It goes through two dead hops to Kassa."

"Are we going back to Kassa?" Jorgun asked hopefully.

"Not right now." She patted his hand, distracting the big man.

Kyle forced himself to stop watching her slender, ivory fingers. "This next hop could be dangerous, Prudence. Maybe we should leave some of the crew behind."

Garcia snorted dismissively. "You're not stranding me on this microwave oven of a planet. And if you leave dummy here, he'll take his hat off and cook his brain."

Jorgun reached up to his head with both hands, stricken with shame. "I forgot where my hat is."

"Jor, it's okay. Garcia, shut the . . . shut up. Nobody's getting left behind. We're just transporting goods. It's our job. If we do our job, nobody will look twice at us."

"And the uniform here? What's his job?"

"Security," Prudence answered, before Kyle could say anything. "He's recently retired from Altair police, so we took him on as a security officer. It's a standard chair. Nothing suspicious in that."

"Chair?" Kyle wasn't sure what she meant.

Garcia laughed. "Yeah, he's convincing because he's so damn familiar with space travel."

"It means a seat on the bridge," Prudence said. "Any decent-sized passenger liner has a security officer at the bridge level. The point is, it's not unusual for a ship to have someone with your qualifications as part of the crew."

"Is he going to take my chair?" Jorgun was having a miserable night.

"No, of course not, Jor. You're nav." Her hand rested comfortingly on his shoulder.

Kyle watched her easy familiarity, wondering what it would feel like.

Jorgun recovered quickly, pulling out his sunglasses and putting them on with a grin. "Except when I pretend to be captain."

"Maybe you should stop pretending." Garcia was back to grumbling. "You couldn't make any worse choices than the current one."

Prudence ignored him. "We better not play that game on this next stop, Jor. I think I can handle it."

Kyle didn't ask, but Prudence explained anyway. "Sometimes it's easier if they think Jorgun is the captain. As if the size of the man was more important than the size of the ship."

In Kyle's opinion, their next stop would require every trick up their collective sleeves. But Prudence obviously wasn't going to expose Jorgun to a charge of fraud. On a place as regulation-obsessed as Monterey promised to be, innocent games could be dangerous.

"Did you hear anything about spiders?" Kyle asked Garcia. He'd listened in while Prudence had talked with her fellow captains, but all they seemed to care about was the safety of node travel and the prices of cargo. The concept of war and planetary devastation didn't seem to connect with them. Maybe the rank-and-file spacers had a different view.

"I heard it laughed about. Nobody around here takes Altair Fleet very seriously. They figure Kassa was some kind of retaliatory raid by another colony. All this talk of spiders is dismissed as fancy-pants in gold braid justifying their pensions."

A compelling enough excuse. Few planets cared to maintain a fleet, and this explanation would only reinforce their self-identified wisdom.

Prudence frowned. "If they want to stir up panic, why aren't the local news services backing the official story? Especially here, where they have more control."

"Because they don't want panic here," Kyle explained. "Panicked people want to change things. They don't want change, because everything's already going according to plan. They want misdirection away from this sector."

She put it in her own words. "The web only trembles where the spider isn't."

The restaurant had rolled up its front walls, exposing the indoor tables to the open air. Solistar took full advantage of the brief twilight, while it was safe to be outside but not yet bitterly cold. Without a blanket of vegetation, the naked face of the planet froze in the dark and burned in the day.

On a vid screen hanging on the wall inside the restaurant, a comedic skit was mocking Altairian panic. One of the characters was plotting to make a fortune selling insecticide, while the other one kept trying to demonstrate his giant-sized bug-swatter.

The placidness of Solistar society, the absolute lack of concern, was unnerving. In the stillness, Kyle imagined the spider so close he could hear it breathing.

All of them felt it. Garcia took refuge in his glass, drinking a local concoction called *araq*. The waiter had sold Garcia on it by swearing three shots would leave an ordinary man incapacitated for three days. Prudence withdrew into herself, silent and unreachable, just when Kyle needed her most.

Only Jorgun was immune, complaining about his dinner like a cranky child one minute, laughing at the vid the next. As Prudence struggled to moderate the big man's flittering emotions, Kyle began to see the comfort Jorgun gave to her. The simple giant required her, by virtue of his handicap, to focus on the here and now, the immediate and concrete. The cloying danger of imagined spiders could not compete with the pressing disaster of fried protein cakes stamped in the wrong shape.

Kyle dealt with his anxiety the only way he knew how, by fixing other people's problems. He bullied the waiter into hand-cutting a new slab of protein to the five-pointed stars that Jorgun wanted.

"You'll spoil him," Prudence complained.

But she didn't send the new cakes back.

SEVENTEEN

Anvil

Five days of Kyle and she was ready to scream in frustration. She seriously considered taking him to bed, just to put an end to her fantasies. He was a man, no different from any other. He had a life back on Altair, family and friends, a place to live and a job to do. He wasn't going to walk away from all that to live on her ship and fulfill her childish dreams of romance, marriage, and family.

But alone in her stateroom, with the lights out, she kept remembering him sitting on the edge of the bunk in a towel.

When the alarm started beeping, signaling that they would be dropping out of node-space in a few minutes, she breathed in relief. The unknown dangers of a possibly spider-infested planet would torture her less than this unmanageable desire.

The entrance was anticlimactic.

An automatic beacon logged her ship's name and assigned them a berth in the spaceport. That was it. No bullying, warnings, gossip, or even advertisements.

"They don't have any cartoon channels," Jorgun complained.

Kyle leaned over Jorgun's console and brought up a screen.

"Tourist information . . . one page. Wow. They don't have anything."

"Of course not." Prudence was studying her sensor readouts.

"There's no sightseeing, because there's nothing to see. The atmosphere is breathable, but opaque."

"You mean cloudy?" Kyle stared at the reddish, featureless blob on the main screen.

"No, opaque. The atmosphere is not transparent to light. So the surface of the planet is always dark."

"Earth-fire," Kyle muttered under his breath.

Prudence shared the sentiment. Of all the places to live, this was the worst she'd ever seen.

"A great place to play hide-and-seek," Jorgun said.

Kyle and Prudence stared at each other. A great place to hide an entire alien fleet, if you wanted to. A whole surface of a planet under a blanket.

"We'll have to land with just GPS and radar. Traffic Control already gave us a vector that will take us straight to the spaceport." She ran it through her own navcom. "A clean one, too. They didn't stint on computers."

As an experiment, she nudged her controls. The new course would cost her a little fuel and force her to orbit the planet once instead of landing directly. After only a few minutes, she was rewarded with a screeching siren.

"Warning! Course is not optimal. Unauthorized flybys of the planet are forbidden. Please correct your course and disable all radar imaging hardware."

So the neglect was illusionary. Someone down there was watching their every move.

The comm screen presented her with an option to view the relevant subsection of the local law code. Idly, she tapped it open. Instead of a welter of legalistic gibberish, there was a simple declaration.

You are not anointed to view the face of the Divine.

"Look at this," she said to Kyle.

He came over to her console, leaning comfortably close. "Holy crap . . . what the Earth does that even mean?"

"Local regulations are the super-cargo's department." She tapped the screen again, sending the image to Garcia's console.

Garcia thought it was funny. "You want me to interpret this?"

"If doing your job isn't too much trouble."

"It's pretty obvious, *el capitan*. The value of religious rules is that you can't question them. They don't want you looking around, and they don't want to explain why. I'm gonna go out on a limb here and suggest that maybe they don't want you to find their super-secret alien base. But hey—that's just a guess."

She kept them on the straight and narrow after that. The ten-hour trip from node to base dragged on, a hundred times worse than the five days they had spent going through the node. Those days had been drifting in perfect safety, where nothing could touch them. This felt like a long, slow fall onto a bed of knives.

The spaceport was absolutely dismal. The atmosphere wasn't any more dangerous than a heavy fog, so they didn't get a gangway tube like on Baharain. Instead, she landed on a concrete platform illuminated by arc lamps, and she and her crew had to walk the fifty meters to the squat, gray building. Of course it was gray. Why paint it when it would always be in the dark?

It took them fifteen minutes of wandering around the warehouse-like structure to find a clerk. He seemed put out that they would disturb him from the vid he was watching.

"Where do we unload?" Prudence demanded.

"Didn't you read the regs? There's a spot marked on yer landing pad. Yer bleeding responsible for transferring yer cargo inside the painted lines. After that, the machines will take care of it."

"Machines?"

"Yes, Captain, machines. They've got an automatic cargo handling system here. It breaks a lot, but that's not yer problem. Just get yer cargo inside the lines."

Prudence was flustered. Her crew weren't longshoremen.

"What if we wanted to hire some help?" Kyle asked.

"Ha." The clerk snorted derisively. "You'd have to go back to Solistar for that. None of these bloody monks is going to lift a finger for yer."

"These monks? So you're not from Monterey?" Kyle made his interrogation sound like idle conversation.

The clerk stared at them. "Do I *look* like a monk?"

"We don't know what monks look like," Kyle answered.

"That's the bleeding point, innit?" The clerk laughed at them. "If you know what I look like, I can't be a monk. The masks, see? You do know about the masks? Tell me you at least know about the masks."

Kyle grinned good-naturedly, accepting the ribbing. "The monks wear masks all the time, right?"

"Bloody yes. Even when they're doin' it, right? Or so they say. Not that anybody's ever seen two monks doin' it. Not that anybody's ever seen a female monk. They hide 'em, don't they. But who cares? Who wants to do it with a bird in a mask? Probably as ugly as a fish."

"What if we wanted to see a monk? I mean, talk to one."

"Then you need to see a brain-fixer, don'tcha? What would you want to do that for? They don't come out here, and you can't go in there. Better for everybody, innit?"

Prudence intervened. "Surely they must come out to the spaceport sometimes?"

"Only when there's a problem. And I get paid to see there ain't no problems, don't I? So no. They don't."

The clerk pushed the button on his screen, starting the vid up again, and went back to ignoring them. Out of ideas, Prudence and her crew wandered back to their ship.

"I'll get the lander out," she told them. "We can use it as a forklift. But there's still going to be a lot of heavy lifting."

Garcia groaned as if she had just kicked him in the stomach. "I don't get paid enough for this. Oh wait, that's right, I don't get paid!" Prudence gave him room and board, but he'd chosen a percentage of all their deals instead of a salary. Lately they hadn't been making a lot of deals.

"I'm sorry, Garcia, but think about it. This place is the dullest, most uninteresting planet we've ever visited. It practically screams, 'Nothing to see here!' This has got to be a clue."

"It's a clue, all right." Kyle's face was grim. "If I were in charge of Fleet, I'd order a planetary bombardment based on nothing more than that clerk's bad attitude."

Garcia always had to snipe at other people. "But you're not in charge of Fleet."

"No, I'm not," Kyle retorted. "So we need more evidence, and for that we need a plan. In the meantime, we have to act like we know what we're doing. Jorgun, you and Garcia start lifting, and I'll go think of a plan."

Garcia spluttered while Jorgun and Kyle laughed. Somehow Jorgun had understood Kyle was joking. Prudence wished she could trust him so instinctively, assume that he would always do the right thing, the noble thing, the good thing.

She envied Jorgun's simple faith in people.

It took them seven hours to empty the ship. The lander did most of the work, carrying the sealed crates twenty meters to the unloading zone, but human muscle had to put everything on the lander and then take it off. They were limp with exhaustion, even Garcia, who had worked harder than she had guessed he was capable of. Either he was motivated by Kyle's example or he had figured out that they couldn't get off this accursed planet until the job was done.

Prudence hadn't done any lifting, but she was as exhausted as they were. Seven hours of making the lander dance had drained her. The craft was intended to travel from orbit to ground and back.

It was bulky, slow to respond, and unequipped with mirrors or side-viewing cameras. One wrong twitch of the controls and it would crash into her ship like a drunken cow. One really wrong twitch and it could crush one of the men. Through the mass of the vehicle, she wouldn't be able to feel it, wouldn't notice the resistance of a human body being pulped against unyielding ground or hull. The knowledge sat on her shoulders and whispered terrible things in her ears, until she wanted to weep with tension. But tears would only blur her vision. So she didn't.

She was as grateful as the men when she tucked the lander into its bay for the last time.

"Now what?" Garcia flopped on the loading ramp, a bottle of whiskey in one hand. Surprisingly, he hadn't opened it until they were done.

"I send the signal, and we see what these machines do." She pressed the button on her pocket comm unit, telling the *Ulysses* to broadcast the message to the spaceport.

Kyle borrowed Garcia's bottle for a drink. "Think of it as a free show. The ballet of the machines."

"What's a ballet?" Jorgun had opened a hot-drink, and was waiting for it to warm up.

"A very boring evening," Kyle answered.

Garcia laughed and took his bottle back. "Join us, *mon capitan*." He took a swig before offering it to her.

For a change, she did. The whiskey burned her throat, but once it was down the hatch it felt warm inside. She was so tired of cold planets.

A rumbling sound. From the spaceport came a squat ground car, a massive box on six wheels with protruding fangs of steel. It wheeled up to the stack of crates, drove around them three times, and then sat thinking for two minutes.

"You weren't kidding," Garcia said. "This is boring."

The machine finally creaked into action again. Driving its

forks under a stack of crates, it lifted them carefully, backed up, and drove off.

Before it came back, a different one showed up. Prudence could tell the difference because this one had a bent headlight frame. The new machine instantly made a selection, grabbed a stack of crates, and left.

"That's pretty damn clever." Kyle was impressed.

Garcia wasn't. "Another reason not to employ a workingman."

"Somebody's got to maintain those machines, Garcia. Wouldn't you rather be paid to fix machines than move crates?" Kyle sounded like an ad for an Altairian educational institution.

"Not everybody is cut out to fix things," Garcia said cryptically.

It took Prudence a second to realize who he meant. Jorgun was sitting quietly, obviously tired, sipping his drink. It occurred to Prudence that he must be enjoying having done an equal share of the work. For once, he had been just another one of the guys, doing the same job.

"Me, now," Garcia continued, "I'm cut out for drinking."

Kyle got up and walked over to the crates. Pushing one that was on top, he moved it to a precarious balance. Coming back to the ship, he winked. "I guess that means I'm cut out for making trouble."

The first machine returned, and stopped, almost as if it were affronted. After a brief moment of staring, it raised its forks and slid them under the offending crate, picking it up by itself. Then it trundled off.

Garcia snickered. "Maybe you need to find a new career."

Ignoring the barb, Kyle went out and moved another crate. Coming back, he pointed to Jorgun's drink container. "Are you done with that?"

"Yeah, I was going to throw it away." He stood up to go into the ship.

"Let me have it. And get another one, okay?"

"Sure." Jorgun smiled and handed over the empty can. "Do you want one, Garcia?"

"Bring me one of the black ones."

Prudence sighed. The black drinks were mild stimulants. When Garcia started mixing them with his booze, he could drink for hours without passing out, getting more and more irrational. On those binges Prudence preferred to stay awake as long as he did. "Bring me one too, please," she called out.

Jorgun came back before any of the machines, passing around his bounty.

The second machine trundled up. It stared at the uneven pile of crates with a little eye, no larger than a data pod, attached to a rod sticking up from the middle of the machine.

Kyle slipped up to the machine and dropped the empty can over the sensor.

There was a gentle rattle as the sensor spun in a circle. Then a red light on the body of the machine lit up, and the engine turned off.

Garcia rolled on the ground, shrieking in laughter. "You killed it! With a plastic can! Who needs Fleet when we have cans?"

In the foggy light, it was hard to tell, but Prudence thought Kyle might be blushing. "It was a bit of a letdown," he admitted. "Somehow I expected . . . more."

"Aren't you breaking a law?" she asked. "I thought we agreed we were just going to look around."

"The clerk said monks only come out when there's a problem. So let's make a problem. It's either that or go home empty-handed."

"If we could get Jor to drink faster, we could conquer the whole planet." Garcia collapsed into howls of laughter again.

Jorgun blushed, but he finished his can in one pull.

"Better let me do it, Jor. We only need one lawbreaker here." Kyle took the can from him.

When the other machine returned, it ignored the disabled one.

While it was glaring at the crates, Kyle disabled it the same way, with exactly the same result.

Prudence consulted her pocket comm unit. "We don't have clearance to take off. We're grounded until that cargo is in the warehouse."

Kyle shrugged. "Then we wait."

They had to wait three hours. Garcia fell asleep on the landing ramp, despite the cold. Jorgun brought out some blankets, giving one to Prudence and draping another one carefully over Garcia's chubby body. Then he sat on the ramp with a portable screen and headphones, watching a cartoon.

Prudence and Kyle drank stimulants, and waited. There was something comforting about being together without talking. It felt like he was accepting her, without asking for anything. Like being herself and being there was enough.

Just when she felt ready to talk, when the silence had stretched on to where she was comfortable and ready to open a tiny window into herself, a light flared in the distance.

A transporter descended on them from the air, cutting through the fog with powerful headlamps. It was smaller than Prudence's lander, hardly bigger than a ground car. To shrink the gravitics to that size had to be outrageously expensive.

"Showtime," she whispered, and Kyle blinked awake. She hadn't noticed when he'd dozed off, but he was instantly alert. He woke up without moving, without reacting until he understood what the situation was. The reserve frightened her, because she recognized it. That was the way she always woke. It made the easy confidence of the last three hours feel irresponsible.

A man got out of the transporter. In the brief and incurious glance he aimed at them, they could see that he was wearing a simple mask of purple silk. It was plain compared to the extravaganza Dejae had worn in Kyle's pictures.

"Hey," Prudence shouted at him. Grabbing Jorgun's portable screen, she tapped it into the local network. "Hey, we've been waiting on your damn clearance. The cargo's right there, but it won't clear us. I should charge you for the downtime." She stomped over to him, hiding her nervousness with anger. "Damn it, clear us already."

She held the screen out to him, expectantly.

He looked at her. Angry, shamefaced, annoyed, unperturbed—who could tell through that mask? When he turned away and stepped toward the machines, she moved to intercept him.

"Damn it, I'm serious. You can see the cargo's all there. Clear us for takeoff already. I'm not going to wait while you fool around with your stupid machines."

Kyle came up behind her, his too-casual stroll a beacon of threatened violence and anger.

The monk might have rolled his eyes, or glared, or something else entirely. Prudence found the lack of a human face or voice disorienting.

He reached out for her screen, tapped it a few times, and it turned green.

"Thank you," she mumbled. She didn't know what to do next. That was as far as her plan had taken her.

"You got a voice, buddy?" Kyle could sound like a real low-life thug, when he wanted to. "The lady was talking to you. Say something."

"If you compel me to summon law enforcement, you will be extremely unhappy with the result." The monk's voice was blurred and distorted, filtered through electronics.

"Not as unhappy as you," Kyle said. In his hand was the pistol Prudence kept hidden on the bridge of the ship. She'd hired Kyle as security, and then not told him a damn thing about her security procedures, plans, and backups. Apparently he'd figured some of her tricks out by himself.

The monk looked down at the wide barrel of the weapon. The mask could not conceal his reaction this time. His authority deflated like a pricked balloon.

"I want some answers, and I'm willing to kill for them. You understand this, right? You understand that I know about the spiders, I saw the dead on Kassa, and I will blow your fucking head off without hesitation."

This wasn't the "look around" plan that they had agreed on. But Prudence didn't say anything. She wanted those answers too.

"If you injure me, an automatic alarm will dispatch law enforcement. You understand they will not hesitate to kill you, correct?" The monk was trying to put on a brave front, but even through the electronic distortion she could detect his quaver of fear.

"You understand if they show up while we're talking, you'll be the first one dead, right?" Kyle shot back.

The monk nodded, his mask rustling softly.

"Good. Then as long as we understand each other, let's have a little talk. But first—get rid of this." He reached up and tore the mask off, in one quick action, before the monk had time to flinch.

Prudence almost fainted. In the background she could hear Garcia swearing in shock. Incredibly, Kyle's gun hand didn't move a centimeter, even though she knew he had to be as stunned as the rest of them.

Standing in front of them was a visibly terrified Veram Dejae.

But this one was half the prime minister's age.

"Another Dejae!" Kyle barked sardonically. "Where do they all come from? Is there a factory somewhere?"

The monk said nothing.

"There is . . . not twins, but clones," Kyle stuttered in disbelief. "There aren't two Dejaes. There's a whole planet of them!"

"Cloning isn't possible," Prudence objected. It was one of those technologies that was always just around the corner. Every time they made an advance they discovered another critical detail they had overlooked. Like the minotaur's maze, there were always more corners ahead.

"Impossible for you," the monk said.

She was impressed that he could manage a sneer even while his lower lip trembled in fear.

Kyle glared suspiciously. "What do you mean, for us?"

"Our process only works on our genetic code. It won't work for you."

"What are you talking about? You're as human as I am."

Prudence understood. She explained aloud, so that the monk would know he couldn't get away with half-truths.

"He means they did it the hard way. By trial and error. They don't know how to clone humans, they only know how to clone Veram Dejae. Brute force, not science."

Prudence knew she had scored a direct hit, because the monk didn't say anything.

Kyle shrugged his shoulders again. "But why? Why even bother?"

"Why not?" snapped the monk. "The First Master, the original Dejae, recognized himself as the ultimate expression of genetics. Why not reproduce? Why not fill the galaxy with the best human, instead of with random genetic trash?"

The arrogant insanity broke something in Garcia, who stopped swearing and bolted into the ship. Prudence could not tell if his flight was in horror or rage.

"And the aliens? What part do they play in this lunatic scheme? Who is master, man or spider?" Kyle leaned in closer, with increasing menace.

The monk didn't retreat. His megalomania was greater than his fear. "Dejae is master, of course. Man is alone, and Veram Dejae is alone among men. The creatures you fear so much are merely our tools."

"But they weren't good enough." Prudence was thinking out loud. "You tried to brute-force their design, too, and it didn't work.

You knew the spiders couldn't take the galaxy by strength alone. So you sent clones out into the *okimune*, to control RDC, and Altair, and Earth knows where else."

Poor little gods. Like the cargo-handling machines, none of their creations could quite live up to their expectations. Everything they made was only a shadow of the genius they had claimed for themselves.

"But why? What is all of this for?" Kyle still didn't understand.

Prudence did. Kyle could not see it. But she had seen Strattenburg, and after that her eyes had been opened to the depths of narcissism that still lived in men's souls. Prudence could comprehend the scope of their plan, the madness that made *different* a capital crime. She had seen it firsthand, breathed the wreath of murderous genocidal smoke.

"They want Altair, Kyle. Professor Jandi told me that Altair was like a vat. A blank medium you could grow any kind of human on. That's why it's so rich, so populated. And that's why the clones want Altair."

She saw the realization creep over his face.

"Fifty million Dejaes . . ."

"You're spoiled," the monk said. "You treat Altair like your private park. That planet could support fifty *billion* humans. With a hundred times as much luxury as we have here."

"That wouldn't leave room for any non-Dejaes," Prudence said. Because she knew that narcissists could never share.

"We're not going to murder them," the monk said contemptuously. "We're not savages."

Kyle growled. "No, you'll just squeeze them out. The League is just another one of your tools. You'll use the League to squeeze humanity into a coffin, and then you'll throw the League in after them and nail it shut." He had finally found the secret he had been looking for, but Prudence didn't think he was happy about it.

"And the aliens are the tool you use to control the League.

There will be other attacks, on other planets. More people will die, and more planets will join the League. The war against the spiders will go on and on and on, until there's nothing left of the governments that took up arms in self-preservation. No matter how much power the League gets, the attacks will continue, so they'll ask for—and receive—even more power. Until they have it all. Then you can institute population controls, or diseases, or whatever you want, until there aren't any native humans left at all." Kyle was doing his interrogation thing, where he laid out a plan so cleverly that the criminal wanted to claim ownership of it. She'd seen him do it to Garcia during one of their card games.

The monk shrugged. "It's worked before."

"Not this time. You didn't plan on us."

"What are you going to do?" The monk seemed genuinely curious. "You must know that the minute you leave this planet, I will report you, and you'll never make it to the node. If you kill me now, then you won't even break atmosphere before they shoot you down."

"What if we take you with us?" Prudence asked.

"Fuck that," Garcia shouted, coming down the loading ramp.

Prudence swore under her breath. He had the splattergun again, and he was drunk as hell.

"Fuck that. Let's just kill the Earth-damned thing right now." Garcia stumbled closer, raising the gun to his shoulder.

"Garcia, put that down!" she ordered.

"It's not even human, Pru! It's a goddamn clone, and it killed Kassa, and it called me and you and everybody in the whole universe genetic trash!"

Prudence chose to overlook the fact that Garcia had called Jorgun that very same thing not too long ago. Probably that was exactly why Garcia was so angry. "He is human, and he's not lying. He hasn't lied to us yet, Garcia. He's not lying about the automatic alarm."

"Then why hasn't he triggered it? Why aren't they already here?"

The monk spoke down his nose at Garcia. "Our society, like any other, attaches different values to different individuals. Being young, I am not particularly highly ranked at this time. Thus, they will not negotiate for my life."

"What the fuck does that mean?" Garcia glared at everyone.

Kyle answered. "It means if he trips the alarm, they'll show up, shoot everything that moves, and sort out the bodies later. It's how police forces without oversight tend to operate."

"Exactly," agreed the monk. "And for the same reason, you cannot take me on your ship. They would detect my leaving the planet and simply destroy your vessel."

"The alarm isn't in there just to protect you, is it," Prudence said to him. "It's there to stop you from running away, too."

Again, the monk said nothing.

"It's a Mexican standoff," Garcia said, and then he laughed. "You know how you break a Mexican standoff?"

"Garcia, I don't even know what a Mexican is," she said wearily. From now on she was going to ration his liquor. She couldn't take these wild mood swings anymore.

"I'll tell you how, Pru. You get yourself one crazy-assed motherfucker of a Mexican. You give him a bottle and a gun, and then you run like hell."

"We can't do that." Kyle was disagreeing with the plan, and Prudence hadn't even figured out there was one.

"You know I'm crazy, right?" Garcia was talking to the monk. "You know I'm drunk enough to do something really goddamned stupid, right?"

"Yes," the monk answered. "I believe you capable of the most irrational behavior."

"Jorgun." For the first time Garcia's voice was commanding, not arguing. "Get me another bottle. Then get Pru on the ship, and get out of here. You've got until I fall asleep or the bottle empties. I hope it's enough."

Their roles reversed, Prudence found herself suddenly trying to wheedle. "Garcia—we can't leave you here. They'll kill you."

"Not necessarily," the monk said. "He's pliable, and too stupid to lie. They may simply enslave him."

The monk was already beginning his negotiations, already trying to talk Garcia into putting down the gun and making a deal. The monk was sober, brilliant, and armed with facts. He would con any ordinary man out of the gun thirty seconds after the ship was out of sight.

But this wasn't any ordinary man. This was Garcia.

"I'll tell 'em everything, Pru. You know that. In the end I'll tell them all your secrets. But not until the bottle is empty. I owe you that much."

Her vision was getting blurry. There were tears in her eyes.

She wanted to thank him. For the first time since she had seen him getting beaten up in that tawdry bar back on Antonio, suffering the results of a complex con he was too drunk to pull off, she wanted to grab his big brown head and kiss him.

But she couldn't. Garcia was doing his own negotiations, playing his own part. He had to make the monk think he would give in, like any sane person would. He had to stall, just on the edge of surrender, for as long as he could. He had to look like the weak, pathetic, incorrigibly dishonest human being he had been for his entire life.

Prudence couldn't wreck that by treating him like a hero, even while he was being one. She couldn't trust herself to say anything. She watched Jorgun, white-faced with confusion and fear, hand Garcia the bottle. Then she walked away.

"We can't do this, Prudence!" Kyle seemed frozen in place, unable to move.

"Do you have any better ideas?" she snapped, without turning around. Without stopping.

"Get the fuck out of here, dummy. And you too, Jorgun." Garcia laughed wildly again. "Go, motherfucker, or I'll shoot you myself!" Screaming rage followed his mirth without pause.

Prudence knew he wasn't merely acting. Garcia had a lifetime's worth of rage to carry him through the next few hours. And Prudence had a lifetime's worth of practice in running away.

Openly crying, she ran up the loading ramp.

T he bridge was cold and austere. In her command chair, she could function without emotion.

Jorgun sat quietly at his console, afraid and uncertain.

She didn't bother to ask about Kyle. Either he had come aboard, or he hadn't. There was nothing she could do about it.

"Requesting permission to depart." Amazing how steady her voice was. Amazing that she had said those words, and not what she was feeling.

Requesting permission to abandon my family to certain death.

The automated control system gave her an exit vector. She let the *Ulysses* follow it, even while she argued with the machines.

"I'm carrying no cargo. Give me a vector that wastes less time in-system."

Cursing, she saw that the machines on Monterey had already taken that into account.

It was harder to not cry when she didn't have anything to do.

Ten minutes, and they were out of the atmosphere. It seemed like hours. How long had it seemed for Garcia?

A light on her console. Another ship, making contact. She sat, paralyzed with fear, unable to respond.

The console relayed the message anyway.

"This is the Altair patrol boat *Launceston*, hailing the *Ulysses*. Acknowledge, please." Captain Stanton's voice washed over her like the dregs of an incomprehensible dream. Did he follow her around from disaster to disaster, like some tardy herald of woe?

"This is the *Ulysses*," she answered, feeling unreal. "Captain Falling speaking."

"May we ask if Altair is on your current itinerary, Captain?"

It was the kind of question that had only one answer.

"I think we could arrange that, Captain. Is there something you'd like us to deliver?"

"We have a surveying report we'd like to send back. Nothing exciting, but regulations are regulations. You can collect a moderate payment for it, of course." The report would be a cryptographically sealed data pod. Fleet vessels scattered these little pods all over the local sector. Theoretically it was a backup system, in case the ship in question disappeared. Since no Fleet vessel had ever disappeared, Prudence was pretty sure they used the capsules as a way to smoke out who could be trusted and who couldn't. She'd never been tempted to crack one of the pods, since she was positive it would just contain a note that said something pithy like "Espionage doesn't pay."

"We'd be happy to oblige you. Can you meet us at the halfway point?" They would have to match velocities to do a physical exchange. If they did it halfway to the node, she could still pick up enough velocity to make the trip on the other side in a reasonable amount of time.

"Negative, Captain. We're not at the Solistar node. We just came over from X785-C844."

The dead node. The one that led to Kassa. Going that way would get them back to Altair in one less hop. She had just enough fuel to get there, running without cargo.

"Captain . . . was it quiet over there?"

"Dead as a doornail. That's why they call them dead nodes." Stanton's voice was not suited to mockery. Then she realized he wasn't mocking. He knew, and he knew she knew, there was reason to suspect what others took for granted. They had both been at Kassa.

There were monsters hiding in the dark places, after all.

"Captain Stanton, have you cleared," she beat at her screen, pulling up a node-chart, "X784-D12?"

"Where? Oh, you mean the inward link?" Inward was an arbitrary designation that meant "toward home." It wasn't the kind of term tramp freighters used. "Yes, we came from there. If you wanted to go to Kassa, it would be a short trip."

"That suits our plans perfectly, Captain Stanton. I'm contacting Traffic Control now and informing them of our course change. We hadn't considered it before, because of the risk. But if you say it's safe, then we can shave a hop off our trip."

They were oh-so-careful to talk in generalities, to explain everything in simple terms. It was a tight comm beam, and encrypted to standard privacy, but both of them were assuming they were being overheard.

"We can do better than merely say it's safe, Captain Falling. Our mission takes us back the same way, so we can go through with you, if you'd like."

Would she like to be escorted by a fusion-powered warship? Would a girl like to be escorted to the dance by the captain of the football team? "That would be very generous, Captain."

"I'm sending you the latest orbital data, for both nodes. Pick your optimal transit velocity, Captain. We'll match you."

That was potentially a lot of fuel Stanton was willing to expend to make her life convenient. She hoped it was merely because he was trying to impress her, like lonely men in deep space often did, and not because he was worried about something dire.

Monterey Traffic Control was not happy. The machines beeped and complained, threatening her with fines for filing false course information. She brushed them off. Free navigation was still the law.

There was a pause in the warnings, and then they went away. That might mean that a human being had taken charge, or it might mean the machines had exhausted their limited threats.

A human being. There was one down there right now, on the planet, making this all possible. She put her hands to her eyes, to hold back the feelings that poured through her.

"Anything?" Kyle asked softly, from the entrance to the bridge. She didn't know how long he had been standing there.

"No." No news was good news.

"Remarkable that the *Launceston* showed up," Kyle mused. "Nice to see an old friend."

"They're not *my* friends."

Kyle grinned. She could tell by the sound of his voice. "One thing I can tell you after my two weeks on the *Launceston* is that Stanton is as anti-League as it is possible to be, and still hold a commission in Fleet. He's a friend to both of us."

"Why are they here, Kyle?" It was too suspicious to let go of.

"For the same reason we are, Prudence. Fleet isn't stupid. There are too many threads pointing this way. Stanton is out here looking for clues."

Stanton came back on the line. "Captain Falling, we've examined your course, and we feel it would be best to handle the delivery on the other side of the node, if that's acceptable to you."

Apparently Stanton found Monterey system as unpleasant as she did. She doubted his opinion would be improved by learning that the planet was crawling with genocidal clones.

"Of course, Captain. We'll see you on the other side, then."

"Acknowledged, *Ulysses*. We'll match with you after exit, while you're doing your cross-system flight. Give you more time to adapt, if there are any problems. Regulations require commercial vessels to try and avoid course corrections during node approaches."

"Understood, *Launceston*." Stanton and his regulations. For once she appreciated them, knowing how handy they might be in the next few hours.

———

An hour passed. Then two. After the third hour Prudence began to consider nominating Garcia for sainthood.

The comm channel lit up again.

"*Ulysses*, this is Monterey Traffic Control. We would like you to return to the spaceport to answer some questions."

A human voice, but not recognizable as Dejae's. Traffic Control didn't stint on its filters. The monks on Monterey had been concealing their identity for a very long time.

"I'm terribly sorry." She was, but not for them. For Garcia. "We've already passed turnaround. We can't abort now. It's not physically possible." Garcia had bought them the time they needed.

"We understand that. However, this is a serious matter. We are dispatching a patrol boat to follow you through the node. We require that you reverse velocity on the other side, and return with the vessel."

"I don't think I can. I've already plotted a vector through the next node, and my current velocity presumes making that hop." She'd been running on maximum acceleration since liftoff. They would streak across X785 like a meteorite, unable to stop before the next node even if they wanted to. There was no margin of error. She was trusting the orbital data from the *Launceston* with their lives.

"Our vessel is equipped with grappling lines and fusion power. It will assist you with velocity management."

They wanted her bad.

"If you cannot correct your course, then you will be required to abandon ship and board your crew on our vessel."

Really bad.

"Well, if it's that important, I guess we'll have to." She signed out.

After a few minutes, they called back.

"*Ulysses*, we note that you are continuing to accelerate. This is not acceptable. Begin your deceleration now, or we will be forced to ask the *Launceston* to intervene."

"I'm sorry, Monterey. The *Launceston* just chewed me out on the regs for course corrections during node approaches." That, of course, had been the point of Stanton's little lecture. "I'm not going through that again. We'll see you on the other side. *Ulysses* out."

She turned off the comm.

Kyle was grinning, in a very unfriendly way.

"What are you so happy about?"

"They're trying to stop us. That's good news."

"How do you figure?"

"It means we can still hurt them."

EIGHTEEN

Hammer

Four long days, but not long enough. He didn't want them to end. Not because there was trouble waiting for them on the other side. The Monterian ship would be only hours behind them. The *Launceston* might well feel compelled to enforce the law. There were many bad things that would start happening once they left the node. But those were not the reasons Kyle found himself resisting the passage of each hour.

Being with Prudence, a part of her crew, a part of her ship. A part of her family. They were together without friction, without suspicion. For the first time in his life, Kyle wasn't playing a role, wasn't trying to present the image he thought others wanted to see. There was no reason to try. Jorgun didn't care, and Prudence couldn't be fooled. And the absence of Garcia drew them together, like a hole in the ground that needed to be filled.

He wanted to win through to the next node for the most selfish of reasons. Because then he would have more time in node-space. Only two and a half days, but beggars could not complain.

The ancients had been right. Heaven was a place in the sky, where nothing bad could touch you. But not for long; never for long enough.

"Listen to that." Prudence played a warbling hiss for him through her comm console. She'd been analyzing the data on his blue pod for the last five hours. He'd helped her with the technical settings, but mostly he'd sat next to her and soaked up her presence.

"I'm not a computer," he said. "It doesn't mean anything to me."

"It doesn't mean anything to the computer, either. But it shouldn't be there. It's not cosmic radiation or planetary comm. And it's at the right time. This signal was sent out by the invading fleet, on a wide beam, throughout the whole system."

"Why would they broadcast their presence?" He kept asking why a lot. Everything these monks did was ass-backwards and upside down.

"I don't have a clue. It's an encrypted signal. But Altair should have computers that can crack it."

"I'll hand it over to the *Launceston*, then. They'll get there sooner than we will."

"Yes, they will," she said cryptically.

A yellow light on her console turned on, accompanied by a gentle but insistent tone. It was the worst sound Kyle could imagine. It signaled the end of their vacation.

"Normal space in fifteen minutes. Put on your best smiles, boys. You need to convince the *Launceston* to give you a ride."

A cold panic washed over him. "What?"

"Think about it, Kyle. I can't stop that patrol boat from catching us. What I can do is put Jorgun and you on the *Launceston*, out of their reach. I'll surrender, and take the *Ulysses* back to Monterey. It will be four more days before they find out they were swindled. You'll be safe by then."

"I'm not leaving you, Prudence."

"It's not your choice."

"You can get on the *Launceston* with us."

She turned her face partly away. "I'm not leaving my ship."

"It's just a ship! It's not worth dying for. With the information you have to sell, Altair will buy you a new one."

"Kyle, it won't work. If I'm not on the *Ulysses*, they'll know something is up. They'll attack the *Launceston*."

"So what? It's armed. It can fight."

"But it might not win."

Kyle stared at her, unable to rationally cope with the prospect of losing her.

"Kyle, we can't take the chance. You have to warn Altair before it's too late. You don't understand. *You don't understand.*"

"Psychotic clones are trying to take over my planet. What part do I not fucking understand?"

She stared past him, into some distant memory.

"The monks think they won't kill anyone. But when they have complete power, they'll forget. They'll get impatient. There will be problems . . . and genocide will look like a solution. In twenty years, Kyle, there will be ovens."

He reached out, to hold her, but she pushed him away, tears pouring down her face.

"I can't lose you and Jorgun that way. I can't lose another family to the fire."

"You can't stop it by dying!" His fingers were numb, all feeling and strength gone out of his hands.

"They might not kill me right away. And if you win, then you can rescue me. You can be my knight in shining armor." She said it with a wan smile, the kind of smile that would have comforted Jorgun. It didn't comfort him.

If wresting Monterey from its orbit and casting it into the sun with his bare hands was what it would take to win Prudence back, he would do it.

But there had to be an easier way.

"Fake a malfunction. Let the *Ulysses* drift. While they're boarding we'll escape on the *Launceston*."

"They're not that stupid, Kyle. For Earth's sake, stop making it hard on me. On us." Jorgun was whimpering at his station, confused but understanding enough to know something bad was going on. "This is the best plan. I've thought about it for days. It's what we have to do."

"I can't do it, Prudence."

"You have to! They will kill you, Kyle. They'll turn you over to Rassinger, and he'll kill you, whether Altair wins or loses. And what hope would I have then, locked in my cell, alone on Monterey? How could I bear the days, knowing you could never come for me?"

Stop it. Stop saying that. He thought the words, but could not speak.

Impossibly, she dried her tears. Impossibly, she stood without breaking, while the world spun around Kyle, colors and shapes turning harsh and unreal.

"Go pack your bags. That's an order."

Jorgun went, unable to disobey her. Kyle had nothing to pack. Everything he wanted would be remaining on the *Ulysses*.

"Take care of Jorgun for me," she whispered.

The light turned red, and they were in real space. It didn't feel any different. The evil had already touched him.

Stanton, of all unlikely sources, gave him a reprieve. The *Launceston* didn't want to play along. When Prudence hailed them to arrange a passenger transfer, Stanton refused.

"I'm not going to abandon my assigned patrol route to ferry your passengers, Falling. Monterey can't board you for a few questions. If they want to talk to you, they can bloody well follow you to Altair."

She tried reasoning with him. "Captain, I don't think you understand the gravity of the situation. They won't take no for an answer."

"This is neutral space. Altair law is as equally valid here as Monterey law. If they want to pick a fight, I'll give them one." Stanton obviously had spent too much time floating around in empty space looking for something to shoot at.

"They will pick a fight, Captain. We know something they don't want you to know. At any cost."

Now she had his full attention.

"What would that be, Captain Falling?"

So she told him.

He was too professional to display any reaction over the comm link. As a soldier, he was supposed to be used to bombshells. "Do you have any proof?"

"Not a lot." Prudence looked flustered.

Kyle shook his head in sympathy. Obviously she had expected her mere word to be sufficient to shake governments. A short vid of a man in a mask on one planet, and a tall tale of the same man in a different mask on another planet, and she thought Fleet would follow her anywhere.

Luckily, she had a well-trained police detective on her side. Kyle held up the mask he'd ripped off of the monk, safely bagged in plastic. He'd already gone over it with a magnifying glass and found what they needed. One single hair, stuck on the inside of the mask. A slender thread to drag a fleet by, but DNA did not lie.

"Yes," Prudence answered the radio, relief in her voice. "We have some vid files, and the physical evidence to back it up."

"Let me see those files now." Stanton was still suspicious, as he should be. Between that and the way Stanton had bailed them out of Monterey, Kyle was struggling to maintain his dislike of the man.

Prudence offered them all her secrets. "We also have a recorded signal we could transmit to you. It was taken from a solar observation post on Kassa, at the time of the attack. We don't know what it means. Maybe your comp can break the code and tell you something useful."

"Acknowledged, Captain. Send it all over while we close for boarding." The *Launceston* had already matched their velocity and was drifting only a few kilometers away, but it would take another hour to safely close the gap with the ships. "I suggest you prepare to abandon ship, Captain Falling. We can't afford to let you fall into enemy hands. We'll be taking you and all your crew onboard."

Tapping her console, Prudence sent all of their hard-won data over in an instant. Before Kyle could start breathing again, she started arguing.

"If they see the *Ulysses* drifting, they'll know to focus on the *Launceston*. I could distract them, make them think you don't know yet."

Stanton didn't answer, presumably watching the vids she had transmitted, so Kyle argued for him.

"Prudence, they'll assume we talked. There's probably a dozen ships burning through that node right now. It will only take one to hunt down the *Ulysses*."

She shrugged him off, speaking into the microphone. "Stanton, I think you should reconsider."

Still no answer.

Her jaw took on that subtle hardness it wore when something was wrong. Kyle was elated that he could see it now, that he knew every line and curve of her face so well. The emotion jangled with his grief and fear, clanging discordantly.

"*Launceston*, reply please."

Silence.

On the screen that showed the depths of space, a white light flared and died.

"*Launceston*, reply. *Ulysses* hailing the *Launceston*. Reply, damn it!" Prudence tapped furiously at her console.

Kyle ran over to Jorgun's console and started working the comm controls.

"They're still there," Prudence said. "If they had blown up, there would be debris and gas. They're still in one piece."

He couldn't raise anything on any channel.

"I'm going to take us closer." Prudence started moving the ship, nudging it towards the *Launceston*'s last position. "If they have casualties, they might need us."

Two frantic minutes passed, but Kyle didn't stop checking every possible wavelength. And then he found something, a single quiet voice in the dark.

"Pru—I've got a signal. It's a suit microphone. Somebody in a space suit wants to talk to us." He flicked it to her chair.

"This is the *Ulysses*. Do you read me?"

"Captain Falling. How nice of you to wait." The voice was faint. Kyle turned up the volume.

Prudence let her worry show. "Stanton, are you okay? What happened?"

"Don't you already know, Falling? Wasn't this part of your plan?"

Now she bit her lip, angry, confused, and scared all at the same time. Kyle wanted to hold her, to wrap his arms around her. Instead, he listened.

"What on Earth are you talking about?" she asked.

"You've disabled us, Falling. Right down to the life support. Not that it matters. On this vector, without course corrections, we'll pass our turnaround point before our air runs out. We're doubly damned."

"Stanton, stop being an idiot. I didn't do anything to you!"

"That recorded signal you chose to share with us, Falling. It's a viral code. It burned through our boards like acid. Every system on the ship went haywire until we pulled the emergency plugs. It even tried to trigger our self-destruct sequence. But I disabled that months ago, when that idiot Daspar came on board. Didn't want my ship blown up because somebody wanted an asinine League officer dead. Never got around to reconnecting it, sorry to say. It's a regs violation. Be sure to include that in my file, Falling."

So Stanton had finally met a regulation he didn't like.

"I didn't do that." Prudence looked ready to cry again, and Kyle watched helplessly, wanting to comfort her. Knowing that he could not. "I mean, I didn't know it would happen. Damn it, didn't you listen to my story? Why would I tell you all that if I was working for them?"

Stanton had his own question. "Why didn't your ship burn out when that virus went through it?"

Finally, something Kyle could say that would matter. He pushed his microphone button. "Because this ship wasn't made on Altair. You know that. You remarked on it back at Kassa." And an unkind remark it had been, looking out across that field of refugees to the homely little freighter with ungainly lines.

"Daspar." Stanton let his displeasure at the ironic coincidences of the universe show through in his tone. "Of course you're there, too."

"He's on our side." Prudence defended Kyle, making him feel warm inside. "The League tried to kill him. Several times. You can trust him, Stanton."

Kyle bathed in the feeling, enjoying it despite the terrible circumstances. Prudence was defending him. Prudence. Him.

Out there, in the dark, Stanton was wrestling with momentous decisions, trying to decide who to trust. "So that's why they didn't disable us on the other side. You filed landing papers; they knew their trick wouldn't work on your ship. And I was too close to the node."

There wasn't anything they could do to help him, but Prudence tried. "We can match your vector, Captain, and take you and your crew on board. And then make a run for it . . ."

"Negative, Captain." Stanton's voice was strong again. He'd made his choice. "That plan has a zero percent chance of success. Your ship is not fast enough. I was lying, earlier, about how bad it was. Trying to buy time. We have physical backups on board. Regs call for us to be prepared to purge and reprogram our system in six hours. We can do it in three."

For once, Kyle appreciated the man's obsession.

"We can't run, Falling. We've lost the vector for that. But we'll be ready for a fight when they come through that node."

"What if they send a fleet?" Prudence, who had moments ago been prepared to stay behind and face the enemy alone, was trying to talk Stanton out of it. Kyle thought that was very sweet of her. Futile, but sweet.

"They don't know you have that recording. So they don't know we'll be immune by then. They'll try to disable us, first, with a radio beam. That will cost them at least one ship. The rest will have to fight us honestly, and that will buy you time."

"How are you going to become immune in three hours?"

Stanton chuckled. "The old-fashioned way, Captain. I'm going to take a hammer to our external comm feeds. We'll be incommunicado after that, so don't expect us to say good-bye."

"I don't feel right, leaving you in a disabled ship."

"Don't worry about us." His voice was stern. "There's something vastly more important you need to do. Half of Altair Fleet is hanging off of Kassa, waiting for the aliens. If they attack with that viral code, the fleet will be destroyed. You have to warn them immediately. Even three minutes of warning will spell the difference between battle and disaster. The enemy could already be on their way, from some other node."

Half of Fleet destroyed in a single battle? The government would collapse. Dejae would be given any powers he asked for.

"Will they believe us?" Prudence asked. Kyle smiled in appreciation. She only made mistakes once.

"Yes, they will, because they already have reason to. We all noticed something while they were handing out duty assignments. They sent the experienced ships, of course, and kept back the new ships, the ones with noncitizen crews. But they also kept back the ships with League officers on them. We knew they were sending the rest of us to the front lines to die first. We just thought it would be a fair fight. The half of Fleet at Kassa isn't just any half, Captain Falling. It's the half that is still loyal to Altair."

Like all criminals, the monks had finally outsmarted themselves. They had gathered all the uncontrollable elements together and sent them into exile, where they could destroy them with one blow. But they had not expected Prudence.

Stanton sent his last transmission. "Go and save my brothers, Captain Falling. Save Altair."

The *Ulysses* crossed the system in dreadful silence. They had no way of knowing if or when the enemy had come through the node. Or how many. Their sensors were not powerful enough to scan across the entire system. And the *Launceston* was in self-imposed comm blackout, so it could neither send them warning nor boast of victory. The life-and-death drama behind them would play out invisibly.

Likely they would not even see their pursuers until seconds before they died.

Prudence drove Jorgun and Kyle like a slaver, making them transfer every nonessential piece of equipment to the main cargo bay.

"Don't we need this?" Kyle asked, shoving on a squat, dense air recycler.

"Not if there are only three of us." Prudence was right next to him, so close they could not help but touch now and again. The sensations kept Kyle going, long after his muscles were ready to quit.

Jorgun pulled from the other side, putting the dead weight back in motion.

"Are we going to leave this at the spaceport?" The giant wasn't entirely clear on this "flyby" concept.

"I think she's going to give us a break, Jor. She's going to dump it in space. So we can just open the cargo doors and let it float out." At least, he hoped that was the plan.

"No," she said. "I'm going to dump it while we're in the next node."

Kyle stopped pushing. "Isn't that kind of dangerous?"

"Not as much as screwing with our mass during the entry."

Jorgun pouted. "We won't be able to play volleyball with all this junk in the cargo bay."

"We're going to seal off the cargo bay, Jor. And vent it. Air is mass."

That meant they would spend the rest of the trip confined to the living quarters. Kyle couldn't really complain. It would mean more contact with Prudence. She wouldn't be able to sneak off and brood like she was prone to do.

"It's not that much mass, is it?" Kyle asked. Not because he was objecting, but because he was trying to show he could learn about space travel.

"I'm not just going to vent the cargo bay," she admitted. "I'm going to take a torch and cut it off."

Kyle was stunned. "What?" She might as well cut off her own arm.

"It's mass. Every kilo we lose is three seconds less travel time to Kassa. I can accelerate faster, and decelerate from a faster velocity. It adds up."

"You're going to cripple your ship?" He was surprised at the level of his own outrage.

"It's just a ship. It's not worth dying for. I'm hoping Altair will buy me a new one," she parroted at him.

He'd been studying spacer manuals since he came on board. "Won't dumping mass in the node fry us?" Things that didn't go through the node with exactly the right velocity came out the other end as a spray of cosmic particles.

"Stop pretending to be a pilot. The scrap won't deviate from our velocity enough to matter. Once we leave the node we'll accelerate away from it. And it won't be making course corrections, so it will pass out of the system and be lost to space. So take a good look around. This is the last time you'll see any of this junk."

She spoke like a surgeon about to remove diseased organs, but she could not disguise the way she gazed on the bits and pieces of her home.

"It's going to look kind of funny without a cargo bay." Kyle tried to imagine it from the outside, and failed.

"It will fly faster. That's all that matters."

The physical labor kept them occupied. It was a surprise when the alarm sounded, warning that the next node was imminent. Kyle found himself grinning with anticipation. For the next sixty hours, they would be safe again. And wonderfully close.

Prudence spent most of those hours in a space suit, in the cargo bay, with the doors locked. She wouldn't let Kyle accompany her.

"Somebody has to stay on the bridge in case of an emergency," she said. "And it can't be Jorgun."

So Kyle spent all his time on the bridge alone while she and Jorgun dismembered her ship. During the six-hour breaks she allowed herself for sleep, she locked herself in her stateroom. Mealtimes were monosyllabic.

Kyle tried not to feel rejected. This had to be hurting her emotionally, in ways she wasn't ready to share yet. After this system flyby they would have five days in the final hop to Kassa. The work would all be done, the danger would be past, and they would have time to talk. To make plans. To think about a future without spiders and clones.

He was almost excited when the alarm turned yellow, and Prudence dragged herself wearily to the bridge. True, there was some risk that the enemy would catch up to them here, but they had changed the parameters of the game. They had a fighting chance.

Watching through the screen as the real world came back into focus, the light reaching their sensors no longer distorted by the physics of the node, he marveled at the serene majesty of the starry sky.

Then he frowned.

"What was that?"

A star had winked out. He was sure of it.

Prudence looked up from her calculations.

Another star blossomed, a tiny light in blackness, and died in a heartbeat.

"A course correction," Prudence said. "That was a course correction."

Another. Then two more, far apart.

"We're too late. Their fleet is in front of us."

There was nothing they could do. Kyle knew enough about piloting to see that for himself. The enemy was halfway across the system, heading for the only node the *Ulysses* could hope to enter. Prudence could not change her mind now. Her course had been calculated and set days ago. Even with the ship stripped to the bone she had too much mass to turn around.

They could not hope to remain undetected. Prudence had to run her gravitics at full power or accept certain death at the hands of a null-vector. They could not hope to evade. The enemy had fusion boats. They were not ruled by the distant whims of planets and stars.

Out of the majestic black sky came the ugly voice of their defeat. "Prepare to be boarded. Any resistance will be met with lethal force. Instantly."

That the enemy had sent a ship to capture them, instead of simply sending death, was not particularly comforting.

"Let me do the talking," Kyle begged. "I can try to make a deal. I still have contacts in the League."

Prudence said nothing, small and still on her useless command chair.

"I'm scared," Jorgun said.

She went to the giant and put her arms around him.

The ship lurched, clanging with contact. The enemy was not gentle. They would never be.

The sound of the air lock cycling. Boots tramped in the passageway. Kyle stood on the bridge, between the entrance and Prudence and Jorgun, trying to shield them with his body.

Men in uniforms came in. Men with guns. Ugly men, without masks. Not clones, but refuse, bits of trash recruited from the cesspits of many worlds, selling out their own kind for a paycheck and a chance to hurt somebody.

"Get down! Get down on your knees and put your hands in the air!"

There was no need to make Kyle kneel. He presented no danger to them, and they knew it. They did it because they could. Because they enjoyed it.

Kyle knelt. "I am a League officer. Do you understand? These people are working for me, on League business."

The lead soldier struck Kyle in the face with the butt of his rifle, knocking him to the deck. He could taste blood in his mouth. The negotiations had not started well.

The men swarmed past him, pulled Prudence and Jorgun apart. They beat Jorgun to his knees.

They stared at Prudence.

"This was worth the trip," one of them said.

The leader grinned. "Let's have a better look." He stepped forward and grabbed Prudence's shirt, tearing it open.

"League officer!" Kyle tried to scream, but the soldier guarding him kicked him in the gut.

Prudence stood like a statue. Beautiful. Immobile. She looked past the men, to some distant, invisible place.

Then Jorgun, simple Jorgun, stupid Jorgun, had to see the last puzzle piece.

"These are the people that took Jelly away, aren't they?" he asked Prudence.

"Shut the fuck up!" screamed the guard standing over him, beating down on the giant with his rifle.

Prudence turned away from him, tears in her eyes. Kyle tried to lie for her, to tell Jorgun to shut up and be still, but he was still gasping for breath.

"Stop that," Jorgun said to the man beating him.

The man shrieked in outrage, and beat harder.

"Earth, just shoot him already," said their leader.

"You hurt Jelly," Jorgun said.

The man beating him stopped and turned his rifle around, bringing the barrel to face Jorgun.

Jorgun stood up.

The man unconsciously paused, disoriented by the giant's height.

Jorgun picked him up by the head and shook him like a rag doll. Kyle could hear bones snapping like toothpicks.

"Do something!" screamed the leader.

Two men leapt on Jorgun. One bounced off like he'd hit a wall. The other one stuck, trapped in Jorgun's arms.

Screaming a mindless, blubbery wail, Jorgun ran across the deck with the man in his grasp, charging the knot of soldiers. The leader dodged out of the way, and Jorgun and his passenger collided with the wall, bouncing off of it and into a heap on the floor.

The man he had been carrying flopped in unnatural ways, emitting a strange quiet keening sound.

The leader started kicking at Jorgun. The rest of the soldiers piled on Jorgun like wolves on a deer, trying to separate him from his impromptu battering ram. Only two men remained, one by Prudence and one looming over Kyle.

Prudence stood perfectly still. Immobile. The man guarding

her could not help himself. Inexorably his attention slipped away from her, to the battle raging on the deck. Kyle kept coughing, even though he didn't have to anymore. He very carefully did not look at Prudence, but looked away, at the fight.

And then she moved. One quick step. She reached out and touched the guard's head, and the man fell silently, a marionette with its strings cut.

Kyle's guard noticed. As he swung his rifle around, Kyle scrambled over the ground to his feet. He hit the man below the knees with his shoulders, sending him crashing to the deck. Two heartbeats and he had climbed on top. While the thug was still getting his bearings, Kyle struck. One punch and the man's head bounced off the floor. Disappointed that he did not have time to hurt the man more, Kyle sprang to his feet.

A burst of gunfire peppered the wall above the knot of fighting men. A warning shot from the rifle in Prudence's hands. But the tangle of men was inseparable. She could not shoot without killing them all. They ignored her.

The tramp of feet, too many feet. Through the entrance stomped a spider, huge and hairy and grotesque. Where its mouth should be were twin barrels. Grimly, mechanically, it sprayed the wrestling men with needle-fire, reducing them to hamburger.

Prudence unleashed her fury on the monster with deadly aim. The needles ricocheted futilely off, cutting only rubber and cloth, revealing gleaming metal underneath.

Kyle wrestled the gun out of Prudence's hands and threw it to the deck.

"We're unarmed! Don't shoot!"

He hugged her, covering her. Waited for the storm of needles. Someone else came into the room.

"What made you think the spider would show mercy?" he said, in Veram Dejae's voice.

"I knew you were controlling it remotely." Kyle's answers were all that could save them. He forced himself to let go of Prudence, to turn around and face the clone.

The Dejae wore a mask, a glittering affair of gems and gold, but it could not hide his annoyance. "How did you deduce this?"

"I saw a spider, on Baharain. When you let the machine drive, it walks smoothly and quickly. When you have to make it do something intelligent, it moves like a robot."

"Intriguing. Stand away from her."

Kyle obeyed, instantly.

More men came into the room, looking shocked.

"Strip them. Bind them. Put them on the ship. Can you handle that?" The Dejae's voice was dangerously casual.

"Yes, sir." The new leader leapt to obey. But as he and his men approached Kyle, they were careful not to block the spider's line of fire.

"I wanted to do it all with robots," the Dejae explained to Kyle, while two men tore his clothes off and a third glared at him from behind a rifle barrel. "I was outvoted. I was told that human judgment was still invaluable. When I find servants who can successfully carry out a simple task like capturing two unarmed men and a girl, I'll consider changing my opinion."

"Good help is hard to find," Kyle agreed. He realized he was trying to keep the Dejae talking, so it would think of him as human. A wasted effort. The clone already thought of Kyle as human. That was the problem.

The men wrapped his wrists in sticky tape. Like the idiots they were, they bound his hands in front of him, not behind his back. But he wasn't going to do anything. Being naked was a kind of binding on its own.

The men moved to Prudence, ripped the clothes from her body. Kyle tried not to look. He could not bear to see how beautiful she was.

Kyle offered more from his dwindling supply of facts. "We're wanted on Monterey, for questioning." When he had nothing left to give, they would kill him.

"You do get around. But you can relax for a few days. We have some business to deal with before we return home."

They marched them past the bodies, his feet squishing in the blood. They dragged them through the blasted air lock, threw them to the floor of their fusion transport. He caught Prudence awkwardly as she fell. She lay in his arms like a sack of potatoes.

Men stood around them, glaring. The Dejae ignored them, his spider marching at his side. At least the Dejae was not going to let them rape her.

Yet.

Kyle wondered if the Dejae would keep her for himself. Kyle began to hope he would. It would be better for her.

The ship moved underneath them.

"Target is cleared for attack," the Dejae said from the bridge. A wall-sized screen showed the *Ulysses* drifting in space as they accelerated away from it. The freighter did not look as ungainly as Kyle had feared. With the cargo hold shorn off, it looked like a dragonfly, lumpy and angular but rendered delicate.

Lights sparkled around the *Ulysses*, and then steam as its air was vented from a thousand holes. At the same time a dark, tubular shape streaked through the screen's vision. A fighter, making a close pass.

In its wake the *Ulysses* came apart in pieces, like shredded lettuce. The main generator exploded, a ball of flaming gas welling up from the remains. When it cleared, there was nothing left. The corpse of the *Ulysses* had been dismembered and cast upon the void.

With Jorgun's body. And Kyle's dreams of home and family. And maybe Prudence's soul.

She still had not spoken, not a gasp, not a whisper.

Ridiculously, he feared for her state of mind.

NINETEEN

Shattered

She took comfort in the feel of his body against hers. Insanity, yes, but it was the only comfort left. She could not speak to him. Even if she trusted her voice, even if she could talk without revealing the medallion hidden in her mouth, there was nothing to say.

Like a rabbit caught in headlights, she remained perfectly still, staring at nothing. The men leered and whispered terrible things, but acknowledging them would only make it worse.

It would be bad enough as it was. They had already taken almost everything from her. Her ship. Her crew. Her family, past and present. Soon they would take her dignity, and then they would take Kyle away and kill him.

Of all of these losses, Kyle seemed the greatest. She had not had time to be with him. Their life, the hopes and dreams it promised, was not just cut short. It had never begun.

She had never even kissed him.

All the sacrifices she had made had been in vain. All the time she had spent dismantling her defenses to let Kyle in had been wasted. All her efforts had been futile. Jandi had been right. But to think on that was to surrender to self-recrimination. And there was no room for that. Grief squeezed out all other emotion, and spilled over her body, coating every sensation with a glaze of unreality.

With nothing else to do, she watched the main vid screen. They were approaching another ship. She could judge its immense scale by the tiny fighters buzzing around it. An opening appeared in the squat, tubular behemoth. A carrier, then: a ship that bore other ships as cargo, like a chinchilla fish carries its babies in its mouth. The fusion boat that had captured them did not seem equipped for node travel, nor could those little fighters manage a node on their own. They lacked the mass necessary to create a stable bubble in the node.

Before they had captured her ship, the gravitics display had told her of the existence of this one massive vessel, and of dozens of other smaller ships, probably a screen of destroyers. In a fair fight, Altair might stand a chance.

But of course they had their secret weapon. The carrier would paralyze her prey and release the swarm to feed. Altair Fleet would be rendered helpless for hours, while the spiders bled them with sprays of steel needles at near-relativistic speeds. Even the idiotic robotic fighter pilots would be capable of total victory in such a one-sided battle.

A warning from Prudence, and Altair could crush this monster under its heel. But in silence, its poison would destroy a foe ten times its size. The remnant of Altair Fleet would be loyal to Dejae and afraid to move. While it did nothing the clones would build more ships, extending their web across the sector until they could defeat planetary fleets without cheating. In a hundred years Altair would be a sea of Dejaes, and the sky would be blotted out with their ships. Then they would be unstoppable. The entire galaxy would be wiped clean of humanity and replaced with Dejae.

It might be an improvement. Presumably the Dejaes treated each other better than ordinary people did. Under the rule of clones, there might not be any more Strattenburgs.

Remembering the frightened young monk on Monterey, she knew it was a false hope. The clones were not better people than people.

The boat shuddered as clamps seized it. Its gravitics whined and died, and she could feel the lock cycling as the air pressure subtly changed.

"Take them to holding. In one piece." The Dejae spoke the order to his men, and swept out.

The spider remained, watching them impassively.

Glaring, the men pulled her and Kyle to their feet. They were not gentle or modest.

One leered at her, his hand slapping her buttock. "Don't worry, pretty little thing. The monks won't touch you. But they'll let us show you a good time, before they space you as a waste of mass."

"Fuck you," Kyle said, earning a beating. The soldier punched him in the face several times while others held his arms.

"Knock it off," their leader said. "He has to be able to talk."

Dragged through the corridors, they came to an elevator. The ship was built on the vertical, instead of the normal horizontal. Like an old rocket ship instead of a surface vessel. Prudence wondered why. Passive grav-plating didn't care which way you laid it. Maybe the monks had not trusted their opaque sky, and had built their ships in deep holes in the ground, like missile silos, easier to conceal than shallow pits. Or maybe they were just crazy. Not every action had a reason. Not everything made sense.

The brig was small, with only two guards. The clones obviously didn't intend to take a lot of prisoners. Kyle and Prudence were forced into a bare room, with solid steel walls. Chains hung from the ceiling, and there were bloodstains on the floor. Their bound hands were held high above their heads while a chain was looped between them and locked. Now they stood, naked and helpless, but after enough hours their legs would give out. Then they would dangle. After enough hours of that, their lungs would collapse, and they would die.

The leader of the guards explained the bloodstains with a grisly smile. "The monks believe in corporal punishment. They say it improves discipline, but I think they just like flogging. The chain is so you have to choose to stand and take it. If you do something stupid like turn around, they'll flog your front side, including the naughty bits." He leered at Prudence's nakedness. "Not so much a problem for you, missy. But that's good news. Maybe there'll be something left for us to play with when they're done."

"Fuck you," Kyle said, through his bloody mouth.

They didn't even bother to beat him this time. Laughing, they walked outside, and sealed the door.

"Prudence." Kyle sounded so lost and alone.

She shook her head. They still had to wait.

But not for long. Five minutes and one of the guards from the brig came in, the huge steel door whining as it opened and closed.

He walked around them, leering. Trying to intimidate her. Futilely, given the circumstances.

"Jobson and I talked about it, and we decided not to wait on the tender mercies of our employers. I won the throw, so I get to go first."

He took his jacket off and hung it over a camera on the back wall.

"No point in letting that pervert Jobson watch." Prudence marveled at the sensibilities of rapists. "You think about how you want to play this. It'll likely be the most fun you'll have for the rest of your life." He advanced on her warily, his hands open and in front of him.

She didn't react. He grinned, and spoke to Kyle. "Don't worry, you'll get your turn too. The monks are like that. Fine for them, eh, a planet full of men. But Earth if an ordinary man don't get to missing a woman something fierce."

Kyle didn't speak. He must know he couldn't prevent this. He must understand that not provoking the guard had to be the best thing he could do for Prudence.

Yet she could guess how much it cost him to remain silent. To look away in shame and helplessness. She could guess to the billionth of a credit what the cost was, because she had looked away helplessly while they beat Jorgun.

"You can scream or cry if you want." He seemed disturbed by their silence. "I turned the audio off. I didn't want to gag you. You wouldn't be able to tell me how much you enjoyed it."

He stepped in, close, the stench of his sweat overwhelming. She heard cloth rustle and metal clink as he undid his trousers.

Turning her face back to his, to stare him in the eyes, she put one leg up over his hip.

"Eager to get started." His leer was vile, up close. "I like that. It won't make me hurt you any less, but it's a good try. Don't forget to tell me how much you like it."

She pulled him in close and put her other leg over his hip. Now she rested her weight on him, so she could reach up and grasp the chain, instead of hanging from it.

The guard grinned and tugged at his trousers, trying to pull them down without dislodging her legs.

Twisting, she pulled him around, turning in a circle. Focused on the heat of the moment, he did not realize which direction she was leading him.

When his pants fell to his ankles, the belt buckle clanking dully on the steel floor, he grinned at her and leaned in close.

"A kiss, first, then."

She squeezed him tight and stared into his eyes. She let herself hate this man, with all the years of righteous wrath she had carried since a sixteen-year-old girl had traded her family for jars of ashes. Using him as a platform, she swung one leg out and over his shoulder.

Annoyed, he reached up to grab her leg. She flipped the other one up to join it. Locking her left foot behind her right knee, she squeezed.

Stupidly, he spent the first fifteen seconds fighting her, pitting the strength of his arms against the strength of her legs. Only when the lack of air began to weaken him did he think to start hitting her. She struggled with him, twisting and cranking at his neck, trying to avoid his blows while keeping the pressure up. He started pulling away, and now she was fighting just to keep her hold.

They staggered around in a circle, bound by the chain, and she realized she was losing. He kept getting loose enough to catch a breath. Soon his attacks would hurt her enough that she couldn't hold on.

There was a sharp crack. She felt the force of the blow even through the guard's heavy body. He stiffened momentarily, his eyes suddenly focused on some distant point, and then sagged limply in her grip.

They swung together, for an instant, until she let him fall. Lying on the ground at an unnatural angle, he feebly twitched his arms, trying to reach his broken back, while drool spilled from his mouth.

Kyle grinned savagely. "I might have broken a toe." He had kicked the guard in the spine. The guard's attempts to retreat had only brought him within range of Kyle.

Kyle stretched out and put a foot on the guard's throat. She shook her head.

"I know," he said. "They almost certainly have him on a sensor. If we kill him, they'll come. I'll wait until the door opens. I'll give you as much time as I can. But please, Prudence. Say something."

She couldn't speak yet. Instead she released the chain and stood on the ground again, staring up. She would only have one chance. Carefully, her hands opened wide, fingers spread in a net, she spat the medallion out of her mouth.

Wet and slick, it slipped through her fingers, fell to the floor, and began to roll away.

Kyle stepped on it, quick as a snake.

"What the . . ."

Shame at her failure, at muffing the one chance they had to live, washed over her, released by the gift of Kyle's second chance. She sobbed uncontrollably, tears spilling from a breached dam.

"What is this?" Kyle asked wonderingly. Gently prodding it with his toes, he tried to pick it up.

Prudence's heart thudded. If he activated the device unknowingly, the blade would spring out at some random direction and cut off half his foot. She had thought it was impossible, but she remembered Jandi's easy release of the blade.

She tried to warn him, and failed. Now that her mouth was free of the secret it had borne, the medallion that it had hidden while she stood by and let Jorgun's heroics save her life, she found her voice was silenced by grief.

"I don't think I'm flexible enough," Kyle said. Gently he pushed the medallion over to her, avoiding the flopping guard.

She reached out with her foot, her toe brushing his. The contact was electrifying, the promise of hope burning like a branding iron.

Carefully, methodically, she maneuvered the medallion under her foot, until her toes could grip it. Experimentally, she sagged on the chain, letting her taped wrists take all of her weight.

It wouldn't work. The pressure rendered her hands nerveless. She could not hang upside down and transfer the medallion from foot to hand. She couldn't leave one foot on the ground and still reach her hands.

Standing on her other foot, she raised her leg and pointed it at

Kyle. Straining at the limit of her strength, she flexed at the waist and brought her foot to his face.

He smiled at her, absurd in these terrible circumstances, but it made her heart light and feathery. Bending his head to her foot, he took the medallion in his mouth, his breath hot on her sole, his lips soft and wet.

She put her foot down, and they leaned toward each other, straining against their bonds to share their first kiss.

Their lips could not reach. But he pushed his tongue the last few centimeters, and she took the medallion from him, savoring the taste of his mouth on it.

Standing straight again, she flexed her wrists, bringing the blood back into her fingers. Paradoxically calmed by the galvanizing physical contact with Kyle, she took aim and tried again.

Her fingers wrapped around the medallion, snatching it from the air.

No tears this time. She was done with tears.

Flicking the knife alive, she sheared through the chain without effort. Her arms fell, weak from exhaustion and weighted by the loop of metal. She caught herself before the metal clanked on the floor. Or before the knife, still extended, wounded her.

She didn't have room for any more mistakes.

Kneeling to the ground, holding her hands at floor level and twisting them around, she still could not reach the tape. At least she could cut the chain lower down, opening the loop so the metal links could slide quietly into a pile.

Standing, she stepped over to Kyle. Before she cut him free there was one thing that was more important, one thing that was more necessary than saving their lives or the entire galaxy. One thing that had already waited too long.

She kissed him, their lips finally meeting, the heat of their bodies shared, their tongues touching without restraint.

Afterward he stared at her, amazed.

Carefully she reached above his head, extending the blade again. She would have to operate by sight alone, since the knife gave no feedback. Touch would not tell her the difference between tape and flesh.

He stood perfectly still, trusting her. Even after she moved the knife away, his hands did not move. They stayed, locked in place, until she stepped back and nodded.

Released, they flew into action. Kyle knelt over the guard, rifling under his clothes, until he found the sensor patch. It was held on by staples instead of tape. As painful as it must have been going in, taking it out would be twice as bad. Not that Prudence cared about that. Now that Kyle knew where the sensor was, he could safely begin stripping the guard. He got no further than tugging on the trousers before the guard moaned in pain and voided his bowels.

Kyle stood up in defeat. "If we move him, he'll die." Prudence didn't care about that, either, in the long run. But for the next few minutes it was important.

Lying in his own filth, gurgling, the guard wasn't intimidating anymore, merely pathetic. Prudence looked down and allowed herself to pity him. This would be her last memory of the man, and she chose pity over hate.

Kyle was already planning the next move. "Sooner or later, the other guy is going to get worried. He should call for backup, but that means admitting he broke protocol in the first place. So instead, he'll open the door to see what's taking so long. Try not to kill him, Pru. You can cripple him, but try not to kill him." While he spoke, he cut the tape from her hands with a knife from the crippled guard's boot.

He hugged her and kissed her ear. She wanted to melt into his arms and stay there, forever. Instead, she stood against the wall, on one side of the door. Kyle took his post on the other, the knife reversed in his hand so he could club with the hilt. And they waited.

Long, long minutes, but so much easier to bear. The memory of Kyle's embrace clothed her, resting on her bare skin like armor.

The door whined.

"Fucking fuck, Holbing, what the fuck are you . . ." Jobson's voice trailed off into silence as the empty room came into view. Like the idiot he was, he leaned forward to get a better view, his head coming through the doorway.

"Hey," Kyle said.

Jobson turned to look at Kyle. Realizing it wasn't Holbing, he pointed his splattergun at him. Finally realizing the naked man was not a danger, he whipped his head around, just in time for Prudence to reach up and touch his face.

She slid the knife in between his eyes. Just a few centimeters and out again, straight and neat, like she had seen the operation done on old medical vids.

Jobson stood there, staring at her.

"Give me that," Kyle said gently, taking the gun from him. "And that," unbuckling the man's utility belt with its little pockets of ammunition and key cards. "That's a good boy," he said, unclipping Jobson's microphone from his shirt pocket. Methodically he stripped the man down to his underclothes, claiming his trousers and boots for himself. "Now just sit down here and be quiet for a while, okay?" Kyle guided the passive guard into the room, and pushed him to the floor. Jobson, his brain no longer fully functional, stared in amazement at the dull metal floor.

Touchingly, Kyle draped the guard's shirt around Prudence, where it hung like a badly fitting mini-dress. She shrugged her arms into it and fastened three buttons. It was romantic, or would have been, if it had been his shirt. And less sweat-stained.

Kyle had already stepped out of the cell and swept the control room with his gaze and the barrel of the splattergun. Prudence followed him, unconcerned. The room was obviously empty. If it weren't, they would have already died in a hail of gunfire.

Kyle found a leather jacket hanging off a chair. He put it on, but had to zipper it closed to hide his bare chest. Wearing a jacket inside a spaceship looked ridiculous. She almost gave him the shirt back, but she didn't. Not that she cared; but she did not want to expose what he had chosen to keep private.

He fumbled at his new belt, made a selection, and touched a key to the cell door. It whined shut.

"Their shift has to end soon." She let his voice wash over her, grateful that it spared her the effort of trying to speak. "Otherwise they would have spent longer talking themselves into trouble. I can kill the next shift as they come in, but after that, I don't have any more plans."

She walked to the main door.

"No," Kyle said, shaking his head. "The guards suck, but the ship designers don't. That door won't open from the inside. Only from the outside. Those idiots were as much imprisoned in here as we were."

How could he be so sure? She looked at him in wonder.

Grinning, he guessed her question. "I recognized the brand name on the cell key. The brig locks were made on Altair. I'll give them that much: Dejae knows quality when he sees it."

So it was up to her expertise now. Pacing around the room, she tried to guess how the ship would be laid out. She picked a corner of the room, out of direct sight from the main door. Opening the knife again, she cut a hole in the floor itself.

The plating dropped a dozen centimeters, clanking on the grav-plating underneath. Carefully she cut through that, trying to avoid any wires or data feeds.

When she pulled the knife away, Kyle hauled the junk out of the hole. Reaching in, he grabbed the bottom layer of mesh by the steel spine that ran along it.

Carefully she cut around his hands, releasing the ceiling mesh from the deck below them. He pulled it out of the way, glanced down briefly, readied his splattergun, and stepped through the hole.

Watching him fall out of sight was wrenching. The soft thud from below was reassuring only because it was not accompanied by gunfire. She had to force herself to wait three seconds before following him.

She couldn't hang from the edges and let herself down gracefully, because they would be too sharp. She had to step into freefall.

He caught her at the bottom, his hands strong and hard. They were in a storeroom, crowded with half-open boxes of machine parts.

"We're going to the engine room, aren't we," he whispered, his eyes alive with delight. "To cause a right piece of trouble, no doubt." Striding to the door, he opened it, and walked through it like he owned the place.

She followed him as they wandered through the corridors, tapping his shoulder to steer him. They went down three more levels before they encountered resistance. Two soldiers stepped out of a doorway. The older one looked over Kyle and frowned. Kyle's disguise had failed, no doubt compromised by his concern for Prudence's modesty.

"Who the hell are you?" the older one demanded. The younger one raked Prudence's body with a feral gaze, his eyes trapped by her exposed legs.

"R and R delivery. Boss thought you might like to have some fun." Kyle grinned and jerked his thumb in Prudence's direction.

The older soldier glanced at Prudence, and she arched her shoulders back, exposing an immodest amount of cleavage. Surprised, the guard hesitated. Kyle took advantage of his distraction, stepping in close and bringing the butt of his splattergun swinging up in a vicious arc into the soldier's jaw. The man fell against the wall and slid to the floor.

The young one finally stopped staring and started to move. Prudence stepped forward and held the knife at his throat, threatening him. But she had forgotten it had no pressure. The soldier brushed against it, unknowing, and his throat opened under the invisible edge of the knife. Blood sprayed over her and him and the corridor and he stumbled and fell.

Lying on the ground, clutching his throat and losing consciousness, he stared up at her. She remembered the look in his eyes when he had heard Kyle's words, and felt nothing.

"Come on." Kyle pulled at her arm and they ran. Behind them a door opened and voices shouted.

Another elevator. It had a red flashing light and did not open to Kyle's touch. He fumbled through the utility belt, trying card after card until one opened the doors. Inside she found the symbol they had been searching for.

Next stop: Engineering.

The elevator doors opened on a short hall with thick blast doors at the end of it. She knew Kyle's cards would not open this. With the knife she cut a circle in the door itself, ignoring the latch. Kyle kicked the circle and the slab fell into the room. Without hesitation he dived through the hole, rolling on the other side. She heard the splattergun fire once.

Carefully, avoiding the hole's razored edges with her exposed flesh, she stepped through. Kyle chased the engineers into a storage locker, shouting and swearing and waving the splattergun like a cattle prod. There were no bodies on the floor. He must have fired over their heads.

While she threw levers on the main consoles, she wondered on his choice of actions. In a battle for their lives, for the lives of all humanity, he had fired a warning shot. Because he could. Because for this minute he could accomplish his goals without killing. Even if thirty seconds from now he would have to slaughter them like sheep, for this instant he could spare them.

The subtle vibration of the ship, the living deck beneath her feet, stilled and quieted as she killed the main engine.

With the engineers locked away, Kyle went to the ruined door and took up a firing position. Buying her time.

She studied the vast engine room. The heart of all gravitics systems was its inertial mass, a colossal lump of heavy metal surrounded by circuitry. The electronics twisted the atoms, turning their inertia into motion. Gravity and acceleration were the same thing to mathematicians and metal. The heavy core would *fall* upward with the force of a hundred Gs.

A honeycomb of steel pillars radiated out from the mass. The skeleton of the ship. All of the decking, the hull, the outer skin and armor, rested on these pillars. The mass pushed on the pillars and moved the ship. This was the simple design that had carried man through space for hundreds of years. It was practically foolproof.

In this monstrous ship the inertial mass was at least a thousand tons of dense metal, a dull barrel shape welded into the center of the room. Nothing she, or heavy artillery, could do to it would appreciably matter. The acres of circuitry were independently wired. The controls were double and triple backed up.

Practically foolproof.

She stepped off the platform surrounding the inertial mass. There was no grav-plating here. It would only complicate the thrust calculations. Pushing off from the deck, fighting to control the turmoil in her stomach, she sailed up to one of the great pillars that held up the rest of the ship.

It was huge, a meter around. With the knife blade she cut a small hole in the side of the gleaming metal. As she had expected, the tube was hollow. Ten-centimeter-thick walls, but hollow. And why not? Steel was stronger in that shape. These columns could easily support the hundred thousand tons of vessel above them.

She traced a circle around the pillar. All the way around, meeting up at the other side. Kicking off to the next pillar, she did the same, carefully choosing the angle of the cut.

Kyle fired from the doorway. Time was running short.

From pillar to pillar she went, deftly touching them with her atomic edge. Kyle fired again, and she heard return fire from down the corridor.

A dull thump and the screech of a thousand nails on steel. They had thrown a grenade. It must have missed the hole in the door and bounced back at them, because Kyle was still alive. She knew because she could hear his gun firing rapidly.

She finished the last pillar. The mass still rested on its base, anchored in place by power lines and control circuitry and simple inertia. The pillars hung stately, unmoved. From five meters away it was impossible to see the hairline cracks.

Kicking to the floor, she crawled out on the deck, and gravity claimed her again. She ran to a service hatch, cut off the sealing lock, and threw it open.

Kyle sprinted to join her, tossing aside the empty gun, but before he jumped pell-mell down this hole she grabbed his arm. Steering him away, to the other side of the engine, to a different service hatch. This time she cut through the metal of the door, leaving the latch in place. No door-lock sensor would give them away here.

Kyle leapt and she followed. The hatchway was shallow, only a meter. Somehow he had lost his jacket. Squatting, cramped, bundled together, she felt the warmth of his body through the fabric of her shirt. And resented that millimeter of separation.

Voices from above. The soldiers had freed their engineers.

Muffled shouting. The soldiers yelled at them to surrender, but they were at the wrong service hatch. The ruse would buy her and Kyle at most thirty seconds. She spent those precious seconds kissing him. Vibrant, fiery life burned through the fatigue and fear and pain, making her head swim with elation. She had never really felt alive, before. She could not bear to think of losing it now.

Dejae's voice—there was no way of telling which one it was, or any point in trying—barked orders.

"Full thrust! We have a node entrance to make, and your foolish cowardice has cost us velocity."

"Hey." A voice from above. Instinctively she and Kyle looked up. A soldier stood at the lip of the hatch, pointing a gun down at them.

Outside, the whine of the generators as they were brought back on line.

"Hey," the soldier shouted to his fellow mercenaries. "Over here!"

The ship . . . *trembled*.

Metal screamed. The soldier looked up in shock, but that was all he had time for. A thousand tons of metal fell upward with the force of a hundred Earths. The inertial mass pushed on the pillars of the ship. And the pillars, cut to the bone, buckled, slipped, and tore.

The heavy metal core fell through the dainty tubes like a stone through moss. Shot through the center of the ship, smashing everything in its path. Debris and shrapnel whirled in its wake, and the soldier above them disappeared in a cloud of smoke and flame.

Alarms shrieked and died. The lights went out. The only sound left was the whoosh of air rushing out into space.

Prudence cut beneath her feet, heedless of disabled alarms and dead power lines now, like a vicious parasitic worm eating its way through the dying ship. They dropped another level into networks of tubes and feeder lines sporadically lit by flickering emergency lights. Prudence led Kyle outward, toward the skin of the ship, trusting to her instincts in the darkness. He followed, trusting her.

At the escape pod hatch, they met another soldier banging on the door, trying to hurry it open.

"This cab's ours," Kyle said, grinning like a lunatic. "Go find another one."

Looking at them in horror, the soldier fled. Prudence and Kyle tumbled into the pod and she pushed the release button. It shuddered, knocking them to the floor, and blew itself free of the ship.

Through the thick glass of the porthole they could see the great ship budding spores as pods evacuated it.

Prudence sat in the pilot's chair and overrode the automatic controls. The node parameters were burned into her brain from hours spent trying to fly the *Ulysses* through them in the optimal path, shaving hours and then minutes from each successive approximation.

The pod wasn't supposed to be flown. It had life support for a week, long enough that if you had to abandon ship while already in a node you'd still be alive when you came out the other side. Dirty, cramped, and possibly homicidal after spending all that time in a tiny room with twenty people, but still alive.

But it couldn't enter the node on its own. It didn't have enough mass for that. And its limited gas propulsion system would never undo all the velocity that was hurling them into deep space. A glance at the vector readings and she knew that nothing could. They were closer than she had thought, already past the turnaround point even for the fusion boats. And they were still on course.

The dead hulk of the carrier was going to go through the node anyway. And the spider fleet would follow it. There were no other choices left. For anyone.

Least of all for Kyle and Prudence. She pushed the pod into maximum thrust, rocketing up the side of the ship. If they hit debris or another pod, they would die. If they attracted the attention of the fusion boats that were trying to rescue the other pods, they would die. If she miscalculated a velocity or a mass number, they would die. If she twitched her hand at the wrong time . . .

Kyle stood behind her, stroking her hair. Waiting for her to be done. Waiting for her, like he had done since he had met her.

She looked at the ship's hull streaking past her and made a

guess. Slowed their velocity. Nudged the pod to start drifting toward the giant corpse.

They floated past the prow of the ship. A used-up party popper, shredded and dark. She pushed the pod in front of the ship, and hit the brakes, adjusting. Watching the solar vector readout like a hawk, waiting for the right instant. When it came, she accelerated again.

And now she was done. They would enter the node just ahead of the corpse behind them, riding in its mass envelope, but with enough velocity to not be sucked back into it, where the resulting chaos would convert them to cosmic radiation. Unless she had calculated wrong, in which case they would hit the node too soon, like a water balloon on concrete and thus becoming a slightly different kind of cosmic radiation.

Kyle did his part now. Leaning forward, he tapped at the pod's comm console, recording a message.

"Virus attack. Shut down all external comm. Validation is Captain William Stanton, service number ZFX86332."

He put it on auto-repeat, and turned the broadcast power to full. Then he set it on a timer, to start in four days.

"I memorized his number when I was trapped on his ship. Yes, I hated him that much."

And then he was done.

They had done everything they could, for the fate of the galaxy.

Kyle opened the supplies cabinet and broke out the drinking water. Wetting a soft cloth bandage from the medical kit, he dabbed at her gently, sponging the blood off. It ran in watery red lines to the drain in the floor. The water from the sponge mixed with her tears, as she wept for all of the things she had lost. Jorgun. The *Ulysses*. Garcia. Jandi, who would be dead by now, by the League's hand or the indifference of heartless nature. Her family, on Strattenburg. Who would always be dead.

Whose ashes were now scattered irretrievably to the void. Whose voices had faded with every year, with every hop. The memory of them had protected her at first, kept her whole and sound while she ran and ran, but each new face she interacted with, only to abandon and never see again, had stolen a piece of that memory, until she had only tatters left. Tatters that could not keep out the cold. And nothing new to sew into a vibrant, living whole.

She looked up at Kyle's face. Battered and bruised, swollen with red and black lumps. When he grinned at her there was a tooth missing.

She reached out and touched his jaw, stroking it lightly with her fingers, trying to convince herself he was real.

"I'll live," he said.

Through the portholes she could see the stars turn into rainbow streaks. They would live.

"I love you," she said.

Then they found they had not done everything they could. There were still things they could do, for each other.

Very good things.

EPILOGUE

The second battle of Kassa was almost as one-sided as the first had been. Altair Fleet, cautious to the point of paranoia, took no chances, and heeded the voice of Cassandra when it came crying to them from the depths of space. Without comm each ship had to fight alone, a single unit instead of a complex whole. But they were ships run by human beings. They *adapted*.

The robotic fighters were confused, diverted, and crushed in detail. The destroyers were pounded into submission. The captured crewmen talked, telling everything, but they didn't have to. After the first mask came off, Fleet already knew everything they needed to know.

Dejae—the prime minister one, that is—escaped them at the very end. They found him at his desk, wearing a beautiful mother-of-pearl mask with elegant diamond studding and a small, neat hole drilled through the forehead. The needle pistol was still in his hand.

The monks' intelligence network was impressive. When Fleet dropped out of the sky on Monterey, they were prepared. Garcia's voice greeted them, his drawl deeply amused at the ironies of fate and happenstance.

"Admiral, the new Dejae Prime asked me to give you a message. *Mistakes were made.* They see that now. And they would very much like to make a deal. They've hired me to talk for them, as they're scared pissless of you."

Fleet responded by sending troop transports instead of fusion bombs. On the way down, they noticed that the main landing pad was cluttered with biological life-forms.

Two dozen naked old men, handcuffed and cowering. They hid their faces, not their bodies, which was pointless since everyone already knew what they looked like.

When Fleet mentioned this curious oversight, Garcia had an answer for them.

"Dejae Prime apologizes for the refuse littering the landing site. He suggests that a brief pulse from your fusion engines should clear the pad."

Barbaric, but blood called for blood. In a flash of light the previous administration of Monterey ceased to be a trouble to anyone. A new era in monk-human relations began, under the unlikely but inevitable governorship of Garcia Mendezous.

The first rule Garcia imposed was the loss of the masks. Never again could the monks hide their nature from humanity. They would not be destroyed; their pipettes and flasks could continue to produce what they had come to think of as their children. But from now on they would have to walk with naked faces among men and each other.

Altair assumed the cost of rebuilding Kassa and reparations for the dead. In exchange they gained the secrets of robotics, extending the strength of their fleet without increasing their payroll. From anyone but Altair's point of view, it wasn't a particularly fair deal, but nobody was heard to complain.

Prudence was offered an admiralty, the head of the scout division. Stanton begged her to take the job, sending her a personal comm from his hospital bed where he was recovering from radiation burns. When she turned it down, they offered her a captaincy and a scout boat. When she turned that down, they bought her a new freighter, a University Exploration commission, and threw in a tax-free trading license to boot.

She was in the process of turning that down, until Kyle caught up with her. Weeks of high-level meetings and state functions had kept him away. She didn't mind. It was her turn to wait for him.

Even though she had been waiting for him her whole life. She just hadn't known his name before.

"I don't want a ship, Kyle. I'll stay here, with you. Altair needs you as much as I do." They had promoted him to the head of Interstellar Intelligence Agency, a new organization charged with rooting out the leftover League cells scattered through the sector.

He picked her up in his arms, spun her around, laughing.

"They don't need me. A stuffed shirt could do this job now. I resigned this morning, Prudence. I came to tell you: I'm coming with you."